The Christmas bow murder

Blonde, attractive and promiscuous Stella Carway is found murdered, a scarf around her neck tied in a bow, her near naked body displayed like a bizarre gift.

Her stormy marriage immediately puts her shifty husband Steven in the frame as her killer. But Chief Inspector Jim Ashworth, swimming against the tide of his colleagues' opinions, thinks this too obvious a solution.

Blackmail, the cover-up of a fatal hit-and-run accident, a passionate lesbian relationship – Ashworth opens up a can so full of worms it would give a crow a coronary in this first crime novel of immense promise.

THE CHRISTMAS BOW MURDER

Brian Battison

This edition published in Great Britain in 2000 by
Allison & Busby Limited
Suite 111, Bon Marche Centre
241-251 Ferndale Road
Brixton, London SW9 8BJ
http://www.allisonandbusby.ltd.uk

A catalogue record for this book is available from
the British Library.

ISBN 0 7490 0475 4

Printed and bound in Spain by
Liberduplex, s.l. Barcelona.

For
PATRICIA, my wife, without whose encouragement, love and
support, this book would never have been written,
and
JOAN MILLER, my sister-in-law and friend who not only
supplied the original idea, but helped enormously throughout.

Prologue

The world exploded before her eyes; planets danced and stars burst. She felt her body pitch forward. It hit something hard, cups and saucers flew and crashed. The sounds of splintering china came to her.

Something soft, smelling of perfume, was pulled tight around her neck.

'No,' she screamed; a scream that hardly left her restricted throat. 'I thought you loved me.'

Then a red mist closed in on her, enveloped her; she crashed into one object after another.

She could feel her eyes bulging in their sockets. Her lungs, starved of air, ached inside her body. Her heart beat a tattoo against her rib-cage. Wave after wave of pain struck as her larynx was forced into her windpipe, blocking it. Her tongue seemed to swell and fill her mouth.

All sound, all smell, all touch faded, came back like a roaring rush in her ears and nostrils, then was no more.

Her assailant allowed her lifeless body to crash to the floor and began to walk towards the french windows, only to return, carefully picking a path through the overturned furniture.

She was lying face down on the expensive carpet. Fingers that were shaking slightly reached for the scarf around her neck and tied it into a bow like those on Christmas presents.

Air rasped from her lungs as her body was turned over. Her unseeing eyes stared at the ceiling as the bathrobe was pulled open, displaying the naked flesh beneath.

In the darkness teeth flashed white in a sardonic grin.

1

Her expression was frozen in the agonies of death. Even hours after the spark of life had departed, the face beneath the thick blonde hair had a purplish tinge to it and the blue eyes bulged and stared in now unseeing terror. The plain blue chenille scarf which had been used to choke the life out of the woman had been tied in a small bow at the back of her neck as if the murderer was presenting the corpse as some sort of bizarre gift.

The body lay on deep-pile fawn carpet; it was clad in a white bathrobe, open at the front.

Chief Inspector Jim Ashworth noted the overturned coffee table, the deep indentations left by the castors of the settee which had been moved during what must have been a violent struggle.

Despite his thirty years in the police force death still disturbed him, still caused his stomach to turn in an attempt to throw up its contents. He swallowed hard,' totally unaware of the mêlée going on around him as the forensic team set to work.

The Chief Pathologist, Bill Warren, was concluding his examination of the dead woman. He was a small bird-like man, balding, and his spectacles had an annoying habit of sliding down his large nose.

Ashworth was glad Bill was on the case for he always delivered the relevant information without the need for prompting, unlike most of his younger counterparts who were fond of using medical terms which meant little to him.

Bill Warren grinned as he stood up. Ashworth towered at least ten inches above him.

'I see from the colour of your face that the old problem is still with you,' Warren said cheerfully. He had a very slight Scottish accent. 'Now, let's see what I've got for you.' He studied his notes. 'Cause of death, strangulation – that's obvious. The macabre touch with the scarf shows a flair for showmanship . . .'

'Or a particularly deep hatred,' Ashworth intoned.

Warren continued. 'Also a nasty blow to the back of the head. Blunt instrument. The force used must have stunned the victim.'

Ashworth's gaze took in the disturbed furniture; that and his raised eyebrows caused the pathologist to offer an explanation.

'I think the blow would have stunned the woman just long enough for her assailant to get the scarf round her neck and begin the job. Then my guess is the woman recovered – out of sheer desperation – and began to fight back.'

'Without much success though.'

'Yes, but she did put up quite a struggle. See the bruises on her legs and torso – they were caused by making contact with the furniture.' He paused. 'As you can see, the lady was not a natural blonde.'

Ashworth ignored the coarseness of that remark as his eyes swept over the shapely body and the thick thatch of brown pubic hair.

'But no signs of sexual assault,' Warren said. 'Or indeed any sexual activity immediately prior to death – which took place around midnight. I'll be more definite about that tomorrow but an hour either side, you can rely on that.'

Ashworth again took in the room. Expensive furniture – mostly dark oak reproduction – took its tasteful place beneath the quality prints that lined the walls. Just what you'd expect for one of the town's leading estate agents, he thought.

He looked now towards the open lounge door and saw Detective Sergeant Owen Turner gesticulating for Ashworth to join him.

The old adage that a plain-clothes police officer looked more like a copper than one in uniform did not apply to Turner; he was a tall, good-looking man, smartly and expensively dressed, and there was always a touch of the cavalier about his neckties; today's was bright red. His hair was light brown and, contrary to today's fashions, was worn long over his ears and lent a softness to his features that belied his thirty-five years.

Ashworth picked his way through the moving bodies and reached the comparative quiet of the hall.

'Morning, sir,' Turner greeted him.

'Morning. What have you got?'

'Not much. The cleaner found the body and called us.' Anticipating the next question Turner continued. 'She's next door with one of the neighbours being fed tea laced with whisky.'

'Lucky devil,' Ashworth joked then added soberly, 'Is she all right?'

'I think so. She's getting on a bit but she seems a tough old bird.'

'Good. No sign of the husband?'

'Not yet, no. We've contacted his office but he's not in yet.'

'Right, I'll go and see the cleaner. Which way?'

'Next house, right-hand side.'

Ashworth opened the front door and stepped out into the pale sunlight of the late October morning. He was glad of the waxed-cotton jacket he had on for there was a light layer of frost on the lawns of the open-plan front gardens.

Most people, given the circumstances, would have taken the shortest route across the grass but Ashworth respectfully used the drive as he purposefully made his way to the house next door.

His hand had barely touched the knocker on the white double-glazed door when it was opened by a woman in her thirties. She was dressed in a blue leisure-suit and a red-checked apron which more or less matched the frilly curtains of the kitchen into which he was led.

'There's a policeman to see you, Amy.'

The woman's tone suggested that Amy was, at the very least, senile.

She was seated at the table, a small, frail woman with thin,

11

brittle-looking grey hair. Her face was lined and haggard. Timidly she pushed her chair back and began to rise. There was alarm in her watery eyes.

Ashworth stepped forward. 'There's no need to get up, Amy. You don't mind if I call you that?'

She shook her head and wearily sank back into the chair, wrapping her wizened hands around a mug of tea that smelt strongly of scotch.

The lady of the house excused herself and Ashworth sat down to face the old woman. 'All right then, Amy, just tell me in your own time and your own words what happened.'

'Well, I turns up to do me cleaning like I does every day,' she started hesitantly. 'Spot on eight it was 'cause I'm always on time. I lets meself in – I've got me own key – an' as soon as I stepped into the hall I knew something was wrong. Couldn't place it then but I've been thinking about it since . . . there was no noise, you know, radio on or crockery being put in the sink. And when I sees the state of the lounge I thought they'd had another of their shenanigans, that's what I thought.'

'They had a lot of fights, did they?' Ashworth asked gently.

'Well, I never seen none, not to actually witness, but I'll tell you something, when they was both in you could cut the atmosphere with a knife.' She took a sip of tea. 'I used to say to meself, they've got all this an' they still can't be happy.'

Ashworth glanced around the kitchen, which was identical to the one next door and probably identical to all the others in the crescent with its fitted hob, oven, units and all the modern appliances it was possible to own, and he reflected that indeed wealth was no guarantee of happiness; often it had the reverse effect.

'So then you found Mrs Carway,' he coaxed.

'That's right. Gave me quite a turn, I can tell you.' Ashworth thought that remark must be the understatement of all time but said nothing.

Amy was saying, 'Lying there nearly naked like that. I think I screamed an' then I said to meself, now you just pull yourself together, Amy Perrin, and phone the police. Well, I knew I shouldn't touch anything in the house so I went to the phone

12

box on the corner but it'd been vandalized so I thought I'll just have to knock up Mrs Jeffries which is what I done.'

Ashworth felt an overwhelming urge to hug this frail old lady. 'You did very well. I just wish everyone could react so coolly in a crisis.'

Amy seemed pleased and her tired face broke into a weak smile. 'Well, Hitler's bombs couldn't drive me and me late hubby out of our home and after that there's not much left to frighten you.'

Mrs Jeffries came in then and made tea. Amy studied the large man sitting opposite. At first he had frightened her; his face was so fierce, heavily lined, his short black hair still thick and his slightly hostile brown eyes clear and bright, but he seemed a kind enough soul.

Mrs Jeffries served the tea; the same again for Amy – and, my, she did feel it was doing her good – and an undoctored cup for the chief inspector, then she excused herself.

'How did you get on with Mr and Mrs Carway?' Ashworth kept his voice at a conversational level.

Amy sipped her tea; the scotch was finding its way around her veins, relaxing her. 'Oh, I didn't get on with madam much. I don't think anybody of my class could. She really thought she was it. But him, he was a completely different kettle of fish. I've always said he's so good-looking he should be on the telly. And he's so charming . . .'

'I've heard he's a bit of a ladies' man.' This was a shot in the dark.

'As well he might be.' Amy leaned forward confidentially. 'But madam was no better than she should be.'

With that they terminated the interview. Ashworth extracted an assurance from Mrs Jeffries that she would take Amy home in her car; he, in turn, had to promise Amy that should the need arise – as it undoubtedly would – for him to speak to her again he would not visit her home in a police car – 'The neighbours, you understand.'

Once again he stood in the quiet crescent with its large box-like houses, all built to the same specifications, all lacking character and personality. The sunlight was warmer now as so

13

often happens in late October when high pressure dominates; the days can be pleasantly warm and sunny, the nights bitterly cold.

After checking with Turner as to whether the elusive Mr Carway had turned up – he hadn't – he got into his Sierra. The engine fired at the first turn of the key and he began his journey back to the station.

The traffic was light, patchy; most of the people who lived on the estates had long departed for work. Somehow Ashworth could never connect all of these estates that had sprung up over the years with his Bridgetown. To him Bridgetown was the busy high street bustling with shoppers, and the hundred or so houses and cottages that surrounded it; the rest was just something the Planning Committee had added on to attract wealthy people into the area.

His car sped over the stone bridge with its seven arches which spanned the River Thane and from which the town derived its name. Along the road, some hundred yards ahead, lay the old police station which was now a warehouse. Legend had it that in years gone by a band of some twenty Cavaliers still loyal to the King had held off two hundred Roundheads for four days from that building, and Ashworth could well believe it with those thick stone walls and solid doors. One of the worst things that had ever happened to him was being moved from that old building into the glass monstrosity that was now the police station. In hot weather it was like a boiler-house, in cold it seemed to allow the arctic chill to pass through unhindered. In winter it needed heating constantly; in summer the air-conditioning was rarely switched off and still, as he had rather venomously told the Police Committee, the damned place was cold when you wanted to be warm and bloody boiling when you wanted to be cool. It hadn't won him many friends, a fact that did not particularly bother him.

The car purred through the council estate. Most of the houses were now privately owned, had been since the mid-1980s, leaving the ones that remained within the council's domain looking more like council houses than ever before.

He pulled the car into the yard at the back of the station and parked it. Once inside he shunned the lift and walked up the stairs to the third floor. He was slightly breathless by the time he reached his office and hardly had time to enter before the telephone rang. Skirting round the neat desk he picked up the receiver.

'Yes,' he barked.

'Sir, it's Owen. The missing hubby's turned up.'

'Now that's good. How'd he take it?'

'He's in shock, sir. His doctor's with him now.'

'Is it genuine shock?'

'Seems to be. If it's not he's a good actor.'

'A lot of criminals are, Owen. You nearly finished there?'

'Just about. The body's gone. Forensic are just tidying up. I think the fingerprint people are in for some overtime. The cleaning lady came back for her carrier bag; she looked about three parts cut to me.'

Ashworth smiled to himself.

'Anyway,' Owen continued, 'she said the dead woman had had some sort of party here yesterday afternoon – about ten people apparently.'

'That's all we need. Right, Owen, get yourself back here.'

2

The next day the exterior of No.39, The Crescent, home of the deceased woman, Stella Carway, looked the same but the interior smelt of death; that strange pungent, stale, almost rotting odour that descends on a property where a death has recently occurred.

Ashworth knew that Steven Carway was in the house before being informed by the constable on the door; the driver of the panda car parked outside the house had told him he was waiting for Carway to collect a few belongings.

Ashworth and Turner now stood in the kitchen waiting for Carway to be escorted downstairs. Slight shivers touched Ashworth's spine as he wondered what type of man could return to the house where his spouse had been brutally murdered such a short time ago.

Turner must have been reading his thoughts for he said, 'He's a cold fish, sir, coming back here. Why didn't he send someone for his things?'

Any reply Ashworth might have made was cut short by the appearance of Steven Carway. He was indeed a handsome man, somewhere in his mid-thirties. The classic features, immaculate dark business suit, black hair gelled and slicked back, lent him the appearance of a television star.

'Gentlemen, I'm sorry to have kept you waiting. Please, do sit down.' His manner was smooth. Selling property would come easily to him, Ashworth thought as he and Turner sat at the large refectory table.

Ashworth's eyes never left Carway, who had gone to stand by the sink. He noticed there was shock in the man's eyes, bewilderment even, but no grief, no sorrow. He said, 'I'm sorry we have to bother you at a time like this, Mr Carway, but we do have to ask certain questions.'

'Of course.' Carway took a packet of cigarettes from his jacket pocket. 'Closet smoker,' he said. 'Have been for years, but today I can't seem to leave them alone. I do hope you don't mind.'

The lighter clicked as Ashworth stole a look at Turner who was carefully scrutinizing Carway.

Ashworth asked, 'Could you tell me where you spent the night – '

'The night my wife was murdered?' Carway interrupted. 'Yes, I spent it at the Coachman's Hotel in Bridgenorton.' The look that passed between the two policemen prompted him to go on. 'I know it's only twenty miles away but I had a meeting early evening with David Easeman, an estate agent there. We had dinner and a fair bit to drink so I stayed over.'

There was a slight pause before Ashworth asked, 'By yourself, were you, sir?'

Carway smiled rather sadly as cigarette smoke curled from

his lips. 'Completely,' he said. 'I went to my room at nine o'clock, had a couple more drinks and went to bed.'

'Thank you, sir. These are questions we have to ask, you understand.'

Carway stubbed out the cigarette as he muttered, 'Of course. Yes.'

Outside Ashworth and Turner exchanged glances. 'There's a lot he's not telling us,' Turner ventured.

'Yes, but what he's told us so far is the truth, I'm sure of that.'

He glanced along the crescent. An autumnal mist had descended and distant trees appeared as no more than dark smudges on a white swirling background.

Turner asked what to do next.

'Interview neighbours,' Ashworth replied gruffly before stamping off towards No.37, the house in which he had interviewed Amy the day before.

He raised the brass knocker and let it fall. He heard activity inside, then footsteps hurrying towards the door which was opened by Mrs Jeffries.

'Good day, Mrs Jeffries. I wonder if I might come in for a chat?'

'Oh yes, please do.' She seemed flustered as people often do when dealing with the police. She stood aside to allow him to enter and then showed him into the lounge which, again, was identical to the one next door. Ashworth noted the same wallpaper emulsioned with the same pastel shades – the builder must have bought a job-lot to keep costs down – that gave a tasteful air to the rooms but lacked any sort of permanence, any stamping of individual taste on the dwellings. No doubt the owners of most of the houses in the crescent saw the large three-bedroomed detached houses as merely a temporary pause on the ladder of life. This in turn made him wonder about Steven Carway; successful, seemingly rich – why should he stay in such a house? He took the question and filed it away in his mind.

Mrs Jeffries, who insisted he was to call her Jean, was an

17

extremely pretty woman. She was more formally dressed than she had been the day before, in a black skirt, and white blouse, and her face beneath the mass of red hair had received considerable attention from the make-up box. Ashworth guessed that many of the other women in the crescent would be taking similar pains with their appearances this morning due to the presence of the police. Remembering the watery tasteless brew of the day before he refused her offer of tea.

'Well, how can I help you, Inspector?'

Ashworth shifted his weight on the settee. 'Tell me all you can about the Carways.'

Jean Jeffries sat down in the easy chair facing him, her knees tight together, feet to one side. 'There's not much to tell. Stella – Mrs Carway – kept pretty much to herself, didn't have much to do with any of the women in the crescent.' She put heavy emphasis on the word 'women' in case Ashworth missed the point. 'Wouldn't give most of us the time of day.'

'And Mr Carway?'

Mrs Jeffries smiled. 'Oh, he was different, really charming. God knows why he married that woman. I can tell you, Inspector, there are quite a few along here who have set their caps at him.'

'And is he responsive to any of these women?'

'No,' she replied ruefully.

Ashworth pondered whether Jean Jeffries had been one of the setters, and whether perhaps the garment being set was a little more intimate than her cap. 'And Stella Carway, did she remain chaste?'

Mrs Jeffries cast her eyes downwards, partly thrown by Ashworth's old-fashioned way of asking if Stella Carway went in for extra-marital affairs but mostly because she was reluctant to speak ill of the dead.

'It would help us a lot, Mrs Jeffries . . . Jean, so tell me anything you know.'

Ashworth knew that he seldom had to remind witnesses it was an offence to withhold information from the police; most only sought an assurance that they would not be thought of as gossips and once that had been given would quite happily gossip all day. Jean Jeffries proved to be no exception. His 'This won't go further than the two of us' brought the response he wanted.

'Well,' she began, 'I did hear a lot of things but there is one thing I actually know for fact – she was having an affair with her gardener.'

'The gardener?'

Mrs Jeffries giggled. 'I'm sorry, that was a rather bad way to put it. He isn't a retired man . . . that's how most people see gardeners, isn't it? He's young, quite dishy really, about mid-twenties. People say he's a schoolteacher who can't get a job.'

'And you know for certain that he and Stella Carway were having an affair?'

'Oh yes.' She was enjoying herself now. 'I was in the kitchen – our window overlooks their side bedroom – and I just happened to be looking out. I glanced up and there they both were in the bedroom.'

'There could have been some quite innocent explanation for that,' Ashworth ventured.

Mrs Jeffries leaned forward conspiratorially and in a lowered voice said, 'And what else would they have been doing? Stella was in her underwear, just bra and pants, and the man, well, I don't know what he'd got on, he was farther back in the room, but I do know that he was naked from the waist up.'

'Not spraying the roses, that's for sure,' Ashworth commented drily.

Mrs Jeffries hardly paused. 'And do you know what she did when she saw me? Brazen as you like, she pulled the curtains, glaring at me as if I was in the wrong.' She sat back, full of righteous indignation.

Despite endless probing the woman could think of nothing else that would be of help. She was showing Ashworth out when the quiet of the crescent was disturbed by a car with a faulty exhaust loudly speeding along it.

Mrs Jeffries' brow creased. 'Oh, Inspector, I've just thought of something else.'

*

19

Some half an hour later Ashworth emerged from Mrs Jeffries' house to be met by Turner strolling from the opposite direction. They stopped at the Ford Sierra parked outside the dead woman's house. The metal handles of the car doors were still cold to the touch although it was now approaching lunchtime. Turner settled himself in the driver's seat and Ashworth climbed in beside him.

'Right little bed of illicit passion,' Ashworth observed as he reached for the seatbelt.

With practised ease Turner divided his attention between the road, the mirror and Ashworth. 'Well, the general consensus seems to be that Stella Carway went to bed with anything that remotely resembled a male, sir.'

'Yes, doesn't it? But that's the women's opinion. I'd like to get a male view on it.'

The car slowed as it approached the crossroads that bordered the estate. 'Did anybody offer any proof?' Ashworth asked.

'No, just gossip and hearsay.'

A car passed in front of them on the main road. Turner checked that the road was clear then accelerated and crossed it. 'Lots of talk about the gardener, though – a young chap.'

'Yes, I know, and I think we can take it that he was indeed Stella Carway's lover. Did you get his name?'

Ashworth laughed inwardly, taking great pains to keep his face deadpan straight as he caught Turner's frosty glare. The young sergeant was good at his job, very good, and any prompting that suggested he was not thorough annoyed him. Ashworth did it constantly.

'Of course I did, sir,' Turner replied with an icy edge to his voice.

'Good,' said Ashworth.

The lane along which they were now travelling contrasted strongly with the estate they had just left; this was still rural England with its fields now neatly furrowed and its trees losing their foliage. The first cottage that heralded the bridge came into view.

Turner steered the car into a corner. 'I also got his address.

He lives on the estate the other side of town – has a flat there.' Turner had far too great a social conscience to refer to it as the council estate. 'Do you want him brought in?'

'In view of what I know, yes. He's become our chief suspect.'

Turner knew it was useless to try and get more information from his superior; he would offer it when he was ready, which on this occasion was when they were comfortably installed in the Old England Café and lunch had been ordered: shepherd's pie for Ashworth and chicken curry for Turner.

The waiter placed the plates on the blue-checked tablecloth and vanished. The first forkful of meat and potatoes had been chewed and swallowed before Ashworth spoke.

'What's the gardener chap's name?'

'Believe it or not, Rory James,' Turner replied between mouthfuls of curry.

'Rory. Ah well, his parents did have a strange sense of humour.' Ashworth took a sip of coffee. 'Well, undoubtedly Rory James and Stella Carway were lovers. Jean Jeffries saw them in circumstances that can't be explained any other way. She saw quite a lot in fact, once her memory was prompted. Apparently, two months ago Stella started going out two days a week, leaving around eight a.m. and not returning until ten, ten thirty at night. Mrs Jeffries could be exact because Stella's Metro had a dodgy exhaust which made a hell of a noise and according to her when Stella went out or came back no one in the crescent could fail to notice.'

Ashworth's knife and fork made scraping sounds on the plate as he rounded up the last of the pie. 'Now, what we have to establish is where she went.'

Further scrapings gave Turner the opportunity to interrupt. 'Was Steven Carway at home the evenings his wife was out?'

'That we don't know because he always puts his Merc in the garage – his wife left her Metro on the drive – so it's quite possible he could have arrived home at a time when Mrs Jeffries wasn't just happening to glance out of the window.'

Having established that the shepherd's pie was well and truly gone Ashworth turned his attention to his coffee. 'Our gardener friend also came in for a good deal of scrutiny. It seems he was in the habit of buying Mrs Carway chocolates.' He studied the coffee.

Turner knew that something vitally important was about to be divulged. The maddening slowness of its disclosure infuriated him but he said nothing.

Ashworth swallowed what remained of his coffee and returned the cup to its saucer. 'And these chocolates always had little bows on the box, as Mrs Jeffries put it, like they do at Christmas to make them look more romantic.'

'Hardly proof – '

Ashworth held up his hands. 'No, there's more. Rory James was seen leaving the dead woman's house . . .' He paused. '. . . at eleven p.m. on the night of the murder.'

Turner leaned forward, his face intense. 'But that's the time of death. Why don't we just bring him in?'

The waiter circled; now the lunchtime trade was slowing he could shower his attention on the customers that remained. They both declined a sweet but ordered more coffee.

'Not as simple as that, I'm afraid,' Ashworth said as soon as the waiter was out of earshot. 'Someone let him out of the house. Mrs Jeffries said this Rory James was walking down the drive when she heard the Carways' door shut.'

Coffee was served; its aroma filled their nostrils. 'Go on then, Owen, give me a theory,' Ashworth said as he heaped five spoonfuls of sugar into his coffee.

Turner watched incredulously as his quicksilver mind began to function. 'Right. Stella Carway and Rory James were having sex. Steven Carway comes home, boots James out and then strangles his wife.'

'What about the car, the Merc? Steven Carway always puts it in the garage. Up and over metal doors make a lot of noise – the couple in the house would have heard.'

'But, sir, you're assuming that Steven Carway happened on the scene by chance. What if he suspected something was going on and sneaked back to the house? It would explain Stella Carway's near-naked state when she was found.'

'Yes,' said Ashworth doubtfully, the doubt shown by the

long-drawn-out vowel sound. 'But wouldn't there have been some sort of fight between Carway and James?'

'There might well have been.' Turner pushed his point. 'Who's to say the furniture in the lounge wasn't overturned by the two men fighting?'

Ashworth was still doubtful. For Steven Carway to come home, throw the boyfriend out, murder his wife and tie the scarf in a bow to incriminate the boyfriend, he would have needed a certain amount of blind faith, not to mention iron nerve, and in Ashworth's considered opinion Steven Carway was a man who would ruthlessly plan any enterprise in which he was involved, leaving nothing to chance. As for iron nerve, only time would tell, but somehow Ashworth doubted that Carway possessed it.

3

Chief Inspector Ashworth drained the last of the tea from the plastic cup. At this time of day – mid-afternoon – the police canteen was usually full: the evening rush of crime and motoring offences had not yet begun, the following late-night alcohol-fuelled brawls and violent crimes were yet to come into their own. Certainly this was a time to be savoured. The quiet before the storm.

With the sounds of good-natured banter ringing in his ears – most of it crudely directed towards the WPCs – Ashworth made for the door.

Feeling rather vulnerable, as he always did whilst walking along the glass-sided corridors, he went to his office. He paused, hand on handle, for a few seconds and listened to the drone of Owen Turner's voice coming through the woodwork, then he pushed open the door.

'Ah, this is Chief Inspector Ashworth,' Turner said as he entered the room. The young man to whom the statement was directed looked up. He was young, twenty-five, with long dark

23

curly hair; his face was swarthy, handsome in a gypsyish way. Although the man was seated it was obvious that he was tall, possibly over six feet, and well proportioned physically.

The young man held Ashworth's eyes; there was a mocking arrogance shining in his own.

Ashworth stood at his desk to face Mr Rory James directly. Turner stood up and as Ashworth started to speak he hitched himself up on to the corner of the desk, facing and to the right of James.

'And you must be Mr Rory James, sir,' Ashworth said.

'That's right, Chief Pig, and maybe you can answer the question your minion here is having such difficulty with.' His voice was well modulated, bordering on cultured. 'What am I being accused of?'

Ashworth smiled. 'Well, sir, the only thing we could accuse you of at the moment is being very rude.' His voice was easy, gentle. 'Which, of course, is your prerogative, but I do wish you'd not exercise it quite so loudly.'

Rory James was a man who used ill manners to annoy, to gain the upper hand. Ashworth had no intention of getting annoyed – yet.

'You were Mrs Carway's gardener, is that correct?' It was Turner who fired the question.

'Not the norm for a gardener, are you, Mr James?' Ashworth interrupted before James had a chance to answer.

'Here we go, man. When are you people going to realize that you're not clever? As well you know by now, I was a schoolteacher who got caught smoking pot with his pupils. Tut, tut, can't have that – get rid of the man,' he mocked.

'As it happens, Mr James, I did not know that, but fascinating as your past must be, save it for your biographer . . . I'm not interested,' Ashworth said drily. 'You and Stella Carway were having a love affair.'

James threw back his head; white even teeth gleamed in his dark face as he laughed. 'A love affair.' He exaggerated the words. 'Where the hell are you coming from, man? The 1930s?'

Well, yes, I am actually, Ashworth thought, the late '30s anyway. 'What would you call it then?' he asked pleasantly.

'We were having sex together. You know . . . sex.'

'Yes, Mr James, my memory is still functioning well, thank you.' A hint of a smile touched Ashworth's lips. 'So you were having sex together.'

'Yes, that's right. Three times a week.'

'And you felt nothing for her?'

Again the teeth flashed in an insolent smile. 'You must be joking, man. With a body like hers, I feel.'

Ashworth thought of Stella Carway's body, ice cold, the limbs frozen in rigor mortis, and James' flippant attitude finally made his patience snap.

'Right, Mr James, I assume you go out of your way to annoy people,' he said evenly. 'Well, with me it's worked. I want some answers and I want them now.'

James' face contorted in mock terror. 'Don't take me down to the cells and beat me . . . please don't.'

Ashworth fought for his self-control. He studied James until the pulsating anger inside him was brought into harness. 'No, I wouldn't do that, Mr James, you've been watching too much television.'

He stood up and stared down at Rory James. 'But what I can do, and by God, will do unless you start to co-operate . . .' His voice began to betray his ruffled temper. '. . . is take you down to the interview room and make this official. I've got enough to hold you on, at least overnight, so you just think on.'

Some of the colour drained from James' face. 'Okay, man,' he said. 'Don't get heavy.' He was trying desperately to regain his composure. 'I'm quite willing to answer your questions.'

Ashworth placed his hands on the desk and leaned forward. 'Good. Now, you were in the habit of buying Mrs Carway presents, such as boxes of chocolates with little Christmas bows on them. Right?'

James' face clouded in puzzled concentration. 'I don't know what you mean.' Then realization crept over his features. 'Oh, I bought Stella a box of chocolates for her birthday in September but I don't know anything about Christmas bows. Hang on though, I got them through a friend at a cash-and-carry . . .' A woman friend no doubt, Ashworth thought. 'They could have been old stock or even stock they'd got in for this Christmas. What's the significance?'

Both detectives stared at him and he became noticeably uncomfortable under their gaze.

Turner broke the silence as he stood up and walked behind the desk to open a drawer. Taking out the blue chenille scarf he said softly, 'Recognize this?'

'Yes, sure, it belonged to Stella. She used to tie her hair back with it,' James said, almost casually.

Turner said quietly, 'It's the murder weapon. Someone used it to choke the life out of Stella Carway.'

They scrutinized the darkly handsome face before them, searching for some kind of fear, or revulsion even, but nothing was forthcoming.

Ashworth jumped in quickly. 'You were there on the night of the murder.'

Again a slight pallor crept into James' face and his adam's apple jumped in his throat as he swallowed. 'Yes,' he replied tonelessly.

'What time did you leave?' Ashworth snapped.

'Around eleven.' James was now looking from one to the other, all arrogance gone.

Turner hardly gave him time to stop speaking. 'Do you know what time Stella Carway was murdered?' Not waiting for a reply he went on, 'It was around eleven. Are you sure she was still alive when you left?'

James came near to breaking. 'Yes, yes, yes,' he cried, emphasizing each word with a cutting stroke of his hand. 'What are you trying to say?' Again he studied their faces. 'Look, Stella phoned me at six and said Steven would be away for the night, would I like to come round?'

'That's just how she put it? Those were her exact words?' Ashworth asked.

James sighed. 'Do you want to know what we did in bed, for God's sake?' His re-emerging arrogance evaporated before the chief inspector's stony glare. 'Her exact words were, "Steven's tom-catting tonight, do you want to come round and service me?" That's what she called it . . . servicing . . .'

26

Ashworth and Turner exchanged a glance which was not lost on James.

'And did you . . .' Ashworth paused. '. . . service her?'

'Long and hard, Inspector. Do you want to know in which position?'

'Okay, I've got the idea. I'm not quite as naïve as you might imagine,' Ashworth said sarcastically. 'And?'

James looked puzzled and then the question clicked in his brain. 'I arrived there about eight and left at eleven.'

'Why did you leave? After all, the husband was away all night.'

'Chief Inspector, I know my sex life must seem bizarre to you but I'd had what I wanted. Why stay?'

Ashworth walked to the window. This all fitted in with what Mrs Jeffries had told him. Someone had let James out of the house and that someone could only have been Stella Carway.

The only thing Ashworth did like about this new police station (it had been ten years since the move and yet he still thought of it as new) was the view it afforded of the town. The mist was already beginning to descend again and already the expressway that skirted the old town was shrouded in it; lines of orange light danced before his eyes.

'Why Stella Carway?' he asked softly, hoping to throw James with the ambiguity of the question.

However, James homed in on the meaning. 'I'm an attractive guy,' he said immodestly. 'Women go for me. Look, I know you don't want my life story but I got into trouble when I was teaching. It wasn't just the pot . . . I was caught with some of my pupils. They were over sixteen,' he added hastily. 'Anyway, that was part of the reason I lost my job. A married woman's a good bet for me, especially a rich married woman. Yes, great, they might think they're in love with me but when it comes to the crunch, when they have to decide whether to stay with wealthy hubby or run off with a penniless gardener . . .' He spread his hands wide, indicating that he had made his point.

Ashworth watched him for some time. 'Was Stella Carway in love with you?'

James shook his head and looked pensive. 'No, Stella was

emotionally cold. In that department she was the coldest woman I've ever met. I don't think she could even love herself.'

Little remained but for Ashworth to politely thank Rory James for helping them with their enquiries and watch him disappear through the door.

'Well, what a fascinating insight into the latter-day Romeo,' Ashworth remarked as the door clicked shut.

'Why do you think he lied, sir?'

Ashworth's brow furrowed. 'About the sex, you mean? I really don't know. Our Mr James, by his own admission, only wanted one thing from Stella Carway on the night she was murdered and from what our Chief Pathologist has told us, he didn't get it.'

'But she must have let him out of the house at eleven.'

'No, Owen, someone let him out.'

'But who else could it have been?'

'If I knew that, I'd be arresting that person and Mr James for murder.' He pondered for a moment. 'Isn't it strange, Owen, that although Stella Carway appears to have had many lovers, none of them seem to have felt any love for her. Nobody has shown the slightest grief at her demise. I didn't know Bridgetown was harbouring so many sleazy little affairs,' he concluded heartily.

'Not all affairs are sleazy,' Turner snapped. 'Some people may be deeply in love.'

'All right, Owen,' Ashworth said, taken aback. 'I was only trying to lighten proceedings a little.'

Ashworth viewed his sergeant's stony expression. Over the last few weeks he had noted – no, sensed – a tenseness in Turner. His usually placid nature had often given way to spells of tetchiness when his prickly remarks caused resentment, especially in those lower down the force than himself. Ashworth had wondered if the cause of this had its roots in Turner's home life but did not mention it, for as long as Turner performed his duties to an acceptable standard his private life remained sacred territory.

These thoughts jogged his memory. 'Oh, I forgot to tell you,

Sarah's invited you and Karen for dinner tomorrow. We can talk over the case after we've eaten.'

Turner's brow furrowed. 'Yes, all right,' he said rather reluctantly.

The response disappointed Ashworth for although he and Turner had only been working together for six months they had fallen into the working pattern that he favoured; much of their work and a good deal of their discussion was carried out over a drink or a meal.

Turner's mood lightened. 'What next?'

'In the morning I want you to go over to the Coachman's Hotel and question the proprietor. We need to know more about Steven Carway's life. That remark young Romeo James made about Carway tom-catting . . . I think we'd better find out who wronged whom in the first place.'

Turner studied his watch then excused himself and left the office.

Ashworth picked up the telephone and dialled a number, drumming his fingers on the desk-top until the connection was made. 'Hello, Mr Carway, it's Chief Inspector Ashworth here. Sorry to trouble you, but I wonder if you could come and see me tomorrow. Yes, sir, at the station if that's convenient. Three o'clock will be fine, yes. Goodbye.'

The receiver had hardly settled in the cradle when the telephone rang again.

'Yes?' Ashworth snapped, his mind still focused on the next day's interview with Carway.

As David Hodges' voice filtered into Ashworth's ear the image of the man came into his mind; small, mouse-like, a man who had looked fifty for the whole of the twenty years that Ashworth had known him and who was probably only now approaching that age.

Hodges' one obsession was fingerprints; they were the central pivot of his life. It may well be said that no one is indispensable, but Hodges would have been hard to replace. His rather absent-minded manner often led people to believe that he was taking liberties with them when the fact was simply that his brain was

29

a long way ahead of his speech. He also had an irritating habit of ending sentences with 'something like that' and this lent a certain ambiguity to his most definite of statements.

'Hello, Jimbo,' Hodges said. 'What do you want first, the bad news or the really bad news?'

'What happened to the good?' Ashworth asked as he realized that fingerprints were not going to be the saviour in this case.

Hodges ignored the question. 'You could have had every villain in Bridgetown in the Carway house for all I can tell you. Prints all over the place. Most of them smudged or overlapping. Some clear ones . . .'

'But none known to us?'

'Yes, something like that,' Hodges confirmed.

'The car's the same, I take it?'

The slowness of the reply irritated Ashworth. Hodges made a sound that remotely resembled a chuckle as he said, 'The last time the interior of that car was cleaned was when it left the assembly line. Same story . . . covered in prints but none of the distinguishable ones are on record.'

'So, I'm up the creek and the paddles are still in the boathouse.'

'Something like that, Jimbo.'

Ashworth thanked him and replaced the receiver. He knew there were times in an investigation when one needed to push, to probe, and times when one needed to sit back and let things happen. The latter course was the one he must now take. There was nothing that could be done about Steven Carway until the next day.

He picked up the local newspaper from his desk. The murder was the lead story. A blown-up photograph of Stella Carway dominated the front page.

Pulling open his desk drawer he took out the original of that photograph; it was slightly out of focus and Stella's features were not easily distinguishable. The newspaper had tried hard but given the bad quality of the original, plus the fact that 35mm film does not take kindly to being enlarged, the resulting copy was fuzzy and extremely bad.

The national newspapers had wisely reproduced the snapshot in its original form but even so Ashworth doubted if any member of the public would be able to tell what Stella Carway had looked like from either picture, which was why he was surprised when Sergeant Martin Dutton poked his head round the door.

'Got something for you, Jim. Someone from Morton seen in the company of the murder victim a couple of weeks ago.'

Ashworth smiled. 'Come on in, Martin.' He liked the uniformed sergeant, who had joined the force some twenty-odd years ago to 'make a difference' and who, remarkably, still clung to that philosophy. Ashworth had, on many occasions, tried to persuade him to join CID but Dutton always refused, saying he was waiting for the post of Community Officer to be created as he felt that was where his particular talents could excel.

'Crank?' Ashworth asked as Dutton settled his large frame in the chair facing the desk.

Dutton shook his head. 'Don't think so, Jim, that's why I came to you with it. The informant's a Mrs . . .' He consulted his clipboard. '. . . Muriel Parker. She said she saw a woman by the name of Susan Ratcliffe with the murder victim. Mrs Parker's husband is manager of Volume News, a newsagent's and tobacconist's in Morton shopping centre, and this Ratcliffe works for him. That's why she's so sure.'

'Did she say if she recognized Stella Carway from the photograph in the papers?' Ashworth asked as he shot a doubtful glance at the newspaper.

'No, she didn't.' Dutton paused. 'The name Susan Ratcliffe rang a bell, Jim, so I went through records. Nothing there. She's clean. So I rang Morton station, talked to your old sidekick, Mike Blair. He did some asking about and rang me back. No one at Morton knows anything about the woman. Never had so much as a parking ticket or a caution.'

'Thank you, Martin. Very thorough, as always. I don't suppose you've changed your mind about coming to work with us?'

Dutton stood up. A smile lit up his plump, homely face. 'No, Jim, I still don't think hitting them over the head and locking them up is the answer.'

Ashworth did not wholly agree with that view. There were some he knew who would respond to help and kindness, but the majority, schooled on free expression, brought up to believe that the police and courts could do little to control society, would view such a liberal policy as one step closer to the anarchy they saw as total freedom. He could not subscribe to Dutton's view but he had to respect the sincerity with which it was held.

'Pity,' he said as Dutton handed him the details.

As the door closed behind the sergeant Ashworth studied the details, relishing the thought of a trip to Morton to renew his acquaintance with Turner's predecessor, Mike Blair.

Mike was the direct opposite of Turner, forty years old, still single and very much a ladies' man. He was always the life and soul of the party, a man who undoubtedly had the ability to charm the birds from the trees. No one, not even his own mother, could accuse Owen Turner of being the life and soul of any party. True, he had a quiet sensitive charm but he was too introspective to ever be classed as outgoing. Turner was a marginally better detective than Blair but he was nowhere near as much fun to be with.

Thinking of Turner made Ashworth wonder where he got to every afternoon of late. Obviously working on the case; what else?

4

Owen Turner climbed back into his car and sat looking at the red telephone box which stood in the lonely country lane. The call had been hell, sheer bloody hell, but then again they always were.

32

The mist that had descended the night before then thickened and turned into fog was now being burned off by the strength of the sun. Misty white drapes were being pulled back to reveal brown furrowed fields and bare-boughed trees now stripped of their summer splendour.

Channelling his mind back on to work, Turner started the car and resumed his journey.

The manager of the Coachman's Hotel in Bridgenorton was a small, rather effeminate man of around forty-five. He wore a dark smart suit, standard attire for an hotelier.

It soon became apparent to Turner that if he was going to interview this man it would have to be on the move: he seemed incapable of staying in one spot for more than a minute.

Turner followed him behind the leather-covered reception desk. 'Mr Baldwin, can you please tell me if Mr Steven Carway stayed here on the night of October 29th?'

Mr Baldwin busied himself with rearranging mail that had not yet been collected by the hotel guests. 'Look at this,' he said with disgust. 'Almost lunchtime and mail still in the pigeon-holes.' He paused for just a second then said huffily, 'That's right, Sergeant, poor Mr Carway did stay with us that night. I do feel for the man, what with this all over the papers . . .'

He took off again, this time heading for the kitchen door at the rear of the dining-room. Stopping briefly to look at Turner he said, 'I really must check that the kitchen staff are coping with lunch.'

Turner set off in pursuit, quickening his stride in an attempt to keep up with the darting Baldwin. He fired a question at the retreating back. 'Did Mr Carway stay here often?'

An answer was not forthcoming until Baldwin had poked his head round the kitchen door and bellowed orders to an unseen staff. At last he replied, 'Quite often, yes.'

He seemed to pause, hovering on the spot, wanting to move but incapable of deciding which way to go. 'Bar,' he said absent-mindedly.

'Mr Baldwin,' Turner barked, stopping the small man in mid-stride just as he had set off on another foray. 'Will you stand still for a moment? This is a police investigation.'

Baldwin blinked, upset by the briskness of Turner's voice. 'Well, I do have an hotel to run, you know.'

'Yes, and I've got an investigation to conduct, so if you could just stay in one place for a minute we'll both find our tasks a lot easier.'

'Oh, very well.' Baldwin was moving as the words sprang from his lips. Once again he opened the kitchen door. 'Andrew, would you kindly check that the bar is ready to open while I answer this . . .' He looked pointedly at Turner. '. . . gentleman's questions?'

The white-suited Andrew huffed and puffed his way through the door, his expression as harassed and haughty as Baldwin's.

'Right, Sergeant, I can give you a few moments.'

As Turner was not offered a seat he stood, with Baldwin, outside the kitchen door with the smell of partially-cooked cabbage wafting around him.

'So, Mr Carway stayed here quite often.'

'Yes, sometimes as many as three nights a week.'

'Didn't it strike you as odd, the fact that he only lived some twenty miles away and yet he stayed in an hotel?'

'Sergeant, as long as my guests behave themselves and pay their bills their reasons for staying here are of no interest to me.' His eyes kept darting from right to left, his body longing to be where his mind was – in the bar.

'And was Mr Carway always alone?'

'How do you mean?' Baldwin asked with suspicion.

'Did he stay here by himself?' Turner asked pointedly.

'Now look here, Sergeant, this is awful, this . . . this invasion of privacy. Mr Carway is one of my regular guests.'

'Mr Baldwin, this is a murder investigation. Now, did Mr Carway stay here with another person?'

Baldwin huffed. 'He stayed here with various young ladies. I believe they're called escorts.'

'Prostitutes,' Turner intoned.

'They were not prostitutes,' Baldwin flared. 'They were very respectable ladies. The very thought that I would allow tarts to ply their trade in my hotel . . . really!'

'You're none too fussy if your guests are married or not then,' Turner said drily.

'I don't care whether they're married or even in love, Sergeant.' Baldwin's colour rose with indignation. 'I simply want my bank manager to love me.'

'I see,' said Turner, suppressing a smile. 'And on each occasion it was a different girl?'

'Well, nearly always, except . . .' Baldwin appeared to be deep in thought. 'I think these last few times it was the same one. A blonde lady. Always drinks gin and tonic. Oh yes, life and soul of the party Mr Carway is whenever he's in the bar. Good for business too . . . gets everyone mixing in and they drink more.'

It did strike Turner that to keep Baldwin's undivided attention he needed only to discuss the hotel trade, so it was with some reluctance that he changed the subject. 'And was this girl with Mr Carway on the night of October 29th?'

'No. Mr Carway was alone that night. He came in about nine o'clock . . .'

'Did he appear to have been drinking?'

'Not excessively, but then he can hold his drink. And he did drive his car, I remember seeing it in the car-park. But, of course, you can drink and drive, can't you? It's when you get caught you're in trouble.'

'Did he drink in the bar that evening?'

'No, he didn't. He went straight to his room. Yes, I remember, he wanted room service. Room service . . . I ask you! With me being short-staffed as well. He had a bottle of scotch and . . . yes, yes, it was crushed ice.'

'What time did he leave in the morning?'

'It must have been about eight, just after breakfast. They usually take breakfast whether they want it or not, having paid for it.'

Turner thanked him and watched as he scurried away, no

doubt certain that his whole hotel empire would collapse unless he could personally check that the beer mats were on the tables in the bar.

Turner left the hotel and set about checking other parts of Carway's story.

Ashworth had made an earlier start to the morning than Turner but because of the fog his journey had been slower; however, by the time he reached Morton it had thinned sufficiently to allow normal driving.

Relations with the Morton force had been fraught of late due to a dispute over the distribution of financial resources. Ashworth had telephoned Mike Blair the previous evening to clear his visit and had been told rather apologetically that hospitality could be extended as far as the use of the station car-park but no further. Ashworth, remembering that parking facilities at Morton left a lot to be desired, had graciously accepted and promised Blair that he would call in for a lunchtime drink before returning to Bridgetown.

Ashworth was not fond of Morton. It was a thriving town which seemed to have escaped the worst ravages of the current recession. Its main source of employment lay in the food industry. The town housed the main offices of several major supermarket chains as well as four large hypermarkets which served the surrounding areas.

Morton had never in its history been a pretty town and beauty had not come with wealth. Most of its old buildings had gone, long since replaced by a modern main street shopping area made up of breeze-blocks and glass. It always reminded Ashworth of a shanty town, one that could be dismantled and moved should the need arise.

The town centre, which still boasted its sixteenth-century stone cross, was also home to a four-storey shopping precinct that dominated the town's landscape.

All around the bustling centre were the box-like constructions of modern houses with postage-stamp gardens hardly large enough for a cat to pee let alone be swung in.

Ashworth drove around the narrow streets, just wide enough for two cars to pass, looking for Adnitt Close where Mrs Muriel Parker lived. Lost in the maze of identical streets he was forced to stop and ask directions on three occasions. Eventually, acting on the instructions of the third person, he found it: a long narrow road with a crossroads near its end; over the crossroads was a neat trim cul-de-sac where 110 Adnitt Close was situated.

He stopped the car in front of the small semi-detached house and as he got out he saw the net curtains move. The front garden was neat if unimaginative and it took Ashworth but three strides to reach the front door. He rang the bell and the door was opened by an agitated woman with mousy-brown hair; her nervous eyes appraised him.

'Muriel Parker?'

'Yes.' Her voice was taut, highly strung.

'Chief Inspector Ashworth. Bridgetown CID.'

'Oh yes, please come in.' She stood back and he stepped into the tiny hall. 'Come through into the lounge.'

Ashworth followed her into a room which overlooked the road. An estate agent would have called it compact; it was in fact minute. The lounge suite was expensive, red velvet, and far too large for the room. A television set and video recorder stood in the corner and a Welsh dresser completed the furnishings but even with these sparse items the room appeared cluttered.

Muriel Parker seemed to read his thoughts. She said, 'I'm sorry about this place. It's not that we can't afford something bigger – my husband does have a well-paid job – but in Morton there just don't seem to be any larger houses on the market.'

Ashworth looked at the woman. There was hardly any swell of breast beneath her pink twin-set and her shoulders, waist and hips formed parallel lines.

'Please sit down,' she said as she perched herself on to one of the chairs, closing her legs demurely and pulling down her grey skirt.

Ashworth made himself comfortable on the settee. 'Mrs

37

Parker, I believe you rang Bridgetown police station yesterday afternoon and reported seeing Stella Carway in the company of one Susan Ratcliffe.'

'Yes, that's right,' she answered resolutely, her long nervous fingers intertwining. 'It was just over two weeks ago. I'd gone to pick up Terry – that's my husband – and I was parked in Green Street.'

Ashworth had some knowledge of the geography of Morton and said, 'If you were picking up your husband why didn't you use the underground car-park at the precinct?'

Muriel Parker trembled, she blinked rapidly. 'I don't like using it. The things you read about and see on the television . . .'

But with everyone leaving work the car-park would have been overflowing with people, Ashworth thought, and he began to wonder about Mrs Parker's motive.

'Well, tell me what you saw.'

'I was sitting in the car and I saw that Ratcliffe woman . . .' There was venom in her voice as she spoke the name. '. . . walk down the ramp. She'd just turned left at the end of it and a car pulled up and she got into it.'

'You're saying that car was being driven by the murdered woman, Stella Carway?'

'Yes, it was.' She avoided his slightly hostile stare.

'You knew Stella Carway? You'd seen her before?'

'No.'

Ashworth slowly got to his feet. 'Mrs Parker, you're asking me to believe that at a distance of at least forty yards you can positively identify the driver of that car as the murder victim, presumably from a photograph in a newspaper?'

'Yes, yes I am,' she said with a tremor in her voice.

'A woman you'd never seen before and on that occasion could only have seen in profile? Is that what you're asking me to believe?'

Mrs Parker's nervousness became more pronounced as she stated, 'Yes, because that is what I saw. You people are always asking the public to co-operate, then when we do you treat us like criminals.'

'It's all right, Mrs Parker,' Ashworth said as he tried to placate the woman.

He was angry when he left the Parkers' house – he was wasting his time, or more correctly, his time was being wasted for him.

He was still angry when he parked the car at the police station before making his way to the shopping precinct.

Already soft Christmas lights adorned the sides of the shopping avenue and along its centre a row of fat Father Christmases watched over proceedings, resplendent in their sleighs filled with presents.

Although it was only nine thirty the centre was already packed with browsers.

Ashworth had taken this route in his search for the Volume News shop. It was a decision he had started to regret as he was jostled by the slow-moving herd.

The taped choir's rendition of 'Hark the Herald Angels Sing' competed with the less dulcet tones of a small boy who, flanked on either side by his weary parents, was staring at an expensive mountain bike that stood in the window of a large toy store. At the top of his voice the boy was petulantly declaring that he wanted the bike for Christmas and resolutely refusing to move until his parents promised that he could have it.

The two voices of Christmas, Ashworth thought wryly.

He located Volume News on the second elevation; it was situated between a café offering a full breakfast for one pound and a sportswear shop with twenty-five per cent off everything.

The interior of the shop was long and narrow. There were newspapers and magazines on racks just inside the door. Directly opposite was the cash register and cigarette counter. The rear of the shop was taken up by a Pik 'n' Mix display. There were floor-to-ceiling racks that offered almost every chocolate bar on the market and shelves that housed the Top Ten paperback novels.

A woman with her back to the door was tidying the morning newspapers. Her body seemed full and shapely beneath the tight Volume News smock and her peroxide blonde hair showed half an inch of dark roots at the parting.

'Excuse me,' Ashworth said.

The woman turned round and Ashworth could see that her face was heavy with make-up, especially around the eyes.

'Yeh?' she said, her jaw moving up and down as she chewed on gum.

'I'm looking for Mr Parker.'

'Back of the shop. Door marked "Manager",' came the bored reply as she returned her attention to the newspapers.

Ashworth walked to the back of the shop and knocked on the door.

'Come in,' a harassed voice called out.

The manager's office was in fact the store-room with a desk in its centre. Metal storage racks packed with cardboard boxes stood all around the room. There was a strong smell of confectionery and paper.

Terry Parker was sitting behind the desk, one finger poised over an adding machine. He was a dark man with a long thin face; his black hair was parted down the middle in an attempt to conceal his receding hairline but the style only succeeded in highlighting the egg-sized bald spot on the crown of his head. His grey suit was fashionable but inexpensive and he wore this with a wide necktie which contained every conceivable colour and shade in its design.

'Who are you?' His accent held the slight cockney twang that had been predominant in the area since the London overspill of the late '70s.

'I'm Chief Inspector Ashworth. Bridgetown CID.' Ashworth closed the door and moved to Parker's desk, his footsteps sounding on the uncovered concrete floor.

'And what do you want with me?' Parker asked as he went back to tapping the keys of the adding machine.

Ashworth said, 'I'm investigating the murder of Stella Carway. I don't know if you're familiar with the case.'

'We are a newsagent's,' the man said as his eyes skimmed Ashworth's face. 'So I think it's safe to assume I see the newspapers.'

'I'm sure you do, sir.'

The only chair in the room was occupied by Parker so

40

Ashworth stood in front of the desk keeping a tight rein on his steadily rising temper.

'And are you also aware that your wife has informed us that one of your employees, Susan Ratcliffe, was seen getting into a car that was being driven by the dead woman?'

Parker stopped hitting the keys. 'Oh, my God.'

'Is that Susan Ratcliffe in the shop?'

'No, Sue left a couple of weeks ago . . . mostly because of my bloody wife. The woman's paranoid, thinks I'm having it off with every woman I know.'

'So when your wife says she came to pick you up from work and she saw Susan Ratcliffe – '

'She wasn't picking me up,' Parker interrupted. 'She was checking up on me.'

'I see,' said Ashworth. 'Now let me get this straight, what you're telling me is that you don't believe your wife actually saw what she reported to us.'

'No, that's not what I'm saying.'

Ashworth enjoyed watching the man become flustered.

'If Muriel said she saw Sue getting into a car, then she did. It's just that she made a mistake about the driver. Do you understand what I mean?'

'Yes, I think it's becoming clear,' Ashworth said with growing impatience.

Parker sighed loudly. 'That's the bloody irritating thing about Muriel, the interpretations she puts on things.'

'Well, if you give me Susan Ratcliffe's address I can let you get back to your facts and figures.'

'Surely you don't need to speak to Sue after what I've told you?'

'Mr Parker,' Ashworth said, trying to keep his voice even, 'can I tell you what irritates me? When we're fed false information we have to check it out from beginning to end just to make certain that it is false. Now, while I'm doing that I'm thinking of all the things I should be doing and that makes me angry . . . and that's why I want to get this matter cleared up.'

'Yes, of course. It's Bedford Court, that's a block of flats.'

'Thank you, sir.' Ashworth turned and walked to the door.

41

'Inspector, there won't be any trouble about this, will there? Any charges, I mean?'

'It's too early to say but I promise you if there are I'll be in touch.'

Ashworth walked through the shop. The woman with the peroxide hair was now sitting on a stool behind the cash register, painting her fingernails bright green.

Ashworth stepped towards her. 'Hello,' he said with a smile.

'Hi.' She smiled back even though her mouth was working overtime on the chewing gum. 'What's he done then?'

'How do you mean?'

'Well, you're a copper, ain't you?'

'You are observant.'

'I keep my eyes open.'

Because of the make-up Ashworth could not actually tell if her face had flushed at the compliment.

He said, 'Did you know Susan Ratcliffe?'

'Yeh, me and Sue were great mates.' She screwed the top back on to the nail varnish. Ashworth watched, fascinated, as she began blowing on to her fingernails, then she sat back, admiring the colour. 'Mind you, I could kill her for walking out and leaving me to cope with this lot on my own.'

Ashworth glanced around the empty shop. 'Mr Parker seems to think his wife had something to do with Susan's early departure.'

The woman's eyes went blank. 'His wife? Oh, I get you. She used to come in and look daggers at Sue. Thought they were having it off. But that didn't bother Sue. She just got fed up and told him to stick it.'

'And was there any foundation for Mrs Parker's suspicion?'

Her mouth dropped open and Ashworth saw the wedge of gum on her tongue. 'Foundation?' she repeated. 'Oh, right, got you . . . were they having it off?' She giggled and touched his sleeve. 'Here, don't you talk funny.' She sobered. 'No, Sue would have told me 'cause we used to tell each other everything . . . even personal things. He used to try it on but he never got there. Sue wasn't really like that. She's got a touch of class . . . know what I mean? Mind you, lover boy in the back used to

42

call it "delusions of grandeur". It's a scream how funny they turn if you don't fancy them, ain't it?'

'I see. So he fancies himself with the ladies, then?'

The woman pursed her lips. 'And then some. Thinks he's really something. Touches my tits and bum every chance he gets. My old man'd thump him if he knew.' She inclined her head towards the rear of the shop. 'He always says, in the retail business wage rises don't depend on productivity but on how happy you make the manager.' She started to polish her nails on her sleeve. 'He ain't bad really, but he ain't got no style. Know what I mean?'

Ashworth watched the teeth mashing into the chewing gum. 'Yes, I think I know exactly what you mean,' he said quietly.

Bedford Court was a fifteen-minute walk from the precinct. Ashworth glanced at his watch as he walked. It was ten fifteen. If he could get this over with quickly he could be back at the police station for noon which would leave him time to have lunch and a drink with Mike before starting back for the interview with Steven Carway.

He knew that this whole thing was a complete waste of time but what he had told Terry Parker was the truth – he did need to eliminate Susan Ratcliffe from the investigation.

He had already decided not to take any action against Muriel Parker for wasting police time. Obviously her suspicions about her husband's infidelity were not unfounded and Ashworth could well imagine how the constant state of insecurity would play on her mind causing her behaviour to become irrational.

What her motive was could only be guessed at. To cause as much trouble as possible, he presumed, or perhaps she held a forlorn hope that a police investigation would unearth some link between her husband and Susan Ratcliffe.

Bedford Court would not have been included in the 'one to five star' scale. It appeared to be fighting a losing battle to climb back into the 'seedy' category. It had been built of grey stone in the 1930s and was now weather-beaten, covered in decades of grime. The masonry of the three-storey block was crumbling in places and most of the net curtains behind the metal-framed windows appeared as grimy as the building itself. The flats were set back from the road behind a small front garden, the turf of which looked uncared for; cut short but unedged, it threatened to take over the now empty flowerbeds.

From the '30s through to the '60s the flats had been used by wealthy businessmen as a place in which to secrete their mistresses but with the changing attitudes of the female came a reluctance to be clothed, housed and fed in return for their favours; from the '60s onwards women had demanded to be treated as equals rather than simply objects of sexual gratification. The landlords of Bedford Court therefore lost a lucrative source of income and were forced to let to just about anyone.

As Ashworth pushed his way through the revolving door he was greeted by a fresh pine smell which surprised him somewhat. Below the 'Enquiries' sign was a sliding glass hatch. Ashworth walked over to it and pressed the bell. The hatch slid open and there stood the caretaker, a mediocre man, dressed in a cheap green uniform.

'Yeh?' the caretaker enquired.

Ashworth had to bend down to look through the hatch. 'I believe you've got a Susan Ratcliffe in residence here.'

'That's right, mate. Thirty-four, top floor.'

Ashworth saw that the office beyond the hatch was cluttered with cleaning equipment: buckets, mops, vacuum cleaners and polishers. On the table was a large steaming mug of tea. Ashworth had interrupted a tea break.

'Know much about her?' Ashworth asked.

The man's small sharp eyes pierced Ashworth. 'You the law?' he asked, his tone implying that the police were not welcome.

'Not really.' Ashworth leaned forward, his voice dropping to a whisper. 'Private detective.'

The man's eyes widened. 'Oh, I see. What's she done?'

'It's delicate. Tell me, does she have many male visitors?'

'No, not really, not like some of them here.' His eyes twinkled. 'Got you . . . it's the old divorce.'

'You catch on quick,' Ashworth said, realizing that his speech was becoming broad.

The caretaker was overawed at being in the presence of a real-life Magnum and as a result he could not have been more helpful. He said, 'Well, it's always the quiet ones who are the worst, but I wouldn't have put her down as a married man's bit on the side though there's plenty here that are.'

'How can you tell that?' Ashworth asked with mock amazement.

'By keeping me eyes open, mate. Your average married man sneaks in . . . right?'

'Right,' Ashworth agreed.

'Then he tries to get up the stairs without anybody seeing him. And he always stays about an hour.'

'An hour,' Ashworth said, taking it all in.

'Yeh, he can get away with an hour, see . . . working late and that sort of thing.' The man chuckled as he said, 'Beats me though what they do with the other fifty-nine minutes.'

Ashworth laughed. 'What's she like, this Susan Ratcliffe?'

The caretaker thought about it then said, 'Well, a bit stand-offish really . . . pleasant, mind, but I'd say she thinks she's a little bit better than anybody else.' He shook his head. 'I still can't believe she was getting a man in here without me knowing.'

'Does she have many women friends?'

'What's a woman got to do with it if it's a divorce?'

The question took Ashworth off guard but he recovered quickly. 'Just think about it. What usually happens when the novelty begins to wear off?'

The caretaker's brow wrinkled in thought.

'If the bed's big enough, that is,' Ashworth prompted.

The man's jaw dropped open so suddenly that it was a second before the bottom plate of his false teeth followed it. 'What, you mean three of them at it? That's been happening here?'

'Could be.' Ashworth nodded grimly. He reached into his inside pocket and took out the photograph of Stella Carway. Handing it to the caretaker he said, 'Now, do you recognize this woman?'

The caretaker took the photograph and held it at arm's length

45

as he studied it. After a while he shook his head. 'No, can't say I know her but that don't mean she's not been here. I don't take much notice of the women visitors, see, 'cause . . . well, I just never thought . . .' He was reluctant to dismiss the possibility that orgies might be taking place within the building.

Ashworth took the photograph back. 'Thanks. Thirty-four, you said.'

'Yeh, that's right. Better walk though, the lift's on the blink. Look, do you want me to keep this quiet . . . you being here, like?'

'In the circumstances that would be wise.' Ashworth gave the man the benefit of another grim nod before turning and heading for the stairs.

He was quite out of breath by the time he reached the top floor but the masquerade with the caretaker had lifted his flagging spirits. He was still smiling as he knocked on the door of flat No.34. He was about to knock a second time when the door was opened by a tall dark-haired woman. Her tight blue jeans were faded to white in places and the pale blue T-shirt looked almost new and quite expensive.

'Yes?'

'Susan Ratcliffe?'

'Yes, that's right. Who are you?' Her speech was well modulated without being affected.

'I'm Chief Inspector Ashworth. Bridgetown CID.' He produced his warrant card, which she did not look at. 'Might I have a word?'

'Yes.'

'Perhaps inside, if that wouldn't inconvenience you too much.'

Reluctantly Susan Ratcliffe stood aside and allowed Ashworth to enter the flat. There were three suitcases standing by the coat-rack; he could not tell if they were full or not. She made no attempt to invite him into one of the rooms but left him in the hall as she wandered over to the kitchen doorway.

Ashworth watched her closely. Her thick black hair was cut short, far too short for a woman in her middle to late thirties. The harsh style seemed to draw attention to her face which was devoid of make-up. The lines around her eyes and those running from the nose to the corners of her mouth might well have given character to the face but for her set sullen expression.

She said again, 'Yes?'

Ashworth said, 'I'm making enquiries into the murder of Stella Carway.'

Just as Ashworth had decided that she was incapable of answering in anything but a monosyllable she managed to put a sentence together.

'I've never heard of her.'

'She's been all over the papers and TV.'

'I don't watch TV or read the newspapers.'

'Well,' said Ashworth, 'someone has reported seeing you getting into a car being driven by the murdered woman.'

'Then they're mistaken,' she said coolly.

'You're quite sure of that?' He showed her the photograph. 'I'd like you to be certain.'

She glanced briefly at it. 'I've never seen her before,' she said briskly.

'So whoever reported this incident to us is lying then . . . is that what you're telling me?'

'No, that's not what I'm telling you,' she flared. 'Muriel Parker thought she saw me getting into that woman's car because she's bloody demented. I have lifts from time to time, a lot of people do. She's made a mistake.'

Ashworth could well imagine Terry Parker getting on to the phone as soon as he had left, advising Susan what to say. Not that he would be overly worried on his wife's account; the fact that she might be charged with wasting police time would matter little to him, but the thought that details of his private life might be disclosed was another matter.

After a pause Ashworth said, 'You've left Volume News then.'

Susan smiled, it made her look ten years younger. 'I can see why you're a detective,' she said sarcastically. 'Yes, I left because I'd rather be on the dole than have that bloody Parker woman accusing me of having it off with her grotty husband. She was forever watching, checking up, and God knows what

47

else. So, has that answered your question? I'm a very busy person.'

'I'm sure being unemployed must be very time-consuming,' Ashworth said drolly.

Susan stepped past him and opened the front door. 'Thank you for calling,' she said crisply.

Ashworth stepped through the door and turned. He smiled sweetly. 'Thanks for your help. It's been a pleasure talking to you.'

She closed the door in his face.

His footsteps echoed as he descended the stairs. Susan Ratcliffe puzzled him; something about her did not fit. She had been rude to the point of arrogance and it was that arrogance, that show of self-importance that bothered him. Her acid 'Thank you for calling' as she showed him the door had surprised him. The Ratcliffe woman had control, authority, self-assurance, which hinted that she had known better times. Undoubtedly his wife, Sarah, would accuse him of being a snob or too set in his ways to adapt to changing times, would point out that nowadays there were many well-educated people, even some holding excellent degrees, who were packing meat in factories or working at supermarket check-outs. Intelligence and education were no longer passports to a well-paid position and secure future.

Ashworth reached the ground floor where the caretaker was using a polishing machine on the already dangerously slippery linoleum. The man looked up and switched off the machine.

'How'd it go?' he asked.

'I've got enough information to pursue my enquiries, as we say in the business.'

'Got you. So we'll be seeing you again?'

Ashworth's face was deadpan. 'I shall be around.' He tapped the side of his nose. 'Whether you see me or not depends.'

The caretaker was impressed. 'Right,' he said as he watched Ashworth leave the building.

*

The bar of the King's Arms was not being over-patronized which probably explained the barman's dour expression when Ashworth ordered half a pint of non-alcoholic lager. However, he brightened somewhat when Mike Blair said he would have a pint of ordinary lager and became positively chatty as they set out ordering lunch.

Ashworth had informed Blair of his wasted journey as they walked to the pub.

'I don't know, Mike, there's something odd about the woman, something that doesn't fit,' Ashworth said as they sat down with their drinks.

Blair studied the mask of concentration that was Ashworth's face. He was well aware of the general consensus that his ex-Guvnor was a plodder, past his sell-by date, although this was a mistake made only by people who viewed Ashworth from a distance, not by those who had worked closely with him. Even so, it was with reluctance that Blair now had to admit that the six months spent away from the great man allowed him to view Ashworth objectively and without emotion. Ashworth was a small-town copper trapped in a town that had been expanding for the last twenty years and where the crime rate was only now beginning to reflect the national average. Ashworth was in grave danger of being swamped by the growing tide of lawlessness.

'Not much we can do about not fitting in nowadays,' Blair said gently as he took the head off his lager.

Ashworth sipped his non-alcoholic drink. He had heard some of his colleagues put forward the opinion that this stuff would have been better left inside the horse and although the choice of words was not his own he entirely agreed with the sentiment.

He put the glass back on the table. 'Well, the woman's on the dodge and there has to be some explanation for that.'

'I'd have great difficulty convincing my Guvnor of that. She's only left her job, after all.'

Ashworth chuckled. 'Ah, Stonewall Maris never did possess an imagination.'

Blair laughed as the barman served lunch. Ashworth had

49

chosen a dubious ham salad and as this was put before him he eyed Blair's two cheeseburgers with envy.

'He speaks well of you too,' Blair said as he unfolded a paper napkin.

'Yes, I bet he does,' Ashworth commented drily.

Blair bit into a burger. 'What is it with you two anyway?' he asked as he wiped grease from his chin.

'Long story. Goes back a long way.' Ashworth stabbed a piece of lettuce with his fork as he watched Blair take another mouthwatering bite. For quite a few years now Ashworth's waistline and digestive system had refused to tolerate excesses of any kind so he munched his lettuce and tried to comfort himself with the fact that it was nutritious.

Blair viewed Ashworth's crestfallen expression. He knew what was coming and dreaded it. He tried to think of a topic of conversation and had indeed started to talk about the English cricket tour in India when Ashworth interrupted him.

'You couldn't spare me a couple of your people, could you, Mike? Just for surveillance?'

'Come on, Jim,' Blair pleaded. 'Maris would chew my balls off if he knew I was helping you and I haven't got enough people for my own enquiries.'

'No, you come on, Mike, you owe me a few favours.'

'Calling in favours is blackmail, Jim.'

'Yes,' Ashworth agreed resolutely. 'You know I wouldn't ask you if I could bring my own people in but Maris would block me and this is important.'

Blair relented. 'All right, but I can't get involved in this officially. I'll get a couple of officers to put in some unpaid overtime.'

'Good man.' Ashworth leaned over and patted Blair's arm.

'What do you want us to do?'

'Just watch.' Ashworth sipped his lager and pulled a face. 'She'll move from that flat today or tomorrow. I just want to know where she goes.'

Blair sighed. 'How do I let myself get talked into these things?'

'It's that junk food,' Ashworth beamed as he waved his fork. 'Slows the brain down, that's a well-known fact.'

5

Ashworth made it back to Bridgetown police station with just fifteen minutes to spare before Steven Carway's interview. His mood was terse as he and Turner sat in the office exchanging the results of their morning's work. He skipped briefly over his own abortive mission but listened attentively as Turner disclosed what he had learned from the industrious Mr Baldwin.

At a few minutes before three o'clock a WPC announced that Steven Carway and another gentleman were waiting to see them.

They were shown into the office. Carway was immaculate in a light grey crisp suit, white shirt and red striped tie. If he was finding the aftermath of his wife's murder traumatic he was certainly not betraying the fact either in manner or in appearance. His hair was perfectly groomed, his eyes bright and shining.

Ashworth recognized the other man immediately as George Gallford, senior partner of Gallford and Tower, Solicitors. He was a man in his sixties, balding, and – compared to Carway – rather seedy in appearance.

The usual pleasantries were exchanged, offers of tea or coffee refused and the four men sat down, Ashworth and Turner on one side of the desk, Carway and Gallford facing them.

Gallford cleared his throat. 'As Mr Carway's solicitor, I trust you have no objections to my sitting in on this interview?'

Ashworth was watching Carway, who sat perfectly relaxed, lips pursed, fingertips pressed together as if listening to a carefully rehearsed speech. 'None at all,' he said. 'I don't feel it's necessary but I certainly don't have objections.'

'Good.' Gallford cleared his throat again. 'You see, my client

51

does feel that there are certain aspects of the unfortunate matter which could portray him in a bad light so we feel they would be better cleared up from the beginning.'

Ashworth and Turner looked at each other; both had substituted 'guilty light' for 'bad light'.

'So,' Gallford continued, 'I'll hand you over to Mr Carway if I may and I shall, of course, interrupt if I feel that would be beneficial to my client.'

'Surely,' said Ashworth, turning his attention to Carway. 'Now, sir, what is it you'd like to tell us?'

Carway looked supremely confident as he said, 'Well, the first thing is, I didn't get on with my wife.'

'Was there any single reason for that, sir?' Ashworth enquired.

A bitter smile touched Carway's lips. 'Yes. She was a cow . . . simple as that.'

Gallford gave him a reproachful look as he jumped in with, 'What my client means is that his late wife indulged in many sexual affairs during their marriage and this caused my client considerable distress.'

'Yes, I see. Thank you for that clarification,' Ashworth said. 'Mr Carway?'

'She had affair after affair. I mean, it didn't matter to me but you could well construe it as a reason for my wanting to kill her.'

'Stranger things have been known, sir, but please continue.'

'It had settled into a way of life with us. We lived under the same roof but that's as far as it went. I did stipulate . . .' His laugh was bitter. '. . . that she was not to have men in the house. The last vestige for the cuckolded husband . . . to make sure the neighbours didn't know.'

'You're aware that she broke the agreement?' Ashworth said.

Carway sighed. 'Many times, I've no doubt, but I didn't kill her, Inspector, I really didn't.'

'You often spent the night at Bridgenorton, sir,' Turner interjected.

'My, you've been digging already,' Carway said with a smile.

'That's what we're paid to do,' Turner snapped.

Carway exchanged a look with Gallford. The solicitor gave him a slight nod and Carway continued to speak. 'Yes, I often stay over at the Coachman's Hotel and, as you undoubtedly already know, I hire girls from an escort agency.'

'Ladies of the night,' Ashworth interrupted.

Turner almost laughed at his superior's old-fashioned terminology; Carway did and there was still a slight chuckle in his voice as he said, 'A man has needs, Inspector, and to me it seems a harmless way of fulfilling those needs.'

'But then things changed, didn't they?' Ashworth said lightly.

Carway was completely thrown by the remark; there was desperation and something akin to panic in the glance he cast at Gallford.

The small slight solicitor tried to regain control. 'Yes, things did change, Inspector. My client formed a relationship with a young lady in his employ . . .'

'And in forming a relationship, he also formed the eternal triangle.' Ashworth drew a triangle on his blotter.

'That is exactly the interpretation my client thought you would put on it. That is why he wants to co-operate with you and clear this whole matter up.'

'I had asked Stella for a divorce, Inspector, and she had agreed.'

'Had proceedings begun?' Ashworth looked at both men, unsure as to whom he should direct the question.

Gallford answered. 'Not as such. However, matters had been put in my hands. And Mrs Carway had agreed, I can vouch for that.'

'Yes, I bet you can,' Ashworth said thoughtfully. 'So, Mr Carway, all you had to lose was half of everything you own. That could be a good motive for murder.'

'No, no.' Carway's voice was raised. He placed his hand over his eyes.

'My client would have lost nothing, Inspector. He and Mrs Carway signed a document before their wedding. In effect, that document stated that in the instance of a divorce neither party had claim to the other's money or properties,' Gallford concluded triumphantly.

Ashworth's manner was dry. 'How romantic. And did your wife have any money or property of her own, Mr Carway?'

'No, she didn't.' The solicitor attempted to interrupt. 'Let me speak, George,' Carway said impatiently. 'My wife had milked some two hundred thousand pounds out of our joint account but that didn't matter to me. I just wanted to get rid of her . . .' His voice trailed off as he realized the implications of that remark. 'But I didn't kill her,' he finished lamely.

'On the night of your wife's death,' Ashworth attacked, 'you were alone at the Coachman's Hotel.'

'Yes, I was.'

'Yet on every other occasion that you stayed there – and remember we're talking about a two-year period here – you had female company. Why not this time?'

'Simply because Carol, my girlfriend, couldn't make it. Her parents were coming to stay. She couldn't very well say, I'll be out tonight . . . I'm sleeping with my boss.'

'Yes, we can see the young lady's dilemma,' Turner remarked. 'So, perhaps you'd like to tell us about your movements that night.'

'I had dinner with David Easeman. We were doing a deal. I had rather too much to drink so when I got to the hotel I went straight to my room.'

'You had too much to drink and yet you still drove back to the hotel?' Turner persisted.

'No, David Easeman drove me, in my own car so that it would be at the hotel in the morning,' Carway explained patiently.

'And you went straight to bed?'

'No, Sergeant, you know full well I didn't. I sobered up a little so I ordered a drink from room service.'

'Thank you, sir, I think that will be all for the moment. Of course, we shall be wanting to see you again,' Ashworth said briskly.

The chief inspector's abrupt way of concluding the interview surprised Turner. Carway and Gallford rose to leave; both looked relieved that the interview had been terminated.

54

They had reached the door when Ashworth spoke again. 'Mr Carway.'

Carway turned, his face now slightly drawn and pale. 'Yes?'

'Tell me, have you any record of the mileage of your late wife's car?'

Carway looked puzzled. 'I don't think so.'

'So you've no way of knowing if the mileage increased greatly over the last two months?'

'No.' A thought came to him. 'Well, she did have it serviced recently and you know how they always put the mileage on the invoice. I could try to find it for you if it would help.'

'It would, sir – thank you for that and for coming in. My sergeant will show you out.'

When Turner returned he found Ashworth deep in thought. 'Well, sir, that looks like our murderer to me.'

'No.' Ashworth slowly shook his head then repeated, 'No. The man's too methodical, even to the point of bringing his solicitor here.'

'That could suggest guilt,' Turner replied stubbornly.

'It could, but to my mind if Steven Carway planned to murder his wife he'd do it in such a way that no one could possibly suspect him. As it is, all paths lead to him. So much so, in fact, that he'd have had to plan it that way.'

'Could well have done, sir,' Turner said. He strongly suspected Carway and was not letting go easily.

Ashworth said, 'Look, it's a simple murder – not at all complex. And you know as well as I do we just haven't got a motive.'

'But we've got enough to bring him in for further questioning,' Turner persisted.

'We have, but where would that get us? He'd request his solicitor and all we've got is circumstantial evidence.'

'Plenty of cases come to trial on circumstantial evidence, sir.'

'And a lot are thrown out of court. I mean, look at us, Owen . . . you think he's guilty, I think he's innocent. Don't you think a jury would be just as divided?'

'But say he got away with it . . .'

'Oh, come on, Owen,' Ashworth said, his smile telling Turner that his theory had fallen on stony ground. 'We're engaged in detective work here, not flights of fancy. What would his odds be of getting away with it? Fifty/fifty? Not good when you're gambling with your liberty. Add to that, the man would need nerves of steel to carry it off and believe me, for all his smooth polish, Carway hasn't got them. He'd go to pieces under pressure.'

WPC Kerrie Stacey interrupted what was fast becoming an argument. She was pretty, mid-twenties, five feet nine, with short dark hair. As Ashworth answered her knock with, 'Come', she entered the office carrying a tray holding three mugs of tea.

'Ah, Kerrie, thank you for bringing the tea.' Ashworth rose from his chair as she placed the tray before him. 'I asked you to bring it up,' he said, 'because I want a woman's angle on something.'

'Yes, sir.'

'Sit down, you know you don't have to stand on ceremony with us. The third cup's for you.'

Ashworth sat down again, reached for his tea and set about piling sugar into it. He said, 'Now, Kerrie, you're familiar with Stella Carway's sex life.'

'Yes, sir, it would seem that the woman did have a lot of affairs.'

'I want to try and get inside her mind if I can, find out what made her behave the way she did.' Ashworth chuckled. 'Of course, in my day it was different, sex was linked to marriage. Things have certainly changed since then.'

Kerrie looked at Turner and blushed. Ashworth assumed that she was embarrassed about discussing the subject in the presence of someone near her own age.

Kerrie cast her large dark eyes downwards as she said, 'I don't think things have changed so much, sir. I think most women are still looking for a relationship.'

Ashworth interrupted. 'A relationship meaning – to use what now seems to be an old-fashioned word – love.'

Kerry nodded. 'The woman would have to love the man and she would hope . . .' She looked again at Turner. '. . . that he loved her.'

'Things haven't changed that much then,' Ashworth said with a grin.

Kerrie went on. 'There are undoubtedly women like Stella Carway, probably always have been, but what makes them tick I don't know.'

'That's the problem,' Ashworth said as he leaned back in his chair, hands behind his head. 'I just don't feel I know Stella Carway yet. If I could only find out what motivated her, what she wanted from life, then I could establish who would have suffered the most harm if she attained those goals.'

'Her husband, sir,' Turner interjected. 'It still all points to him. Stella wanted a comfortable life-style and divorce would not have provided that so I reckon she refused to give him one.'

'Maybe,' Ashworth mused.

The WPC drained her cup and stood up. Ashworth smiled. 'Thank you, Kerrie,' he said. 'Sorry I embarrassed you.'

6

That evening Ashworth parked the Sierra on the gravel drive outside his house. It was six o'clock and a full moon hung on the horizon like a pale silvery balloon. It illuminated the front garden sufficiently to remind him that he had not yet pruned the roses.

As he opened the front door the warmth of the hall hit him. He looked around as he took off his topcoat and hung it in the cloakroom.

He and Sarah had fallen in love with the house the moment they had seen it. Was that really twenty years ago? They had at the time two very fast-growing children and the large four-bedroomed detached house was exactly what they had been looking for. Ashworth smiled as he remembered the trauma of the house purchase. 'It's a buyer's market,' the solicitor had said. However, by completion date they had come to realize that buyer's or seller's markets made little difference to the nervous breakdown territory to which moving house invariably transports one.

It had taken a couple of years to do the place up and very little had been changed since. The kitchen had been updated; Ashworth had fitted the units himself but had left the plumbing and hob installation to more expert hands on the insistence of his wife.

Of course, with the children now grown and flown from the nest the house was far too large but neither he nor his wife could bear the thought of moving for they were now part of the house and it part of them.

Sarah came from the kitchen when she heard him. Ashworth felt the usual surge of warmth at the sight of her but somehow this evening it was more intense. Undoubtedly the things he had learned about the Carways' marriage had made him especially thankful for his solid secure base.

Sarah's smile was warm as he kissed her lightly on the lips.

'Dinner's cooking. Should be ready for seven.'

Sarah had never been a beautiful woman but middle age had lent her an elegant handsomeness. She wore a tweed skirt and green jumper, the colour of which matched her eyes exactly. The grey flecks in her short hair added distinction to her appearance rather than years.

The way Ashworth shunned the newspaper, leaving it lying on the hall table, and the way he made small talk as they walked to the lounge indicated to Sarah that her man was deeply troubled.

Three miles away in Birch Avenue, Karen Turner was also aware that her man was deeply troubled; he had been for weeks now.

They were upstairs in the master bedroom which looked out on to the tree-lined avenue.

'All I'm saying,' Karen said from her seat in front of the

dressing-table, 'is that the bloody storage heater in the lounge isn't working properly.'

Turner rounded on her. 'Look,' he said, 'it's a rented house and I'm not going to the expense of getting people in to look at this and that when we're not staying.'

'Oh, and in the mean time your children can go cold. Is that what you're saying?'

'The kids aren't going cold, for God's sake,' he flared back. 'Why do you have to exaggerate everything?'

'Perhaps because I'm in it all day and you're not,' she replied bitterly. 'Next door's TV coming through the wall all the time . . .'

'For God's sake, stop moaning.' Turner picked up his jacket and stormed out of the bedroom, resisting the urge to slam the door for fear of waking the children.

Karen turned her attention back to the mirror. She was pretty, three years younger than her husband, blonde hair cut and shaped in the latest fluffy style; her usually clear blue eyes were now slightly clouded by held-back tears.

Familiarity, the very act of seeing someone every day, of waking up next to that person each morning, had, no doubt, dulled Turner's awareness of his wife's attractiveness. However, at the age of thirty-two and despite having had two children she could still draw wolf-whistles from men in the street.

Morosely she rose from the stool and began to dress. Knowing Jim and Sarah Ashworth disliked formality she had elected to wear a blue skirt and a figure-hugging white top. She really did not know how she was going to get through this evening. For so many weeks now it had been like this, the sudden flare-ups over trivial things followed by days and nights of long stony silences. Her whole world seemed to be falling apart around her.

Turner put his head round the bedroom door. 'What time's the baby-sitter due?' he asked gruffly.

The ring of the door bell answered his question.

*

The dinner did in fact go quite well. People have a way of forgetting their problems – perhaps being forced by good manners to do so – when in the company of others.

The roast lamb was superb, the crêpes Suzette divine. Sarah, always the perfect hostess, looked slightly embarrassed at the praise being heaped upon her culinary skills, all the time confessing that it was far from her best.

The men retired to the study and Karen insisted that she help with the washing-up, knowing how awful it is to wake up to a sinkful of dishes.

When the dish-mop had been round several plates Sarah asked the question that had been on her mind all evening. 'Is everything all right, Karen?'

Karen paused as she dried a dinner plate. 'Yes, fine.' She smiled. 'Why do you ask?'

'It's just that you and Owen seem a little tense with each other.'

'We're just going through a bad patch, I suppose. What with trying to find a house and everything . . .' She averted her eyes and busied herself with the tea towel, rubbing the plate with such force that Sarah wondered if her intention was to remove the pattern.

'Sorry, Karen, I didn't mean to pry.'

Suddenly, tears brimmed in Karen's eyes, threatening to spill over on to her cheeks. 'You're not, Sarah, it's just that I'm so unhappy. I don't know if it's my fault or Owen's but it's all going wrong.'

'There, there,' Sarah soothed, immediately abandoning the washing-up to pour two sherries.

When they were seated at the kitchen table Karen was ready to open the floodgates and allow her troubles to flow out. 'It just seems everything I do is wrong. I know I go on about getting a house of our own . . . but surely that's normal.'

'Yes, it is,' Sarah agreed. 'But Owen is under a lot of pressure with the Carway woman's murder.'

'That's just it,' Karen said vehemently. 'Why can't he leave all that behind when he comes home, devote some time to the kids and me?'

Sarah had no answer. She had seen the police force wreck many seemingly rock-solid marriages. Of course, the long irregular hours were part of the problem but there was far more to it than that. The very qualities that went to make a good detective could ruin a marriage.

Her own husband was obsessed with work; this was something she had come to acknowledge early on in their marriage. Every piece of every case had to fit into place like some giant jigsaw puzzle before he was satisfied. Solving the crime was not enough, he had to know exactly why it took place. At times this made him difficult to live with. Policemen's wives are born, not made: Sarah had realized that fact a long time ago.

Karen looked up and asked the question that was the real cause of her concern. 'You don't think he's got another woman, do you?'

'I'm sure he hasn't. Owen would never do a thing like that.' Sarah just hoped that she was right.

The study was Ashworth's room. Its original title, fourth bedroom, had long been forgotten.

The solid mahogany desk which had been there for nearly twenty years was so positioned that when he sat in his leather captain's chair Ashworth was afforded a view of the large rear garden with its extensive lawns surrounded by borders crammed with rose bushes and, in summer, French marigolds and *Lobelia erinus*. In the centre of the lawn stood a lilac tree, its trunk old and gnarled with age, yet every spring its boughs were adorned with sweetly perfumed sprays of purple flowers.

The garden was of a size that made it a joy in spring when nature breathed new life into the suspended animation of her cycle. But as spring rolled gently into summer the constant attention it required to retain any semblance of order would bring forth Ashworth's oft-made threat . . . pave the whole damned lot and fill it with potted flowers! It was a threat which, over the years, Sarah had resolutely resisted.

However, on this cold winter's evening – for winter had arrived early this year – the red velvet curtains were drawn across the study windows. The central heating kept the room warm and snug, the wall lights cast shadows around the room.

Ashworth poured malt whisky into two tumblers and topped them up with soda water.

'Well, what have you got, Owen?' he asked as he sank into his chair, passing his sergeant the drink.

Turner sat facing him in another leather chair which, although not as luxurious as Ashworth's, was extremely comfortable. He was noticeably more relaxed here than in the office environment.

'After our interview with Carway I made some enquiries,' he stated, sipping his drink. 'I established that the party Stella Carway had held on the afternoon before her death was a meeting of a local drama group she had once belonged to . . .'

'Once belonged to? Why the party then?'

'They say she was thinking of rejoining.'

As Ashworth watched Turner pause to sip his drink he said, 'You're certain Steven Carway's guilty, aren't you?'

'One hundred per cent. The man's lying through his teeth.'

'He's lying all right,' Ashworth agreed. 'At least about one thing, but that doesn't mean he murdered his wife. Quite the contrary, in fact.' Ashworth savoured his scotch, enjoying the warm path it weaved down to his stomach. 'What did you get from the drama group people?'

'Very little really. I spoke to the secretary on the phone. You know how these theatricals are. The woman only seemed interested in whether Mrs Carway could act, which apparently she couldn't. Anyway, I'm seeing her tomorrow.'

'Good, and what else?' Ashworth laughed. 'Come on, I can tell by your expression you've got something you think is going to startle me.'

'Yes, well I have, sir.'

'For goodness sake, Owen, call me Jim. We've been working together now for six months.'

'Okay, Jim.' Turner could hardly contain himself, he had been waiting all evening to convey this information. 'As you know, Karen and I are looking to buy a house which has brought me into contact with solicitors. Well, to cut a long story short, I've had a word with one who deals in divorce cases and he's told me that these marriage contract things aren't worth the paper they're written on.'

'Go on.'

'Even the pop stars and movie people don't get out of marriage scot-free,' Turner continued earnestly. 'They sign these contracts, you see, but that only gives them a point at which to start negotiating.'

Ashworth's expression indicated that he was interested.

'The husband goes to the wife and says he wants a divorce. The wife refuses point-blank and sets the lawyers in motion. What they do, more or less, is allow the husband to buy a divorce.'

'And what if he won't? What if he simply invokes the agreement?'

'That means that the only way he can get a divorce is to move out of the house and wait. So the very least the wife can walk away with is the marital home.'

'All well and good . . .' Ashworth stood up, indicating Turner's empty glass which was passed to him. '. . . but what would Carway's house be worth in today's market? Eighty thousand? A man like Steven Carway would write that off. Mind you, I did wonder why he lived in The Crescent when he could afford a property costing four times as much. Anyway, don't forget Stella had already siphoned off two hundred thousand pounds.'

The scotch gurgled into the glasses; Ashworth added soda and returned to his chair.

A rather crestfallen Turner said, 'You said Carway was lying earlier on . . . lying about what?'

'He's lying all right, about the two hundred thousand pounds.' Ashworth leaned forward. 'Look at it this way, everything Sarah and I have is in joint names – fair enough, we trust each other – but a man like Carway who felt he had to have a financial get-out clause before he even married the woman . . .' He shook his head and sat back. 'Well, it doesn't make any sense. That their current account with perhaps two hundred thousand in it would be in joint names is ludicrous. Now, a large sum on deposit, that's possible.'

'So you think Carway lied about the money.'

'I know he did.' Turner seemed perplexed. Ashworth expanded on his theory. 'Stella Carway took the money all right, but not from some joint account . . . she stole it.'

'Then why didn't Carway just tell us that?'

'Because it would provide us with the one thing we haven't got. Motive.'

'Then why tell us at all?' Turner asked before draining his glass.

'Simple. Just in case it came to light sooner or later – he probably hoped that because he'd told us half the truth it wouldn't be investigated further.'

'Not very clever.'

'I agree, but it does rather dent your portrayal of him as a cold-blooded killer who'd thought of everything. Rather unlikely, I'd say.'

'Yes,' Turner conceded. 'But I still feel your theory about Rory James is just as far-fetched, and without even circumstantial evidence to back it up.'

'I couldn't agree more, Owen. Rory James is in this somewhere, I'm almost certain, but there's someone else as well, someone we haven't seen yet. And another thing I'm sure of, we haven't got an inkling yet of the real reason Stella Carway was killed.'

Ashworth was getting ready for bed, putting on the baggy cotton pyjamas that Sarah insisted upon because she liked him to have plenty of room in his night attire.

Sarah was already in bed, looking sleepy. Ashworth climbed in beside her and their lips brushed in a goodnight kiss. He was still moving about, trying to find a comfortable position, when the click of the bedside lamp plunged the room into darkness.

After a few moments' silence Sarah said, 'Jim, I think Karen and Owen are having a few problems with their marriage.'

Ashworth grunted.

'You don't think you could stop working him so hard, do you? At least until they find a house. All this evening work must be playing hell with their lives. Three evenings last week and already one this week . . .'

'I'll see what I can do,' Ashworth murmured.

In the darkness he opened his eyes, coming awake abruptly, for to his knowledge Turner had not worked an evening for over a month.

The news that greeted Turner the next morning at the station was that Chief Inspector Ashworth would be in and out all day. He was to carry on with the investigation and if he found that Stella Carway had any really close female friends, telephone their names and addresses into the station; this was one area Ashworth wanted to follow up personally.

Soon afterwards Turner was seated in the front room of No. 9, Farmview Close. The house was Victorian and smelt of damp. Mrs Phyllis Sharman, the owner, was a fussy woman somewhere in her late fifties. Her face was lined and her brown-tinted hair lifeless, but in spite of this she was heavily made-up and her smart dress had obviously been fashioned for someone years younger.

She had seated Turner in a floral armchair that must first have seen the light of day in the 1950s, while she elected to take up a theatrical pose on the matching settee.

'Stella Carway was a terrible woman, dear, just awful. No acting ability whatsoever. She was . . . how can I put it?' She pursed her lips and posed, head tilted back, selected the dagger and plunged it in. 'An exhibitionist. No feelings, you see. No sensitivity. It was all simply show.'

'Did she have any particular women friends in the group?' Turner asked and thoughts of the Art of Coarse Acting came into his mind as he watched Phyllis Sharman place her fore-finger to her pursed lips as if in deep thought.

'There was Ann Thorncroft,' she ventured after her pregnant

65

pause. 'Nice girl. Modicum of talent but lacks the dedication to ever become a real star.'

'Do you have an address for her?'

'Oh yes, dear – apart from being the group's leading lady I'm also secretary and treasurer.'

She reached behind the settee, brought out a black leather handbag which looked even older than the furniture, and rummaged about in it.

'Yes, here it is.' She passed Turner an address book. 'Look under T,' she said helpfully.

Turner flicked through the book, trying to cut out the drone of Phyllis's voice, but mercilessly the assault on his ears continued.

'These youngsters think it's all the smell of the greasepaint, the roar of the crowd. They don't know the half of it. All the hard work that goes on behind the scenes, the administration. Do you know . . .' She leaned forward. '. . . sometimes after a performance I'm still sitting here at midnight trying to balance the coffee money.'

'Yes, I'm sure,' Turner acknowledged. 'Do you know of anyone who would have wanted to see Stella Carway dead?'

'Me for one, dear. Do you know what she had the cheek to say to me?' She paused. If she noted Turner's look of dismay she paid it little attention. 'She said that for me to think of playing the part of Meg in *The Countryman's Daughter* was going beyond the bounds of poetic licence. I ask you . . . just because in the third act Meg has an affair with a man in his thirties.' She leaned forward again, a look of horror on her face. 'She said that to me at an AGM. Well, I soon pointed out to her the wealth of experience needed to play such a part and I also pointed out – and this is what completely destroyed her argument – the parts played by Joan Collins and Elizabeth Taylor who are both far older than I.' Her face took on a pleasant smile. 'Anyway, I played the part and the local paper adored my performance.' She almost sighed the words.

Taking advantage of the lull in the tirade Turner jumped in. 'Did she have any particular men friends within the group?'

Phyllis threw back her head and laughed. 'Is the Pope a Catholic, dear? Look, I don't usually gossip . . .' Her voice dropped to a stage whisper. '. . . but as this is a police enquiry I have little choice in the matter.' She hardly stopped for breath. 'There was John Faulkner. A Conservative councillor, you know. Well, he and Stella had a . . . thing. You'll want his address – it's under F in the book. Then there was Rodney Watson. Now he was a real catch for the group. Worked on a building site. I really did see that as a statement. Theatre is for all people, not just the wealthy. Lovely man. Not overly articulate, of course, but there was real talent in there some- where. He was something to do with the council as well . . . Labour, of course.' She waved her hand dismissively.

'And did he have a thing with Stella Carway?' Turner was glad her reply came in the form of a nod. 'Before or after this John Faulkner?'

'At the same time, dear. Our Stella wasn't choosy. I think she enjoyed the thought of men fighting over her.'

Turner jumped in quickly. 'And did John Faulkner and Rodney Watson fight over her?'

'Frequently, dear. I mean, they were natural enemies in any case, being from different sides of the political spectrum as it were. But when John found out Stella was seeing Rodney, oh dear, it was open warfare. I remember as if it were yesterday. John was standing in the rehearsal room. He looked so gallant. Leave Stella alone, he said, you're not good enough for her. Nice man, John,' she said, mouthing the words, 'but a terrible snob.'

'And that was the end of it? The argument, I mean?' Turner ventured.

'My goodness, no, it went on for weeks. At times you could cut the atmosphere with a knife. Right in the middle of rehearsals for *Paradise is Two People*. I can tell you, dear, I felt like calling the whole cast together and telling them I could well do without it, at that tricky stage when a play is just beginning to grow. You'll want Rodney's address, of course . . .'

'It's under W,' Turner said pointedly. He was eager to get

away now so he stood up and said, 'Thank you, Mrs Sharman, you've been a great help so I won't take up any more of your time.'

'Wait.' Phyllis jumped up; the suddenness, the agility of her movement startled Turner.

'Just for a moment there, when the light caught you as you stood, I thought that's a face that belongs in Shakespeare. Have you ever trod the boards?'

Turner explained that his job, the hours it demanded, made interests and hobbies almost impossible.

'Pity, dear, great pity.'

She followed him along the musty passage towards the front door. 'The group has so many women members but we just can't get the men. I always say I'll give my body to any good male actor who'll stay with the group.'

With some relief Turner reached the front door and turned the Yale lock. He repeated his thanks and hurried along the garden path. On reaching his car he looked back; Phyllis was waving to him, her eyes darting left and right as she took what was in effect a curtain-call for the benefit of the neighbours.

7

'What about female friends?' Ashworth barked into the car phone, waiting for a reply as he listened to paper rustling at the other end.

PC John Medway's voice rose above it. 'Ann Thorncroft, sir. Sergeant Turner did have an address for her . . .' More rustling. '22 Meadow Court, that's her home address, and she works at the Blow and Dry hairdressing salon in the high street, or she did six months ago.'

'Did?'

'Yes, sir, that's the last business address this secretary of the drama group had for Miss Thorncroft. Seems they've lost touch.' There was a hint of humour in the man's voice as he said, 'From what Sergeant Turner was saying, this secretary fancies herself as a reincarnated Mae West. I think he was thankful to get out with his honour intact.'

Ashworth felt there was a certain malicious intent behind the humour, undoubtedly brought on by Turner's lack of popularity at the station, but he let it ride. 'Okay, John.'

'Sergeant Turner did give other information when he rang in. Do you want that, sir?'

'No, it's all right, John, I'll catch up with it later.'

Ashworth replaced the receiver and peered out through the windscreen, his eyes penetrating the fog.

He was parked in the car-park of the Bull and Butcher public house, directly opposite Steven Carway's estate agency, and although it was now eleven o'clock, Carway's Mercedes was still not in its allocated parking space.

Ashworth got out and began walking the two hundred yards to the Blow and Dry salon.

The damp air was heavy with exhaust fumes discharged hours earlier by the rush-hour traffic but denied escape by the thick blanket of fog; it stung his eyes, irritated his throat as he hurried along the busy high street.

People, many with scarves wrapped around their faces, loomed out of the swirling mass, and cars with headlights dipped crawled along, adding their exhaust emissions to the problem.

The quaint old-fashioned sound of the bell above the door gave an opportunity for different smells to assail his senses: the odour of ammonia mingled with perfume and the strange smell that comes from treated hair as it is quickly dried.

The salon was large, with six wash-basins, all occupied by women at various stages of their treatment. The male intrusion into this strictly female domain did not go unnoticed by either clients or staff.

A dark-haired woman began to walk from the rear of the long narrow room which was softly lit to afford the clients a flattering view of themselves in the mirrors.

The woman was tall, perhaps a couple of inches short of six feet, slim, well proportioned; her long hair obviously received daily attention for it was immaculate.

She reached the counter where Ashworth was waiting. 'Yes, can I help you?' Her voice held both confidence and authority.

'I hope so. I'm looking for a Miss Ann Thorncroft.'

Ashworth found it impossible to avert his eyes from her own; they were large and green. He noted her flawless skin to which very little make-up had been applied.

'And who are you?' Even the slight hostility in her voice was not unpleasant.

Ashworth smiled and produced his warrant card. 'Chief Inspector Ashworth,' he replied in slightly hushed tones.

'Ah, yes.' The woman smiled, displaying white even teeth. 'I'm Ann Thorncroft.' The smile faded. 'I suppose this is about Stella.'

'Yes, madam, it is. If you could just spare me a few minutes . . .'

'Well, I'd like to . . .' The friendly open smile was back. '. . . but could you give me half an hour? I've got Mrs Wainwhite half-way through a tint and if I leave it her hair is likely to turn purple.'

'And we wouldn't want that to happen,' Ashworth laughed. 'How about making this rather unpleasant occasion a little more bearable by joining me for a drink? It should make our chat easier.'

'That's nice of you. I'll meet you in the Bull and Butcher in half an hour, shall I?'

'No, I've got a better idea. I'll call back here and escort you to the pub.'

'All right, I'd like that.'

Back in the car Ashworth checked that the Mercedes was still conspicuous by its absence – it was. He picked up the car phone and punched out a number.

A female voice interrupted the ringing tone. 'Carway's Properties. Can I help you?'

'I'd like to speak to Mr Steven Carway, please.'

'Sorry, Mr Carway's not in the office at the moment. He's out with clients. Can I get him to call you back?' This sounded like a well-rehearsed speech, delivered without much conscious thought.

'No, I'm in and out all day myself. I'll call him at home tonight.'

'I'm sorry, Mr Carway will be away on business tonight,' the mechanical voice replied.

'I'll catch him tomorrow then.'

Ashworth put down the receiver with a glow of satisfaction. Good, what he wanted was to catch Carway off guard, away from his solicitor with his carefully considered answers. The bar of the Coachman's Hotel might just afford him that opportunity. All that remained for him to do was ring Sarah and tell her he'd be a little late home tonight.

The oak-beamed lounge of the Bull and Butcher was almost empty. Two elderly gentlemen were playing dominoes at one end of the room as Ashworth steered Ann Thorncroft to a table in front of a roaring log fire.

He held the chair for her to sit. 'What can I get you to drink, Miss Thorncroft?'

'Make that Ann, will you? A vodka and tonic.'

George, the landlord, served him, making small talk about the weather as he dispensed the vodka and pulled half a pint of bitter.

When Ashworth returned to the table with the drinks Ann Thorncroft had removed her black coat; she looked good in a white roll-neck sweater and black skirt.

'Do you mind?' she asked, waving a cigarette packet and lighter as he took his seat.

'Not at all,' Ashworth said, and as the lighter clicked, 'Tell me about Stella Carway.'

Ann looked thoughtful as smoke curled from her lips. 'What do you already know?' she countered.

'Most of the people I've spoken to thought she was promiscuous, selfish, not too well-mannered, and to be honest, not many seem upset by her death.'

A smile played around Ann's lips. 'If this wasn't such a serious business I'd be tempted to make a joke about not

71

wrapping it up, giving it to me straight. No, Chief Inspector, Stella was none of those things. She was kind, sensitive. Maybe life had given her a hard outer shell but it was all a front, believe me.'

'Promiscuous?' Ashworth asked.

It had been two years since he had given up smoking but the curling smoke from Ann's cigarette warned him that the craving was still there.

'Not by today's standards, no.' Ann held his eyes with her own gaze. 'She had lovers, yes, but not to the extent you've obviously been led to believe.'

'I've been led to believe there were quite a few . . .'

Ann threw back her head and laughed; it was a deep throaty sound. 'I can see you've got old-fashioned views on these things.' She sobered somewhat. 'I don't think Stel would have taken lovers if her marriage had been happy, and believe me, she wasn't to blame for that.'

'Go on.'

Ann smiled and sipped her drink. 'I bet I'm shedding new light on this. Steven chases anything that's female. Believe me, I know from personal experience.' Her face took on a mysterious expression. 'What he wanted was for Stel to just sit at home playing the obedient little wife while he was sleeping with anyone he found willing. That's what caused all the trouble.'

Pieces of the jigsaw began to fit into place in Ashworth's mind. That was why Steven Carway wanted the marriage agreement, not because he hadn't trusted Stella, but as an instrument with which to persuade her to fit in with his life-style.

His thoughts were interrupted by the noisy entrance of a group of youths. Numbering around ten, they were dressed in leather, carrying crash helmets.

Some of the colour drained from George's face as he began to take their orders, his expression suggesting that he did not exactly welcome their custom.

The youths proceeded to look around the lounge for a victim. It was a familiar pattern, one which Ashworth recognized and knew was on the increase; they select someone and taunt them until they retaliate, getting beaten up in the process – or to use modern terminology, the victim bottles out, gets gutted then leaves, totally humiliated.

The lack of lunchtime patrons made Ann and Ashworth prime targets.

'Hello, darlin',' one of the youths shouted across. 'Brought your dad out for a drink, have ya?'

The corners of Ashworth's mouth flicked up slightly; the colour drained from Ann's face. 'Another drink?' he intoned softly and when she nodded he said, 'Excuse me.'

The youths jeered and guffawed as Ashworth stood up, impressed neither by his size nor by his formidable appearance; the mob rarely fears the individual.

Ashworth shouldered his way through the crowd. George looked relieved to see him. He said loudly, 'Ah, Chief Inspector, are you looking for a refill?'

Silence pushed over the crowd like an unfurling carpet.

'Yes, George, I am, but I really wanted to warn these young men about the dangers of drinking alcohol and then riding motor bikes.' He glanced around the group, a friendly smile on his face. 'Nasty things can happen,' he went on, 'like patrol cars in the car-park and having to blow into bags.'

Such is the psychology of the mob that as long as it retains its members it soon recovers.

One particularly obnoxious youth, obviously the leader, said, 'An' what if we don't have too much to drink but just stop here an' take the piss at you? You can't do nothin' then.'

Ashworth was still smiling. 'Oh yes I can, young man, I can think of lots of things . . . like having you for disturbing the peace, offensive behaviour . . .' Ashworth's human side took over, the tiny part that had survived the training and enforced regulations. 'And I can kick your arse all the way to the police van.'

He and the youth locked eyes. The rest of the gang, sensing that their leader was in trouble, came to his rescue. 'Come on, Vince, leave it . . . the old boy's a nutter.'

They began to make a hasty, if noisy, departure from the lounge.

When they could be heard singing in the car-park George let out a relieved breath and said, 'Thanks, Jim.'

Ashworth chuckled. Who gutted whom? he thought as George lurched into his well-known speech about things getting worse and how on a Friday and Saturday night he had to hire bouncers; whoever would have thought it could come to that?

George refused Ashworth's money, telling him the drinks were on the house.

Ashworth returned to the table, trying to keep the swagger out of his walk.

Ann smiled warmly up at him. 'You handled that really well.'

'Just a group of kids, they're not really a problem. Now, where were we?'

'You were corrupting me,' she said seductively.

'Corrupting you?'

'With lunchtime drinks.' She laughed, indicating the vodka and tonic water Ashworth was still holding.

'Yes, so I was.' He joined in her laughter as he sat down. 'So I was.'

Ashworth watched her pour the tonic into the glass; as it bubbled and fizzed his eyes appraised her. He found himself thinking what a fine-looking woman she was, mid- to late thirties but with that certain something that would always ensure she was the focus of attention. He felt embarrassed when she smiled at him, realizing she had noticed his scrutiny of her.

Ann lit another cigarette. 'Funny really, talking about Stel has brought it home to me. Before, I felt almost light-headed but it's hit me now . . . she's dead.'

'It's called shock,' Ashworth said gently. 'Now, can you tell me anything else about Stella?'

Ann's brow furrowed as she searched her memory. 'Well, something did happen about two years ago. I don't know what exactly, but I do know it changed Stel; she dropped out of everything, the drama group, our evenings out . . .'

'So for the last two years you saw very little of her?'

'I used to visit her at home but she wasn't the same. She was

74

always withdrawn, depressed, and that wasn't Stel . . .' She stubbed out her cigarette. '. . . because whatever Stel was, she was always fun to be with.'

'Something to do with her marriage?' Ashworth probed.

Ann shook her head. 'No.' Her face was a mask of concentration. 'In fact, it got worse before it got better. I went to see her – oh, it must have been around four months ago – and she was devastated; Steven had asked her for a divorce.'

'And that devastated her?'

'Oh yes, she didn't want a divorce . . . better the devil you know and all that. But then as time went on she got back to her old self . . . right back, I mean.'

'And when was that? When did the old Stella re-emerge?'

Ann took another cigarette from the packet, put it between her lips and paused. Ashworth wondered how anyone who smoked so many cigarettes could have such gleaming white teeth.

'That was about two months ago.' The cigarette lighter clicked and flamed. 'We started going out a couple of evenings a week. Stel was fond of a few vodkas. I remember her saying a few weeks ago: Ann, I've found a way out of it all . . . the answer to all my prayers. You know how people talk when they've had a few drinks.'

'What interpretation did you put on that?'

'I don't know really – that she and Steven had come to some financial arrangement over the divorce, I suppose. You know about the marriage document, I take it?'

Ashworth nodded and drained his glass. Ann, taking this as a cue, drained hers and glanced at her watch.

'Was Stella extravagant with money?'

'Not particularly. Her appearance was everything to her. She had her hair done at least twice a week. Clothes always good but middle-of-the-range stuff, that's about it. She didn't care much for possessions. Well, you've seen her car . . . eight years old. Mind you, she was always backing into something, or smashing the door into other cars when she parked.' She stubbed out the cigarette and glanced again at her watch. 'Look, I really must be going . . .'

'Of course,' Ashworth said. 'I'm being a little inconsiderate. Let me help you with your coat.'

They stood up and he helped her on with it; her expensive perfume danced in his nostrils.

After the warmth of the pub the outside air felt damper, colder than before, seemed to eat its way through their clothing and into their bones as Ashworth escorted her back to the salon; Ann hurried along beside him, attempting to keep up with his long strides.

'I shall need to see you again,' Ashworth said. 'If that won't be too much trouble.'

'Not at all. Why don't you call round one evening? I've just moved into the flat above the shop.'

Stopping outside the salon, Ann stared up into the chief inspector's eyes and just for a moment he saw the message there.

Ann asked, 'Is there anything in particular that you want me to try and remember?'

'Yes, it would be helpful if you could remember the exact time Stella became depressed.'

'Will do.' She produced a card from her pocket and wrote on it. 'This is my phone number. Just give me a ring when you want to come.' She favoured him with a smile that made his heart leap foolishly.

Ashworth watched her walk into the salon. The tinkling swinging bell had slowed before, pulling in his stomach, he walked away.

There was a certain spring in Ashworth's step as he mounted the stairs to his office. Turner was already there, sifting through a pile of papers on the desk.

Ashworth told him of his interview with Ann Thorncroft. 'The answer's there somewhere, Owen. If we can find out what caused Stella to become depressed and withdrawn we've got the key that unlocks this. What have you got?'

'Quite a lot, sir.' He recounted his talk with Phyllis Sharman. 'So, I've turned up two more of Stella's lovers. Oh, and the lab

76

report's in.' He waved a sheet of paper. 'Bill's put the time of death between eleven p.m. and one a.m. but says it's most likely to have been around eleven thirty. And door-to-door have turned up another neighbour – this one living on the opposite side of the crescent – who saw Stella Carway let Rory James out of the house at about five minutes past eleven on the night of the murder.' He glanced up to see what effect this was having on his superior. 'The witness claimed they looked . . . how did she put it?' He studied the statement. 'Very friendly . . . kissing and cuddling.'

'Stella's two lovers – who are they?'

Turner consulted his notes. 'A John Faulkner and a Rodney Watson . . .'

'Is that Councillor John Faulkner?'

'Yes, I believe it is, sir.'

Ashworth sat behind his desk, drumming his fingers restlessly on its surface. 'John Faulkner . . . well, who'd have thought it?'

'You know him, sir?'

'Oh yes, I know John. He and Sarah did a lot of charity work for Help the Aged. John Faulkner . . .' he mused, almost in wonderment. 'And what about this Rodney Watsisname? Do we know him?'

'No, sir, but it does appear that he and Councillor Faulkner almost came to blows on more than one occasion because of Stella.'

'Did they now?' Ashworth's mind dwelt for no more than seconds on how much deeper this case would take them into this maze of illicit relationships. He said, 'Leave Faulkner to me.'

'Shall I see Rodney Watson?'

'No, let's see what I can dig up first.'

Ashworth regarded his sergeant; choosing each word carefully he said, 'I'm going to see Carway tonight. I've an idea he's staying over at Bridgenorton. I thought I'd catch him off guard. Do you want to come along?'

Turner looked defensive. 'Can I give it a miss? I'd like to spend some time with the kids.'

Ashworth had to bite his tongue. What he wanted to say was: Look, whatever it is you're up to don't involve me in it . . . If I'm asked whether you're working, I'll say no. But what he did say was, 'Heard you had difficulties with the secretary of the drama group. Rumour has it you were lucky to get out of there with your clothes intact.'

Turner rose as his temper flared. 'All I said was the woman's mad. Why everybody at this bloody station has to twist everything and make me a joke . . .' He strode to the door, slamming it shut behind him.

Ashworth stared after him for a long time. 'Perhaps because of late you can't seem to take a joke,' he muttered to himself.

8

Ashworth studied the painting again. It undoubtedly represented something to its artist and to lovers of abstract art, but to him it looked as if the painter had thrown different coloured paints at the canvas then walked all over it.

'Mr Faulkner won't keep you long now,' said the pretty young receptionist, smiling at him. She then started a conversation about the weather and other such things in the rather forced manner that surfaces on these occasion. She seemed relieved when her telephone buzzed. 'Mr Faulkner's free now, sir. Do you know the way?'

Ashworth assured her that he did and told her it had been nice talking with her.

The building, now converted into offices, had been built around the time Princess Victoria had ascended to the throne. Over the years it had seen many alterations with stud-partitions dividing its large rooms into many smaller ones. However, some of its original features had been retained, such as the long narrow corridors and the steep winding stairs that Ashworth was now climbing.

John Faulkner was waiting at the top of the second flight. He greeted Ashworth warmly. 'Jim, how are you? And Sarah? . . . I trust the good lady is well.'

Ashworth confirmed that they were both in the best of health as he was ushered into Faulkner's large office.

'Take a seat, Jim.' Faulkner walked round his large light-mahogany desk and settled himself into his executive chair.

Faulkner was a tall, expensively dressed man, darkly handsome. The last time Ashworth had seen him, a couple of months ago, the only hint to his approaching fiftieth birthday had been a slight greying at his temples but now this had mysteriously disappeared, leaving him easily mistakable for a man ten years younger.

'When my secretary said you wanted to see me I wondered if the police were now so highly paid that you needed an accountant to start fiddling your taxes.'

Ashworth laughed politely as he shifted his weight in the inadequate office chair. 'It's a little more delicate than that, John. I believe you knew Stella Carway.'

'Ah yes, I've been half expecting this.' Faulkner sank back into his chair, stretching his long legs beneath the desk, his wary eyes, however, betraying the relaxed attitude. 'I had an affair with Stella, yes. I don't really see why I should have to justify it,' he said before proceeding to do just that. 'I'm single and Stella's marriage had fallen apart years before I came on to the scene.'

Ashworth held up his hand. 'I'm not really interested in the moral issue.'

'No, of course you're not. So, tell me what it is you want to know.'

'I believe you had several – what shall we say? – heated arguments with a Mr Rodney Watson. Were they about Stella?'

A bitter smile touched Faulkner's lips. 'The grapevine is working well. Yes, I did have occasion to tell Watson to leave Stella alone.'

'Why? Was he making sexual advances?'

'No, no, it was deeper than that.' Faulkner's composure was now returning. 'But that did come into it. Stella had a fling with him some six months before our affair.' He bit on his lip, choosing his words. 'As far as she was concerned it was all over between them but Watson wouldn't leave her alone. I don't think it's too dramatic to say that he had some sort of hold over her. I think she was terrified of him.'

'Why do you say that?'

'Well, he kept pestering her, making coarse remarks, suggestive things. I suppose Watson thought it passed as charm but when I took exception to it and threatened to thrash him Stella became very worried and said she didn't want any trouble with him.'

'Maybe she didn't object to his advances,' Ashworth commented.

'No, no, it wasn't like that, Jim. She really was frightened of him.'

Ashworth studied the man, tried to see behind his mask of confidence. 'Tell me about Watson.'

'Watson.' Faulkner's lips almost sneered as they formed the word. 'Well, I suppose you could say he'd been Stella's "piece of rough". Worked on the building sites at the time. Stood for the council but didn't get elected.'

'You say he worked on building sites,' Ashworth said as he scribbled in a notebook.

'Yes, that's right, but he runs his own car repair business now.'

'And when did he start that, do you know?'

Faulkner pursed his lips. 'About eighteen months ago, I think.' He paused for thought. 'Yes, when I was friendly with Stella he'd been off work for about six months . . . smashed some bones in his foot or something, and he simply didn't go back.'

'He'd need money to set up a car repair business,' Ashworth mused.

'Of course,' Faulkner agreed. 'But I presume that builders make good money, and he was already doing car servicing and repairs on the side, so that must be where the capital came from.'

Ashworth changed tack. 'How long did your friendship with Stella Carway last?'

'Not long.' Faulkner sounded wistful. 'Over inside a few months. She kept going off with Watson, giving him lifts home and to be truthful Stella was a disappointment. I'd fancied her for years. I do Steven's accounts. But, I don't know, she'd changed, become really withdrawn, and she was hitting the bottle quite hard which didn't help.' He shot Ashworth a nervous look. After a moment he said, 'Jim, I will do anything I can to co-operate but does any of this need to be made public?'

'I wouldn't think so.' Ashworth watched relief flood into the man's face. 'You're not involved in the case. But I do need to clear one point up – where were you on 29th October, around eleven o'clock?'

'I anticipated that question.' And although he undoubtedly had, and just as certainly had worked out his answer, he still consulted the Filofax on his desk. 'I was at a council meeting. That finished at ten. And I can assure you I was quite capable of murder by that time; the Labour councillors had just blocked the plan for a new ring road. Can you believe that? Six hundred local jobs at risk just because the road was due to go through a field where some obscure poet had planted a tree a hundred and fifty years ago.'

Ashworth hoped that Faulkner would soon arrive at the point.

'So, I went for a drink with Raymond Simms and we worked out a plan to do a deal with the Liberal Democrats; it worked too, although we did have to promise to keep a day centre open that had been due to close.' Faulkner laughed. 'Balance of power politics are crazy, I can tell you.'

'And what time was all that over?' Ashworth asked patiently.

Faulkner's face was momentarily blank. 'Oh, the drink with Raymond? Well, we went back to his place after the pub . . . it must have been around twelve-thirty.'

Ashworth rose, glad to be free from the tight confines of the small chair. 'Well, I won't take up any more of your time, John.'

'Jim, it's been nice to see you,' Faulkner said as he came round his desk, hand extended, fixed smile usually reserved for wealthy clients on his face. 'If I can be of any further help you only have to ask.'

81

Ashworth took the warm, rather damp hand. 'There is just one point, John. You asked me if this needed to go public . . .'

'Yes?' There was a hesitant tone in Faulkner's voice.

'Well, as I've already said, as far as the police are concerned the answer's no, but when the murderer has been apprehended and the trial's over . . . well, the tabloids might just pick up on Stella Carway's bizarre sex life . . .'

Faulkner nervously bit his lip. 'Yes, I hadn't thought of that.'

'Well, goodbye, John.'

'Yes, goodbye.'

Ashworth turned before the other man could see the wicked gleam in his eye.

Turner parked the Sierra half-way along the deserted side street; ignoring advice usually given by the police he left it as far away from a street lamp as possible.

After setting the alarm he pulled up his coat collar against the damp air and began to walk, glad of the anonymity afforded to him by the fog.

It was early evening and his footsteps echoed in the dark. He was filled with an uneasy feeling, stemming from the fear of discovery which mingled with frustration brought on by Ashworth's absence for most of the day; that, and his own unreasonable behaviour when his superior had been in the office, meant there had been no opportunity to discuss the case.

He turned left into the wide well-lit main street. His footsteps quickened as he scrutinized the drivers of oncoming cars.

Suddenly his feeling of unease became more acute; he tried to quell it as he always did by telling himself, You're a policeman, for God's sake, what better excuse can you have? . . . if you're seen you can say you're going to interview someone. It had never helped in the past though and it didn't now. He never felt relaxed until he was in the flats, safely installed in the lift.

Turner listened to the metal cables grating over the pulleys as they propelled him to the third floor.

The door of flat No. 78 opened almost immediately in answer to his knock. He gave WPC Kerrie Stacey a tight smile as he stepped into the hall.

'Owen,' she breathed. 'I didn't think you were coming. How long can you stay?'

Further words were halted by his lips pressing firmly on to hers. She responded, their bodies merging as they embraced.

Terry Parker rang his wife from the Volume News shop, telling her he would be working late, would be on the telephone for most of the time to Head Office. He reminded her of the fracas she had caused two days before with the police and warned against letting her imagination run riot again. He pressed the button to terminate the call then placed two Super Snack bars between cradle and receiver to keep the phone off the hook. If Muriel phoned she would get the engaged signal.

Parker had already moved his car to the multi-storey car-park next door so now all he had to do was leave the precinct by its front entrance then, when he had finished, slip back the same way, return to the shop to replace the telephone receiver so that all would appear normal to the cleaners in the morning. Then let himself out of the side entrance where Muriel would be if she was watching him because it was the only area around the shopping centre where she could park a car and she was far too nervous to stand in the street on a cold dark night.

Foolproof. Parker's step was light as he crossed the empty shopping mall.

He arrived at Bedford Court via a maze of deserted back streets. Once there he had a dread of entering the building. On his few previous visits the bloody silly caretaker had always leered at him knowingly. On this occasion however he was pleasantly surprised; the little man was nowhere to be seen.

Parker toyed with his sparse hair before tapping on the door of flat No. 34.

The door opened a few inches.

'Terry, what the bloody hell do you want?' Susan Ratcliffe demanded.

The tone of the question made no indent on Parker's thick skin. 'Now is that any way to greet an old friend?' he grinned.

Susan swung open the door. Parker saw that she was wearing a tight pink dress which ended inches above her knees. As he edged his way into the hall he said, 'You've had your hair cut short. It suits you.' It didn't, in fact, it made her face look hard, older, but Parker felt it would be a bad tactical move to say so.

'What are you here for, Terry?'

He noticed the cases in the hall. 'You going somewhere?'

'Yes, away,' Susan stated irritably. 'I'm going to start a business a long way from this god-forsaken place.'

'A business, eh? On the proceeds of your pools win, no doubt,' Parker mocked.

'Don't be facetious.'

'Facetious? My, you were serious about improving yourself.'

Parker started to move towards the living-room but Susan blocked his path. 'Terry, you may think you're being amusing but I'm very busy . . .'

'Is this all the thanks I get for covering for you with the police?' he whined.

'What do you mean, covering for me? Your bloody wife did make a mistake.'

Parker grinned. 'Oh yes? Well, shall I just say, I didn't mention that I'd seen you with that woman quite a few times. I recall I saw you both going into a bank in the high street on more than one occasion . . .'

There was panic in Susan's eyes. Parker pushed his advantage. 'So, I thought one good turn . . . get me?'

Susan laughed in his face. 'You really are low life, Terry. You thought I'd go to bed with you . . .? I told the police all about it,' she lied. 'The woman's a friend of mine helping with the business.'

Once again Parker was reduced to begging. 'Oh come on, Sue, ask me in.'

'Piss off, Terry, before I call wifey and ask her to pick you up.'

Parker was glad that Susan slammed the door in his face; rather that than have her watch him skulking along the corridor.

Ashworth had changed his plan; instead of going to Bridgenorton at seven o'clock he went home and ate a light dinner with Sarah. He reasoned that it would be far better to catch Steven Carway after he had spent a couple of hours drinking in the hotel bar; a man deep in his cups could nearly always be relied upon to overlook discretion.

He had taken a strange delight in relaying to Sarah the news of John Faulkner's affair with Stella Carway, induced no doubt by the slight stab of jealousy he had incurred when Sarah began her charity work with Faulkner; at the time she was forever going on about what a lovely man he was and how all the women thought he was so charming.

'Heavens! John Faulkner? I don't believe you.' Sarah's mouth sagged open in disbelief.

'As God is my witness,' Ashworth replied smugly. 'Now he's worried to death in case it gets into the papers.'

'I should think he is,' Sarah said, visibly shocked.

'Look, why don't you come along with me this evening? We haven't been out for ages.'

'Yes, I'd like that,' Sarah said as she carried the dirty dishes through to the kitchen.

Now it was nine o'clock and the car was crawling along winding country lanes. Fog swirled in front of the windscreen; the dipped headlights just about picked out the ghostlike outlines of tall hedges bordering the fields as Ashworth steered the car round a bend in the road.

Thirty yards ahead red brake lights glowed through the fog as traffic waited by the lights at the main junction of Bridgenorton's high street.

The bar of the Coachman's Hotel was warm, snug, and many of the town's residents had sought out its warmth and hospitality this particular evening.

Ashworth chose a small empty table in a corner before going

to order drinks at the dark-wood bar festooned with horsebrasses.

As it was a busy evening Baldwin was having to help out behind the bar. He hurried forward to serve Ashworth. As he got ready the half of lager and sweet sherry he babbled on about the approaching festive season.

Ashworth made polite replies as he scanned the room. Finally he came upon Carway, who had his back to him. He was in the middle of a group; a girl clung to his arm and even in profile her face flashed jealousy whenever Carway paid attention to other women in the group.

Ashworth took the drinks and joined Sarah, discreetly pointing out Carway as he sat down. 'Not behaving much like a man who just lost his wife in tragic circumstances, is he?'

'No,' Sarah agreed. 'And if that's his girlfriend with him, I'd say she doesn't trust him as far as she can see him.'

They watched as Carway drained the remaining scotch from his glass. His face travelled around the group, obviously asking what they would like to drink. This task completed he turned round and looked straight at Ashworth. The smile froze on his face. He whispered something to the girl; she too turned and looked towards Ashworth as Carway disentangled himself from her arm and walked towards their table.

'Chief Inspector, I'm surprised to see you here. Can I buy you a drink?'

'No thanks, we've just got these. I don't think you've met my wife, Sarah, have you?'

'Mrs Ashworth.' Carway inclined his head slightly before returning his attention to the chief inspector. 'Rather a long way to drive on an evening like this just for a drink.' Although he was carrying it well, it was obvious he had consumed quite an amount. 'I shall think you're beginning to hound me if you're not careful.'

'Now why would I do that, Mr Carway? You're beginning to develop a persecution complex.' Ashworth gave him a tight smile. 'But since I have run into you I might as well ask if you've found the service records for your late wife's car.'

'Yes, yes, I have. They're at my office.'

'That's good, sir. I'll get someone to call round for them tomorrow. Now, I'm sure we don't want to keep you from your friends . . .'

Without speaking Carway turned away.

'Oh, there's just one other thing, Mr Carway.'

Carway turned back, an angry expression on his face.

Ashworth ignored it. 'It's about the two hundred thousand pounds you allege your late wife took from your joint account. I'd like a detailed explanation of how that happened. It's not urgent but I would appreciate it during the next few days.'

Carway said, 'Chief Inspector. Mrs Ashworth.'

They watched him return to his friends, once again linking arms with the girl. She turned her head and studied Ashworth until Carway said something to her and she turned back.

Ashworth picked up his glass. 'Right, Sarah, I fancy a couple of malts before bed and I don't think getting breathalysed would look good on my records.'

'I agree with Steven Carway . . . it was a long way to drive just for a drink.'

Ashworth's smile was grim. 'My love, police work is often about knowing when to move. Carway now knows that wherever he is I can turn up and he also knows I don't believe his story about the money. I'll let him think on that for a time and just wait for him to make his mistakes.'

Outside a wind had whipped up; it had a chill edge to it but was helping to disperse the fog.

Ashworth took hold of Sarah's hand, their fingers intertwining. 'Do you know,' he said, 'I feel like a twenty-one-year-old tonight.'

'Well, you'll just have to make do with me,' Sarah laughed, and as Ashworth was opening the passenger door she said, 'Do you think Carway killed his wife, Jim?'

Ashworth made no reply until he was in the car, struggling with his seatbelt. 'No, I don't, in fact I know he didn't, but the lies he and others keep telling me are preventing me from finding out who did.'

*

It was nine-fifteen. Owen Turner arrived home to find his dinner steaming on top of a saucepan and Karen steaming in the lounge; next-door's television was blaring through the wall. He listened to a female voice stubbornly refusing two packets of her old washing powder, declaring her intention to stick with the new one they'd had to force on her the week before.

He took one look at Karen's face then, with a sigh, he left the house. So preoccupied was he with his thoughts that he failed to notice the fog had almost lifted. From the top of next-door's drive he could see their new double-glazed door.

Turner lifted the knocker and allowed it to fall. A few seconds later a shaft of light appeared from the lounge, the hall light came on and the door was opened by a man who tutted when he saw it was Turner standing there.

Turner kept his voice even but made no attempt to disguise the frosty hostility that he felt. 'Excuse me,' he said, 'but could you turn your television down? We can't hear ourselves think next door.'

'Who is it, Pete?' a shrill female voice asked from the lounge.

'It's next-door again,' the man said pointedly. 'If this gets much worse we'll just have to watch the picture and learn to lip read.' He slammed the door.

Back inside the house Turner could hear canned laughter from his own television which confirmed that the neighbour had complied with his request.

He went into the kitchen and took the plate from the saucepan, burning his fingers in the process. A muffled oath sprang to his lips.

Morosely he picked at the lasagne, chasing it around with his fork. He had already eaten spaghetti bolognese at Kerrie's flat and now he could feel the food sticking in his throat, steadfastly refusing to go down.

Turner knew that on this estate, as on many others, being a policeman made him a target for hostility and as he toyed with his food a little scenario went through his mind: the police had withdrawn their services and all the people who had formerly accused them of causing all the trouble in the world, now finding their properties, possessions, even their very lives at

88

risk as the rule of the jungle took hold, were begging on bended knees for the return to law and order.

Turner was an intelligent man, he knew that these flights of fancy where, in his mind, he went forth and solved all the niggling little problems contained in this world, were no more than an escape route, an attempt to steer his conscious thoughts away from the problem that now dominated his life, made his whole existence one of divided loyalties, guilt and intense desire.

He emptied what was left of his meal into the pedal bin, very quietly opened a wall unit, took out a bottle of whisky, poured a liberal measure into a tumbler and topped it up with water from the tap.

How have I got into this mess? he asked himself as he sat at the kitchen table, sipping the drink. There was nothing else for it, he now had to acknowledge that this had developed into one unholy mess.

Was it just sex? This was the question that perplexed him more than any other. No, he felt a fondness for Kerrie; a warm feeling enveloped him whenever he thought of her. However, he had to admit that his feelings for her did spring from sex.

Maybe if he'd been more sexually experienced when he had married Karen things would have been different; as it was, Karen had been a virgin until just after their engagement and he'd had only limited experience amounting to one visit to a prostitute at the age of nineteen and two unsatisfactory incidents involving a former girlfriend. So he had hardly brought a wealth of sexual knowledge to the marriage.

That old saying, you never miss what you've never had, is certainly true. But now he'd had it; Kerrie had shown him another world, one far away from mortgages, houses, bills and other mundane things. When she was beneath him, pushing back, breathing words of encouragement, nothing else mattered.

But even Kerrie had changed. Not many months ago she had been glad to see him for a few hours a week, whenever it was safe for him; now she wanted him all the time, forever saying she couldn't bear to think of him at home with *her*.

Turner felt Karen's presence, looked up to see her standing in the doorway. She stared at the glass, the bottle, then at him. Her expression said more than a hundred words could have done.

'I'm going up,' was all she said.

Damn, Turner thought, how is it she can make me feel that any sort of enjoyment I have is taking food out of the kids' mouths?

Shaking his head, he stared at the bottle and returned it to the cupboard.

Coarse laughter started to filter through the lounge wall, then the drone of the television as the volume crept back up.

Climbing the stairs, Turner felt a weariness unrelated to physical tiredness.

He could hear Karen brushing her teeth in the bathroom as he passed *en route* to the bedroom. Guilt stopped him from looking in on the children. He changed into his pyjamas and waited for Karen to finish before using the bathroom.

When he returned Karen was already in bed. He climbed in, his head hardly touching the pillow before she said, 'What's wrong, Owen? What's happening to us?'

'I just feel down.'

He felt her move and her face appeared above him. She touched his arm. 'Owen, it's been weeks . . .' She waited for some response. 'Owen?'

'I don't feel like it. I'm just too tired.'

Turner heard her exasperated sigh, felt the coldness inside her as she turned her back on him.

Her soft sobs blended in with the night sounds: the sudden rain being buffeted against the window, the hum of traffic, always louder at night, and a distant voice with an American accent telling everyone to freeze . . . this is a stick-up.

Susan Ratcliffe attempted to relax. Her left foot which was jammed down on the accelerator ached and her right foot, as it hovered over the clutch pedal, was suffering from pins and needles.

She checked the rear-view mirror. For the first time since she had left Morton the road behind was clear, but this did nothing to dispel the tight cramp of tension which persisted in her neck and shoulders. For fifty miles she had paid far more attention to the vehicles behind than she had to the road ahead, expecting at any second a nondescript pair of headlights to be accompanied by a flashing blue light and a police siren.

She had lost them. She breathed a sigh of relief. Her guilt was fuelling her imaginative powers, she knew that.

Had they really been watching her? Of course, the one who came to the flat had asked about Stella but she had explained her way out of that. There was no reason at all why the police should be looking for her. The man watching the flat and then the bed and breakfast must have been a private detective hired by Muriel Parker. If he had been police that would mean they knew something about her involvement with Stella Carway, and if they did she would have been arrested by now.

The dazzling reflection of headlights on full beam suddenly filling the mirror startled Susan, bringing a cry of fear to her dry throat. The car, its lights now dipped, was coming up fast, 200 yards, 150, 100. It slowed behind Susan's Fiesta.

Her heart was pounding as the car dropped back, pulled over to the right, drew level with her, then sped past. Its red tail-lights faded into the distance before breath rasped from her lungs.

Susan's car travelled for another mile and then a red light began flashing on the dashboard.

'Shit,' she exclaimed, slowing the car so that she could study the light. It wasn't the oil as she had at first feared, but the petrol warning. That meant she had twenty miles in which to find an all-night petrol station.

'Petrol, petrol, petrol,' she repeated. She could have kicked herself. She had been so careful, buying the car under an assumed name, hiding it in a lock-up garage; why hadn't she thought of petrol then?

A despondent feeling prevailed over her for sixteen miles before the welcoming glow of a petrol station appeared on the right-hand side of the road. Susan was not sure if the Fiesta had been converted to lead-free so she put fifteen pounds' worth of four-star into the tank.

She opened the car door and retrieved her handbag then strolled over to the cashier.

The shop was closed and the till was being manned by a bored-looking youth sitting behind a heavy wire grille, listening to an all-night radio station.

Susan took out her cheque book.

'Pass it over, love,' the youth said. 'The machine can print it, all you have to do is sign it.'

When the cheque was passed back Susan added her signature and was about to push it beneath the grille when she realized with horror that she had used her own name. With trembling fingers she crumpled the cheque and threw it into her handbag.

'I'm sorry,' she said, attempting to laugh. 'I've messed this up. Can you do another one?'

The youth's bored expression remained the same as he complied with her request.

Damn, Susan thought. Pull yourself together . . . you're no longer Susan Ratcliffe.

9

Rodney Watson turned out to be a huge man, six feet in his socks and fourteen stone of bone and muscle. He was about thirty years old, with a pleasant smile and a habit of insisting that everyone should call him Rod.

Ashworth and Turner approached his premises, situated on the north side of town. The yard was filled to capacity by the four vehicles parked on it; beyond was a garage big enough to house two cars.

Watson was sitting in the driver's seat of a battered Ford Cortina. The car door was open; he was turning the ignition key, his lips moving silently as he heaped four-letter words on to the engine that refused to roar into life.

'Mr Draper . . .' he called as they neared, 'can you park in the road? I can't get this cow started. You'll be all right, I get on well with the local fuzz.'

'That's good,' Ashworth said drily. 'We are the local fuzz.' He flashed his warrant card. 'I'm Chief Inspector Ashworth and this is Detective Sergeant Turner.'

Unperturbed, Watson nodded. 'Gents,' he said. He looked towards the heavens; a light rain had started to fall. 'Bleedin' day,' he remarked and continued turning the key.

'You'll never start it like that,' Ashworth said lightly. 'Push the pedal right down to the floor, then turn the key.'

Watson's expression was a delight to behold; undoubtedly he was on the verge of telling Ashworth to mind his own business, but quite unconsciously he had followed the suggestion, the engine fired, nearly caught, then spluttered back to silence. On the next turn the car shook and vibrated as the engine finally started.

'Well, what do you know!' he exclaimed.

Ashworth felt quite pleased with himself and it showed in his voice. 'With these old Cortinas you're likely to flood the engine, but if that little trick doesn't work, try leaving it for an hour.'

Watson's face lit up. 'I've been trying to get this thing started for days . . . had the battery on charge twice.' He ran his none-too-clean hands through his blond hair. 'What can I do for you gents?'

'Do you think we could talk inside?' Ashworth asked, indicating the rain.

'Yes,' Watson said, his hand going reluctantly to the ignition key.

Ashworth said, 'Don't worry, it'll start again, just go easy on the choke.'

Inside the garage it was spartan to say the least. There was a well in the floor, a work-bench housing the tools of Watson's trade, a kettle, a glass jar filled with tea-bags, a bottle of milk and a half-empty packet of sugar.

'It's about Stella Carway, sir,' Turner said as soon as they were out of the rain.

93

'Call me Rod, everybody does.' Watson sat on the front of the bench. 'Yes, poor old Stel.' The smile left his face. 'Bad business. If there's anything I can do, just ask.'

'You were friendly with Mrs Carway,' Ashworth commented.

'Come on . . . Chief Inspector, is it?' Ashworth nodded. 'I was bunking her up, you know that.'

'How a true poet would put it,' Ashworth retorted. He paused. 'People have told us she was frightened of you . . .'

'Frightened of me? Stel? You must be joking. Oh, hold on, I bet you've been talking to Fanny Faulkner. Well, Fanny thinks he's really something with the ladies and he just couldn't get it into that true blue skull of his that Stel preferred me. I'd offer you gents a cup of tea but being a one-man-band I've only got one mug.'

Ashworth gave Turner a look which said there was no point pursuing this line of questioning.

'That's fair enough then, Rod,' Ashworth said. 'Now tell me, you used to service Stella's car for her . . . is that correct?'

'Yes, that's right, even before I started this place . . . but it was all open and above board.'

'I'm sure it was. Now, I did notice on one of her invoices that you once did some bodywork repairs . . .'

'Yes.'

All but the most observant could well have missed the slight shock that registered in Watson's eyes; Ashworth noted its split-second presence, then it was gone.

'Stel was like a demon behind a wheel. Don't think she could get into a car without hitting something.' Watson laughed. 'I had my foot in plaster for six months and she used to give me a lift. Put years on me, it did.'

'I'm sure, Rod. Now, what were the bodywork repairs?' Ashworth persisted.

'Oh yes, that . . . Well, Stel was pulling into her drive and she pressed the accelerator instead of the brake pedal.' His feet began to follow the sequence of events. 'She hit the anchor pedal really hard then but still she went slap bang into the garage door. Now, let's see . . . new bumper, headlight, and a little bit of panel beating.'

94

'And a new garage door, I shouldn't wonder.' Ashworth interjected.

'Don't know about that . . . don't deal in them,' Watson replied cheekily but again the shock came into his eyes. 'Well, gents,' he said, sliding from the bench, 'it's been nice talking to you but I've got a living to make.'

Ashworth watched the man's face closely as he asked, 'Just one more thing, where were you on the night Stella Carway was murdered?'

'Well out of harm's way, mate,' Watson said with a grin. 'Like I told you, I had my foot in plaster for six months, dropped some scaffolding poles on it when I worked the building sites. Well, to cut a long story short, it started playing me up a bit so I had to go into hospital and that's where I was.'

'I see.' Ashworth digested the information which removed Rodney Watson from his list of subjects. 'Now, if you'll just let us have your address we'll leave you in peace.'

'Sure.' Watson pushed away from the bench. 'It's only three doors along the road . . . No. 105. When this yard came up it was just too good to miss.'

Ashworth made a mental note of the address, thanked Watson, then he and Turner left.

As they walked through the double gates into the road Ashworth glanced back. Watson was back in the old Cortina; thick black smoke was billowing from its cracked exhaust. His face broke into a huge grin as he gave them the thumbs-up and watched them depart.

Silently they walked along the street lined with terraced houses, noting No. 105 as they passed.

An awkwardness had prevailed between them through the morning due to Turner's outburst the previous day. They were still quiet as they reached the Sierra parked some thirty yards down the road and it wasn't until the car was weaving through the traffic on its way to the centre of Bridgetown that Turner spoke.

'What now, sir?'

'When we get back to the station I want to analyse those

95

service invoices. By the mileage on them it's obvious that Stella Carway did more travelling than usual during the last two months of her life.'

Back in the office Ashworth spread the invoices on top of his desk, all the while scribbling on a piece of paper.

Turner cleared his throat as he stood, ill-at-ease, in front of the desk. 'Look, sir, can I apologize for yesterday?' he asked quickly.

Ashworth looked up; so engrossed had he been in his thoughts that it took a few moments for Turner's words to register. 'No need for that, Owen. Far better forgotten.' Then, staring intently at his sergeant, he said gruffly, 'You know, Owen, if there's anything wrong and you think discussing it might help . . .'

'No, it's nothing, sir. It's just what with trying to find a house, and our neighbours don't seem able to watch their television unless it's on full blast . . . it's getting us down, that's all.'

'Well, if it's noise nuisance get the environmental health officer in to help.'

'No, it's all right.' Turner's look was bitter. 'Living on that estate and being a copper don't mix and any action I take is likely to make me even more unpopular, sir.'

'Yes,' Ashworth conceded. 'Sometimes it's a little difficult to work out why nobody loves us . . . and for God's sake, call me Jim.'

'Yes, sir . . . Jim,' Turner said awkwardly.

'One day, Owen,' Ashworth laughed. 'One day.'

It took Turner a few seconds to realize what he had said, then he too laughed and with that laughter the depression lifted off him.

Ashworth passed Turner a sheet of paper. 'Look,' he said, 'this is what I've written down.'

The paper was marked off in columns; in the left-hand column he had written STEVEN CARWAY, in the centre RORY JAMES, and in the right-hand column JOHN FAULKNER and RODNEY WATSON.

Turner studied it as Ashworth said, 'Steven Carway's our

only real suspect. Rory James . . . I'm going to see that silly young beggar this afternoon and give him a chance to get himself off the hook.' He spread his hands. 'Faulkner and our Rod both have cast-iron alibis. What did you make of Watson?'

Turner pursed his lips. 'Seemed on the level. I did notice he looked a bit shifty once or twice but I think that can be explained by the fact that when he was doing car repairs on the side he probably wasn't declaring it to the Inland Revenue.'

'Could be,' Ashworth mused. 'Anyway, I should know more about that tonight . . . I'm going to make a date with a beautiful young lady.'

Turner raised his eyebrows.

'Ann Thorncroft,' Ashworth said with a wink.

Turner laughed. 'So, you're coming round to my way of thinking, Jim . . . that we work on Carway.'

'We've got no choice,' Ashworth agreed. 'But we'll be doing it for different reasons: you to prove he did it, me to prove he didn't.'

'Get rid of our only suspect? That's clever.'

Ashworth responded to the sarcasm good-naturedly. 'Glad to see you've got your sense of humour back,' he smirked. 'Now, take a look at these.'

He pushed the service invoices across the desk. The headings on them read: ROD WATSON – CAR REPAIRS & SERVICING – YOU WON'T FIND CHEAPER!! Printed below was the address. Something about it disturbed Turner but he couldn't quite put his finger on it.

Ashworth's voice drove the thought away. 'Now, the service before last showed that Stella's car had travelled approximately two thousand miles in a year. About average for a car that's just a run-around . . . you'd agree?'

'Yes.'

'But now look at the last one, dated two weeks before the murder; the car had covered nearly five thousand miles from its last service. I've worked out that the trips the neighbour saw Stella Carway setting off on every Wednesday and Thursday must have been roughly hundred-mile round-trips. Yes?'

'Yes.' Turner sounded doubtful. 'But the annual mileage of people's cars does fluctuate.'

'Yes, I know, that's why I've worked on the maximum mileage of those trips. Right, if you draw a circle on the map and list all the places . . .'

'That's a lot of territory.'

Ashworth grinned. 'Yes, well, you've got all afternoon to see to it.'

After Turner had left the office Ashworth picked up the telephone and dialled. He was still staring at the name STEVEN CARWAY on the sheet of paper when his call was answered.

'Hello?' a pleasant but impatient voice said.

'Could I speak to Ann Thorncroft, please?'

'You're doing that.'

'Hello, Ann, this is Jim Ashworth. We met – '

'Jim, of course, I remember.' Her voice was now warm and friendly. 'How can I help?'

'I'd like to come and see you. Would this evening be convenient?'

'Of course. Let's see, the salon closes at six. Give me an hour to make myself beautiful. Will seven be all right?'

'Yes, that'll be fine. Look forward to seeing you.' There was a grin on Ashworth's face as he said, 'Bye.'

Mike Blair telephoned Ashworth ten minutes later. The call dispelled most of the elation he had felt since speaking to Ann Thorncroft.

'Sorry, Jim, we've lost her.'

'Don't worry, Mike,' Ashworth replied, trying to keep the disappointment out of his voice. 'I couldn't really expect you to keep tabs on her. What happened?'

'We really did try, Jim. I roped in another DC to help Tim Collins. She moved out of the flat as you predicted and stayed at a bed and breakfast. Tim tailed her there, watched her go in at eleven p.m. He went back at six yesterday morning but she'd gone. I'd have got back to you sooner but I've been up to my eyes in it.'

'Like I said, don't worry. If she's important she'll turn up again. Thanks, Mike, and thank Tim for me.'

The news reinforced Ashworth's suspicions that the Ratcliffe woman was somehow involved in the case. She obviously knew she was being watched and was clever enough to have got away.

But what could he do now? His harsh laugh was tinged with bitterness as he thought of the outcry that would ensue if he requested time and money to find this woman. He felt both impatience and frustration as he leant back in his chair knowing that very soon his Chief would be on the telephone demanding to know why he was taking so long in solving the case.

If the flat had not been on the twenty-third floor Ashworth would have given the lift a miss; it smelt of dried urine and graffiti covered its walls.

As the lift glided upwards he found himself staring at the aerosoled words of wisdom put there by an unknown philosopher: *Warning! I brake for cycle sluts from hell!* He wondered what it meant, if indeed it meant anything at all outside the mind of its creator.

The lift stopped surprisingly smoothly and Ashworth stepped out into the corridor, his footsteps beating a tattoo on the uncovered stone floor.

He was in the notorious high-rise known as Terror Tower. It was one of a pair, built in the 1960s, and this one was by far the worse.

After dark its dimly lit corridors and stairs became a favoured hunting ground for muggers and others who get a kick out of inflicting pain. Even rapes committed within its walls were no longer the headline-grabbing news they had been just a few years ago.

Ashworth stopped outside flat No. 630. There was neither bell nor knocker so he banged on the door with his fist. This brought no response so he banged again, harder this time.

Straining his ears he caught a muffled, 'Go away.'

There was a humorous glint in his eye as he banged a third time.

Sounds came from inside the flat, then the same voice muttered, 'Whoever you are, you're dead.'

The door swung open to reveal Rory James, dressed only in a pair of blue jeans that had obviously just been thrown on for the zip was still undone.

He scowled when he saw Ashworth. 'Jesus Christ, man, what are you bugging me for?'

'Am I to take it that you're not over-pleased to see me, Mr James?' Ashworth did not wait to be asked in.

James was indignant as Ashworth strode past him. 'Hey, where you going, man? What's going down?'

James followed Ashworth into the living-room, which was surprisingly clean and well furnished with modern pine units and two tubular steel-framed chairs with deep comfortable cushions on the seats and backs. The walls seemed freshly painted and coloured posters of James Dean, Marlon Brando, Bob Dylan and Jimmy Hendrix contrasted strongly with their stark whiteness.

All the rebels, Ashworth thought as he looked around.

James was still protesting but now in a quieter tone. 'Give me a break, I've got a happening here. I'm making music . . . you dig?'

'No, I don't dig,' Ashworth said pleasantly. 'In fact, most of the time I've got no idea what you're talking about.'

'Please.' James was almost pleading. 'I've got a bird in the bedroom. She's married and if she knows the fuzz is here . . .' His expression indicated that Ashworth should realize the effect this would have on an erring wife. 'Meet me in the café round the corner in five minutes . . . yeah? I'll answer your questions then. Come on, don't incinerate something beautiful.'

'Okay, on one condition,' Ashworth said soberly.

'Name it, man, it's yours.'

'Drop all the hip talk, will you? You sound like a lyric from one of his songs,' Ashworth quipped, stabbing a finger at the Bob Dylan poster.

*

100

The owner of the café looked up as Ashworth entered, his weathered face breaking into a broad grin. 'Jim, how you doing? What brings you to this neck of the woods?'

Ashworth searched his memory for the man's name. 'Hello, Fred. Oh, just pursuing my investigations as all the telly detectives say.'

He ordered two teas, explaining that he was meeting someone.

'Still like it strong, like when you were on the beat?'

'Just so the spoon stands up in it,' Ashworth laughed.

'Sugar?'

'Four in mine and I'm not sure about the other one.'

Fred said, 'I can't put the sugar out on the tables any more, Jim, it gets nicked . . . and the ashtrays. Wouldn't surprise me if they started carrying the tables and chairs out next.' He passed the teas to Ashworth. 'Don't know what it's coming to, I really don't. It's got so bad round here, I don't let Jean go out on her own any more. Can't you do something about it, Jim? We need more bobbies on the beat.'

This was an all-too-familiar theme with the older residents of Bridgetown, those who had known Ashworth since he was a uniformed officer. Many of them seemed to assume that he had the ear of the Home Secretary at the very least, if not that of the Prime Minister himself, in the delicate area of police funding.

He was rescued from further complaints by the appearance of Rory James. His jeans were now zipped up and he had on a thick sweatshirt, the logo of which proclaimed in large letters: NO SHIT, MAN.

They sat in the far corner of the deserted café and Ashworth studied the young man. He remembered reading somewhere that it was very difficult for a man to assess what makes other men attractive to women. This did not hold true in the case of Rory James. Ashworth could quite clearly see why women would find him attractive, with his dark skin and black hair, his body fit and well developed. As James fingered the gold sleeper in his right ear Ashworth thought that if his own daughter was still at home he would want to keep her well away from Mr Rory James.

101

'Well, Rory, it's been brought to my attention that you've been slightly less than truthful with us . . .'

He had meant about James' declaration that on the night of the murder he and Stella had made love, so he was surprised when James answered, 'Okay, so I didn't lose my job for smoking pot or seducing my pupils . . .'

'Why did you then?' Ashworth was intrigued.

James smiled. 'You really don't know, do you? I never had a job. I'm a qualified teacher who can't find a job.'

Ashworth frowned. 'So why all the stories?'

'It's all about image, man. A teacher who can't get a job suggests a loser. The way I tell it makes me a romantic figure.'

'The way you tell it could land you in a lot of trouble, young man.' Ashworth did not wait for a reply. 'We know you didn't have sex with Stella Carway on the night she was killed.'

James shuddered and inhaled deeply.

'Come on,' Ashworth coaxed.

'Look, this puts me in a bad light, man. I haven't done anything.'

'I know that.' Ashworth sipped his tea; it was so strong it bit the inside of his mouth. 'Witnesses saw Stella Carway showing you out of the house at around eleven.'

James looked relieved. 'So that means I'm in the clear?'

'Yes, so tell me what happened.'

Now certain in the knowledge that he was no longer a suspect, James began to unburden himself. 'Stella didn't invite me as I told you before. I'd been out for a drink and was passing the house. Stella's car was parked in front of the garage which meant her old man wasn't at home . . . so I thought, why not?' He shrugged his broad shoulders.

'What time was this?'

'Around ten thirty.'

'And why not? Why didn't you have sex?'

'I don't know. Stella seemed put out at seeing me. She invited me in and offered me a coffee, and that in itself was unusual because she liked a drink but that night she was stone cold sober.'

'She could have been expecting her husband home,' Ashworth ventured.

James nodded. 'She could have been but she didn't say she was. She was really on edge, uptight, she couldn't get me out of there fast enough.'

Ashworth sensed that the man was holding something back. 'What else?' he demanded.

'There was someone else in the house,' James replied.

'You saw who it was?'

James shook his head. 'No, I didn't see anyone but I heard someone moving about upstairs, just a floorboard creaking but I know there was someone up there.'

'Then what?'

'Stella kissed me goodnight and bundled me out of the front door. And some boards creaked on the landing as she was letting me out.'

'Who do you think that could have been?'

'How should I know? At the time I thought I'd disturbed something, you know . . . I felt quite uptight about that . . . and when I heard that Stella had been murdered I knew it would look bad from. . .'

'From an image point of view,' Ashworth said wryly.

James laughed. 'Hey, man, for fuzz you're not bad. What I meant was – '

Ashworth cut in again. 'What you meant was that if it came out that you'd disturbed Stella with a lover you could have been suspected of returning later and killing her in a jealous rage.'

James nodded. The rebellious arrogance was still there in his eyes and in the set of his mouth but it no longer annoyed Ashworth for he had begun to realize that James was simply a young man with more than his fair share of masculine pride.

'What was Stella wearing that night?'

'Just a dressing-gown.'

'You're sure about that?'

'Of course I'm sure. Hold on, that's just reminded me; when I stood in the hall I could smell . . .' He sat concentrating for a moment, trying to find the right words. 'It smelt like someone had taken a bath, you know, bubble bath, that sort of thing.'

Ashworth shrugged. 'Perhaps Stella had just bathed.'

'No, she hadn't. I know what Stella smelt like after a bath, I'd shared enough with her.'

'Okay then, perhaps she was about to bathe.'

'Then why didn't she either invite me to share it, like she'd done before, or tell me to piss off?'

'What do you read into that?'

As quickly as the thread between them had been formed it was broken and the ingrained resentment resurfaced in James' countenance.

'Hold on,' he said, 'you're the cat that gets fat repressing people. You earn your bread.'

The intelligent, basically nice person had vanished and Ashworth watched as James ran his finger round the rim of his untouched cup of tea.

'Rory,' Ashworth said impatiently, 'why don't you stop doing this rebel-without-a-cause bit and sort yourself out?'

James' eyes flashed hostility and the passion which burned inside him. 'Where are you coming from?' he retorted angrily. 'You've got your safe salary, nice house and big fat pension building up.' He waved his hand towards the plate glass window. 'Welcome to the real world, man.'

Through the gathering dusk Ashworth viewed the dirty littered streets, graffiti-covered buildings, the shops opposite that had been converted from old houses, their masonry crumbling, their dirt-covered façades in dire need of repointing.

James spoke vehemently. 'My dad spent his entire savings helping me through teachers' training college. I still owe money on a student loan. Three years . . . three years, man, I worked day and night to qualify and when I did . . . no job. So, how'd you expect me to feel? Should I just sit back and say nothing while politicians play Russian roulette with people's lives? Sort myself out, man? You're preaching in the wrong market-place.'

Ashworth did not answer; he had no answer. James' words had given him much food for thought.

'Am I clean, man?' James asked sullenly.

Ashworth looked at him. 'Yes, but don't change your address without telling us.'

James' chair made a harsh scraping sound on the floor as he pushed it aside.

'And thanks,' Ashworth added. 'You've been a great help.'

'Okay, top cop. Stay loose . . . and keep out of touch.' James winked, using humour to take the sting out of his last remark.

From the window Ashworth watched him vanish into the advancing cloak of darkness.

He walked slowly back to his car, which was parked in a side street. Three youths were loitering around it. One was a huge black lad with hair so closely cropped it appeared almost shaven; he was dressed in blue jeans and black leather jacket. The others were white, wearing the same 'uniform'. One had a radio of enormous proportions balanced on his shoulder and Ashworth wondered how anyone could walk under such a burden.

The black youth looked up as Ashworth approached, said something to the others and they sidled away.

Ashworth caught the strains of a pop tune he recognized as he got into the car. Different singer but the same song he had listened to almost thirty years before. He found himself thinking, These kids haven't even got their own music to rebel to, only the stuff their parents used all those years ago.

The full significance of what Rory James had told him was now beginning to sink in: the killer had been in the house when James was there, was intimate enough with Stella to be about to share a bath.

Ashworth knew that he must get Steven Carway out of the frame for Turner would, given the chance, build up such a good case against the man there would be no alternative but to charge him.

Turner was a technician, ruthlessly gathering every piece of evidence, and, once he had made up his mind that the suspect was guilty, would go to great lengths to prove his case.

Ashworth possessed the same tenacity but was motivated more by his gut instincts, his ability to get inside people's heads. He had always maintained it was possible to prove someone had or hadn't done something, guilty or not; after all, lawyers spend their whole lives doing just that.

He glanced at his watch: it was just six p.m. There was another hour yet before he was due to visit Ann Thorncroft so he decided to take a drive around the darkened country lanes in an attempt to rid himself of the numbing depression brought on by this particular part of town.

10

The Stella Carway murder investigation was the last thing on Turner's mind.

'Just for an hour,' Kerrie was pleading in hushed tones.

They were standing in a deserted corridor on the ground floor of the police station.

Turner's voice was an impatient whisper. 'I can't. Look, I've told you I can't make it every evening. You knew that from the start.'

'You could say you were working on the investigation,' Kerrie persisted.

'Again? And what if Ashworth phones me at home?' he countered.

Kerrie changed her approach. 'It's only because I love you and want to be with you.'

'I'll try to make it tomorrow.'

Kerrie's face was dismal. 'I don't know how much more of this I can take, sitting there in that empty flat, thinking about you with her.'

'There's nothing between us now . . . there hasn't been for months. Just give me some time,' he implored.

'I don't know how much more of this I can take,' Kerrie reiterated, watching his hard fixed expression before walking away.

The depressing hopeless feeling that was always with Turner of late intensified as he watched Kerrie disappear down the corridor. He knew that in the not too distant future a decision would be forced upon him. He would have to choose between the new and exciting and the settled existence that had fallen into a comfortable routine over the years.

His head pulled him one way while a more basic part of his anatomy pushed him the other.

Ashworth rang the bell and waited. The darkness behind the half-glass door became light and footfalls sounded on the uncarpeted stairs.

Ann Thorncroft opened the door. 'Hi.' Her smile was radiant. 'Come in. Sorry about the lack of carpet but I've only been in a few weeks,' she explained as Ashworth followed her up the stairs. 'So much to do.'

They entered a room at the top of the stairs; it was a large lounge, soft lighting threw shadows on to the pastel pink walls, the flickering light from the coal-effect gas fire danced on the brilliant white ceiling. The smell of paint was very much in evidence.

'As you can see, I'm still working on the place. Come through and have a look at the bedroom.'

Ashworth followed as she conducted her guided tour. Large sheets were draped over the furniture. He could make out the shape of a dressing-table, noticed the bed was a double.

The ceiling was newly painted, brilliant white, but the walls were still bare. Paint pots littered the floor, which was uncarpeted.

'I've got a slight problem here.' She brushed past him; their bodies barely touched but Ashworth felt the sensation of a light electric shock pass through him. 'See here?'

She was bending over by the window, peering at the wall below it.

Ashworth joined her, looked to where she was pointing and saw a small patch of damp coming through the wall. 'Ah, now what you've inherited here is the Bridgetown problem: a lot of the stone that came from the local quarry is very porous, it just breathes in water.'

'Oh dear, that sounds serious,' Ann said, gazing up at him intently.

107

'No, it's not really. You can get something to paint on the wall to stop it coming through.'

Even if he would not admit it to himself Ashworth was flattered that such an attractive woman should be asking his advice. 'Mind you, to do a proper job you'd need to take the plaster off and put it on the stone.'

'I've got a plasterer coming in next week to do the bathroom.'

'There you are then, no problem, I'm sure he'll be able to do it for you.'

Ann looked doubtful. 'He's only a bit of a kid . . . you don't know the name of this stuff, do you?'

'No, I don't offhand, but I tell you what I'll do, if I'm near the DIY supermarket I'll get some and you can settle up with me.'

'Oh, that is kind of you. Now, let me get you a drink.'

They went back into the lounge. 'As you can see, I'm waiting for the furnishings. All I've got at the moment is the three-piece suite.'

She invited Ashworth to sit on the deep-cushioned settee, saying, 'Now, you look like a scotch man to me.'

'Thank you. Just a small one.'

Ann excused herself and went into the kitchen. Ashworth heard cupboards being opened.

'Anything with it?' Ann called.

'Soda if you have it,' Ashworth replied.

'Can't do it. Ginger ale?'

'Thank you.'

Ashworth rose as Ann came back carrying the drinks.

'Please do sit,' she said, smiling. 'It's been years since I've met a man with such good manners.'

Ashworth took the drink and they touched glasses.

'Good health,' Ann said as she settled herself in the large armchair to face him.

Ashworth sipped the drink and found the mix to his liking. 'Did you manage to find anything that could throw light on Stella Carway's depression?'

After a moment's pause, Ann said, 'Oh, yes. Do you know, I'm enjoying your company so much I'd forgotten why you're here.' She got up. 'Excuse me again.'

108

Ashworth began to rise. Ann said, 'No, please stay seated.'

He listened as Ann searched through cupboards in the kitchen, then she returned with a brown cardboard box which she laid at Ashworth's feet.

Kneeling on the floor, she said, 'I was thinking about you all last night.'

'Oh?'

'Yes, while I sorted through all this stuff.' She smiled up at him. 'Drama group programmes.' She rifled through the box. 'I've written it all down. Here.' She passed him a piece of paper.

Her perfume wafted over Ashworth as she sat on the settee, her soft hair brushed his cheek as she leant over to point at a date she had written down.

'There,' she said. 'That was the date Stel became depressed.'

'How can you be so exact?'

'That's easy, it was during our production of *The Bleak Lake Mystery*. Stel had the lead in it and on the Monday she played a blinder, really brought the house down, but on the Tuesday it all went wrong, Stel was all over the place, missing moves, taking prompts . . .'

'What happened on Monday, after the performance?'

'We all went to the pub for a drink. Stel was with Rodney Watson at the time . . . if you take my meaning.'

Ashworth nodded.

'Rod had his foot in plaster and Stel was giving him a lift home.' She rose from the settee. 'I know it's a vile habit but I must have a cigarette.' She crossed to the fireplace and took the packet and lighter from a shelf above it.

Ever since Ashworth had given up smoking, people who still indulged in the habit annoyed him immensely; this was not the case with Ann.

Her tight sweater accentuated the curve of her breasts, the flatness of her stomach. She looked towards Ashworth as she lit the cigarette, almost as if she wanted to seek his approval.

Picking up a large ashtray she paused to collect her gin and tonic, and balancing glass, ashtray and cigarettes, she came and sat next to him on the settee. The acrid smoke burned his nostrils, causing him to blink.

Ann continued. 'Anyway, after the dreadful performance on the Tuesday Stella told us that she'd had an accident in her car the night before. She apologized for being so bad but said she was still a bit shaken.'

'Did she say anything about the incident?' Suddenly Ashworth was more interested in what Ann was saying than how she looked.

'She hit the garage door at home apparently. Got the pedals mixed up or something, that's what she said anyway.'

'And you're sure that was on the Monday?' Ashworth pressed.

'Quite, because on the Tuesday she was in Rod's car. I was feeling really down because of how the performance had gone and I saw them getting into his car. You know how some people are good with cars, can keep anything running, well, Rod's like that, but the fumes from that exhaust when Stel started the engine, it was just black smoke. Well, with these things . . .' She waved the half-smoked cigarette. 'I don't need anything else to irritate my lungs. I was coughing all night.'

Ashworth considered all this while Ann stubbed out the cigarette. 'So that's when Stella changed.'

Ann drained her glass. 'Yes, but it didn't seem like that at the time. None of the events seemed to be linked. Can I offer you another drink?'

'Better not,' Ashworth smiled. 'I'm driving.'

'Pity.' Again she stared into his eyes. 'I was beginning to enjoy myself.'

'Go on with what you were saying about linking things together.'

'Well, Stel stopped coming to the group after that production, just used to drop in from time to time after that. I suppose if I'd given it any thought – which I didn't – I'd have said it was because she couldn't get on with the secretary. And when she started calling off our evenings out I just thought she'd met someone she wanted to be with.'

'But now you see it all as linked?' Ashworth coaxed.

'Yes, I do. Looking at it in retrospect, I think it was the beginning of a very bad time for Stel.'

'What do you think of Rodney Watson?'

'Oh, he's all right . . . until he opens his mouth,' she giggled. 'No, that's not fair, I suppose he does have a certain crude charm, but he's not my type.'

'So what was a woman like Stella Carway doing with him?' Ashworth asked, bemused.

Ann laughed as she pulled her legs up beneath her, relaxing into the comfort of the settee. 'He's a big strong boy, yeh, yeh, yeh,' she replied, giving a passable impression of the ex-boxer, Henry Cooper.

They both laughed.

'No, to be honest, Stel would have been far more comfortable with someone like Rod, or that gardener chap, because she came from much the same background. She'd developed a lot of poise and polish but she came from very humble beginnings.'

'Stella came from a poor family?'

'Poor as in "hide from the rent man" poor. I suppose she always had a bit of a chip on her shoulder about it.' Ann leaned forward. 'Do you know, she couldn't stand Christmas to this very day . . .' She faltered slightly, realizing what she had said. 'She hated it. She once told me she couldn't stand it because when she was young, on Boxing Day all the other kids in the street would be out playing with their toys but she would stay in because she didn't have any. Isn't that sad?'

'Where was this? Where did Stella come from?'

'Rushmeer.'

In his mind Ashworth drew a fifty-mile circle around Bridge-town. Rushmeer was well outside its radius but he still asked the question, 'Did Stella have any family still living there?'

'Well, her parents are dead, her mother died about four years ago and her father years before that.' Ann stopped to think. 'I believe her grandmother's still alive. Look, are you sure about that other drink? The first one was some time ago, and it was only a small one.'

After a moment's hesitation Ashworth smiled. 'Yes, all right then, I'd like another.'

He followed Ann into the kitchen. 'Do you know if Stella ever visited her grandmother?'

Pouring the drinks, Ann said. 'I wouldn't have thought so. She didn't even go to her mother's funeral.'

She handed Ashworth the scotch and leant against the kitchen units, sipping her drink.

'No, I think Stel wanted to leave all that behind. I think it's the reason she married Steven in the first place.'

Ann nodded towards the lounge as the chill in the kitchen caused her to shiver.

'Of course, I'm sorry,' Ashworth said as he followed her back into the warmth.

When they were comfortably seated again, he said, 'Would you say Stella had been frightened of Rodney Watson?'

Ann's expression was incredulous. 'No way. They hadn't made a man that could frighten Stella. Mind you, she frightened a few in her time.'

Ashworth looked thoughtful. 'It's just that John Faulkner said he felt Watson was holding something over Stella.'

Ann thought about that. 'I don't know what it could have been. I know she was mad about John for a time but . . .' She shrugged.

Ashworth went on, 'John Faulkner claims that Rod had something over her and he used it to take Stella away from him.'

'Well, if he's telling the truth, there must have been something, there's no way she'd have preferred Rod to John.'

Ashworth realized that he did not want to leave, dreaded looking at his watch, so to put it off and to pretend to himself that he still had questions linked to the investigation, he asked, 'Was Stella really so attractive?'

For a second Ann was thrown by the change of subject. 'Yes, I suppose she was. When she was dressed to kill she was really stunning. Mind you, I saw her once or twice without her make-up – she really used to pile it on, full eye job, lipstick, the lot – and I'm not being catty but she was really beginning to need it.'

Ashworth picked up the sheet of paper that Ann had given to him earlier. 'So, something happened on 5th November that caused Stella's life to change from the 6th . . . that's my birthday.'

'Really?' Ann did a quick mental calculation. 'That makes you a Scorpio. Oh dear, very deep, hates to lose. I can tell a lot about you from that.'

Ashworth drained his glass as he looked at Ann. 'Tell me something about yourself. From your title I know you're unattached, but surely there's a man in your life?'

'No, I don't need a man . . . well, not as a permanent fixture.' She laughed; it was an infectious sound. 'God, that sounds awful, doesn't it? No, I'm a Cancerian, you see . . . I think with my heart.'

Ashworth did what he had been putting off for too long, he looked at his watch. It was nine thirty. He had been in this delightful woman's company for over two hours; time that had simply flown by.

He stood up rather reluctantly. 'I really must be going. Thank you for the drinks, the information, and the company.'

'Thank you,' Ann said and smiled.

She followed him down the steep flight of stairs to the front door.

At the bottom he turned. 'Thanks again.'

Ann kissed him lightly on the cheek, her lips just brushing his skin; it was the type of kiss one might give to a departing relative but it still sent a tremor through Ashworth's body.

The cold night air hit him as he opened the door and stepped out into the high street. There was a short awkward silence.

Ann broke it by saying, 'If you could remember that stuff for the damp . . .'

'I most certainly will. I'll drop it in for you.'

'I'm in most evenings.'

Ashworth had parked his car some twenty yards away. When he reached it he looked back and for some reason felt a slight pang of disappointment in seeing that Ann had gone in and closed the door.

Next morning at the station was hectic. Ashworth had ordered copies of every recorded incident that had taken place on the night of 5th November 1990, and in the early hours of the 6th. He found that it had not been a quiet night.

He and Turner combed the files. There had been a rape, at least twenty burglaries, an armed raid on an all-night petrol station carried out by a male and a female, so far without apprehension.

'Could have been them, Jim,' Turner joked. 'Bridgetown's own Bonnie and Clyde.'

'Not unless the man had his foot in plaster and limped badly,' Ashworth laughed.

Everyone at the station had noticed his good mood this morning.

'This is interesting though.' Turner drew a report from a file on his desk. 'A parked car badly damaged in Simpson Street. Owner didn't discover the damage until the morning. Red paint found on the bodywork.'

Ashworth considered the map that was drawing-pinned to one of the few parts of the wall that was not glass. 'That's interesting,' he said. 'The drama group's there. Rodney Watson lives here . . .' He traced his finger along the map. 'And Carway's house is here. So, Stella would have passed along Simpson Street before she dropped Watson off . . . and Stella's Metro is red.'

'But it doesn't make sense, Jim. The parked car was damaged, yes, but no one was hurt and yet she was said to be in such a state about it.'

'What action did we take?' Ashworth asked.

Turner studied the report. 'All local garages informed, asked to tell us of any red vehicles brought in for bodywork repairs. No reports came in, and with this little lot . . .' He pointed to the stack of files. '. . . it would hardly have been chased up.'

Ashworth sighed heavily. 'So, we have Stella's car damaged and the only motoring accident reported was that one. If she'd been involved in it there's no reason why she shouldn't have reported it – even if she'd been drunk at the time she could have done it the next morning. No, Owen, we need to know

114

what that car did hit . . . and I'd bet my pension it wasn't the garage door.'

Ashworth pushed the bell for the third time. He looked around the neat garden in front of the small council bungalow. Wintering pansies were already putting on a fair show and here and there spring bulbs could be seen shooting up, over an inch high some of them, their vibrant greens beautiful amidst the dirgeful browns of the borders, but surely to die when the first of the heavy frosts came.

Beyond the garden's low wooden fence, children were playing on mountain bikes, enjoying what little warmth there was to be had from the weak winter sunshine; they were screaming, shouting, generally creating mayhem.

When, after a couple of minutes, there was still no sign of life inside the bungalow Ashworth rapped on the door. This, at last, brought the desired result. A door opened within, shuffling feet could be heard.

'Who is it?' a timid voice asked.

'Chief Inspector Ashworth, Bridgetown CID,' he replied.

Sounds of bolts being drawn across top and bottom of the door, then it was opened gingerly.

Ashworth made his smile warm and reassuring. 'Hello, Amy,' he said.

'Hello, sir.' The little woman looked pale, frozen, even more frail than at their first meeting. She said, 'I give me statement to that sergeant of yours . . . nice young man.'

'I know that, Amy, I've just dropped by for a chat.'

'Well, you better come in then.'

She let him pass, closed the door. He followed her along the passage, his wet shoes sliding on the linoleum. They came to the living-room; its furnishings were sparse: a two-seater settee, matching chair. A car rug of loud red and green check was on the floor in front of the chair; Amy had obviously been wrapped in this before Ashworth disturbed her.

On the plain white wall, above the old-fashioned gas fire,

115

hung a print of a young boy with a tear running down his cheek.

'Bet you was ringing that bell,' Amy said. 'I'm waiting for the council to come and mend it. Like waiting for doomsday.' She tutted. 'Here, let me turn the fire up. I don't feel the cold myself but I know others do.'

Ashworth had enough sensitivity not to say anything.

Amy straightened up and faced him. 'Can I make you a cup of tea, sir? It's real tea.'

'Real tea?' Ashworth intoned.

Amy chuckled. 'That's a joke me and my Tom had. He used to say, Amy, if you ever come home with any of that synthetic tea in them little bags, or any of that cotton-wool sliced bread, I'll divorce you, girl . . . I will, I'll go and live with that Jane Russell.' Her face broke into a huge grin and her shoulders jigged with her silent chuckles.

Ashworth laughed too. 'I'll tell you what, Amy, let me come through and I'll help you make it.'

The kitchen was small – no, tiny would be a more accurate description – and icy. It housed a stainless steel sink, kept spotless, a cupboard underneath, wall unit above; a draining board on a small square of worktop and a cooker; no washing machine, no fridge even, none of the glorious conveniences of modern life.

While Amy talked him through the ritual of warming the pot, shovelling in the loose tea, adding boiling water and leaving it to mash, Ashworth's mind wandered along a path it had often taken during the last few years, since reaching his half-century: what would become of him if anything happened to Sarah? And more worrying, what would become of Sarah if anything happened to him? Would she be forced to live in a rabbit hutch of a house? Would she be able to cope with all the trivial mundane things of life that he had dealt with throughout their marriage?

He comforted himself with the thought that, hopefully, this was all a very long way into the future. Even so, he knew that over the last ten years or so the future had developed an

116

alarming tendency to accelerate towards him very quickly indeed.

'How long have you lived here, Amy?' Ashworth asked as he poured the tea through a strainer into the cups.

'Six years now. It's seven since my Tom went. It got him in the lungs.' She used the word 'it' as so many elderly people do, fearing that the very act of uttering the dreaded word 'cancer' would bring tragedy hurtling its way towards her. 'I tried to stop on in our old house but it was too big . . . too many memories as well, I can tell you.'

Ashworth let her talk, encouraged it, realizing that Amy would very rarely have someone there just to listen.

'So I moved here. Bit small but there's plenty worse off these days.'

Their tea by this time had been sugared and milked and they took it into the living-room.

Ashworth sat on the settee, Amy perched on the armchair. She was saying, 'Had to sell a lot of me furniture but I managed to keep me three-piece suite.' She took a sip of tea. 'The other chair's in the bedroom, no room in here. I couldn't bring myself to part with it 'cause it was Tom's.'

She chuckled quietly to herself, reliving memories that had once been so painful but that were now her only source of comfort.

'The times I've seen him sitting in this chair, putting the world to rights. Sitting there, he'd be, with his packet of Park Drive and a pint of home-brew. They said it was them that killed him . . . the fags, I mean, but I don't reckon it was. When them doctors said he was killing himself he soon told 'em. Going on at me, he said, for having a few fags a day . . . what about all that nuclear stuff in the atmosphere? Course, he spoke his mind, did Tom. I don't know, sir, I reckon all them politicians and doctors are pulling the wool over our eyes, I do. You can't tell me the air out there's as pure as it was when I was a girl.'

'That was a lovely cup of tea, Amy. Best I've tasted in years.' It was too.

Ashworth placed the cup and saucer on the floor beside him. 'Now, Amy, I know you're a very observant type of person and I want you to help me. Can you remember anything about Mrs Carway that you haven't already told us?'

'Like what?'

Ashworth shrugged. 'Visitors to the house? Anything which might seem insignificant to you but could mean a lot to us.'

'Well . . .' Amy's brow became even more wrinkled. 'There was them drama group people, they started coming round again. Rum lot . . . used to kiss and cuddle just saying hello. Then there was this dark-haired woman come a couple of months ago. There was something funny about her . . .'

'How do you mean, funny?' Ashworth probed.

Amy carefully put down her cup. 'Well, I'm a little bit hard of hearing. I'm all right with people like you and your sergeant, people who talk clear, but with some it all gets blurred. Anyway, this woman was saying something about children . . .'

'And why was that funny?'

''Cause madam was hanging on her every word and she couldn't stand youngsters. If she'd had that to put up with . . .' She indicated the noise filtering through from the children outside. '. . . she'd have been out there tellin' 'em to clear off. Her posh talk would soon slip when she got a paddy on her.'

Ashworth was interested. 'What did the woman look like?'

Shaking her head, Amy said, 'I didn't see her face. They was in the lounge and she had her back to me. Oh, and there was a chap – this must be going back over a year now – big, fair-haired man, looked a nasty piece of work. I remember because I let him in and his hands was all dirty, black fingernails . . .'

'Yes,' Ashworth prompted.

'Well, him and madam was arguing about money. I remember it as plain as anything. He said it wasn't enough, Stella, I'll give you till the weekend to get some more.' Ashworth digested this as Amy continued. 'Well, at the time I thought madam must be buying something from this chap, but I did think it was funny 'cause there was no shortage of money in that house.'

'And the gardener chap . . . did you see much of him with Stella?' Ashworth said.

Amy chuckled heartily. 'There was talk of hanky-panky going on between him and madam . . .' She leaned forward, lowered her voice. '. . . and if you ask me there was something going on, but I never saw it, mind, not first hand. He was a cheeky young devil. Used to call me Grandma when he first started but I soon put him straight on that. Told him he wasn't too big for a clip round the ear, I did.' She sat back, smiling. 'Still, he's not a bad lad.' She started to laugh again. 'Do you know, he told me his name's not Rory . . . it's Ralph.'

Ashworth laughed with her, then she was serious again.

'I don't know if that helps you any, sir,' she said.

Ashworth smiled. 'Yes, I think it does. Well, I'd better be off now.' As he stood up a thought came to him. 'Was the job with Stella Carway the only one you had?'

Amy sighed as she collected the tea things. 'Yes, sir, it was. Most people want somebody a bit younger than me. Like my Tom used to say, they go for youth rather than experience in this country.'

Ashworth followed her to the kitchen, stopping in the doorway. 'My wife's the President of the Women's Guild, and I think some of her members might be looking for a cleaner. Would you be interested?'

Amy's face almost glowed. 'Oh yes, sir, I would.'

'Right, I'll put it to her then.'

They walked to the front door. 'Tell me, Amy, have you any children?'

'I've got a son and a daughter. Don't see much of 'em, they've got their own lives to lead . . . can't spend much time listening to me ramblin' on.'

Ashworth thanked her and as the door closed behind him he heard the heavy bolts sliding into place.

He approached the children playing on the grass verge. One boy of around ten was riding his bike in a large circle, handlebars in the air, balancing the bike on its rear wheel. The others were shouting encouragement.

'Excuse me,' Ashworth said pleasantly. All activity ceased as the youngsters regarded him with suspicion. 'Look, there are a lot of retired people in these bungalows and I'm sure they'd appreciate a little peace and quiet. Now, don't you think it would be a good idea to go and play in the park?'

The junior acrobat with the bike piped up. 'Can't mister, our mums say we got to play outside our houses because there's a lot of perverts about.'

Some of the group giggled.

'I suppose your mothers are quite right,' Ashworth agreed. He noticed several women appearing in the doorways of the houses opposite. 'So, do you think you could keep the noise down a bit?'

'Yes, all right.'

The children resumed their games, making slightly more noise if anything. Ashworth sighed as he headed for his car.

Sergeant Turner faced Steven Carway over the desk. He had not been invited to sit down.

Before Turner had even spoken, Carway was angry. 'This is getting pretty close to harassment, you know.'

Turner's voice was even. 'Come on, sir, we do have to pursue our enquiries.'

They were in Carway's office at the rear of the estate agency.

Carway spat, 'I want my solicitor present. Anytime I talk to you people I want my solicitor there.'

'That's fine, sir,' Turner replied easily. 'Perhaps you'd like to come along to the station, phone him from there, and we'll make a day of it.'

'I'll ring him from here.' Carway picked up the telephone, confident in the knowledge that his solicitor would very quickly sort out this irritation.

Turner said, 'As you wish, sir. I'm sure he'll tell you we're perfectly within our rights to ask you to help us with our enquiries.'

Carway's eyes lost their angry glint as he contemplated a day spent at the police station. 'All right, what is it you want to know?'

'Your late wife had an accident in her car about two years ago – hit the garage door, we've been led to believe.'

Turner watched some of the colour drain from Carway's face. 'Yes . . .' He tried to sound at ease. 'I remember something like that happening.'

'So, you have a receipt, sir,' Turner concluded.

'Receipt?' Carway's eyes went to the telephone.

'Yes, sir, for the cost of repairing the damage, which must have been quite substantial.' He read from his notebook. 'New bumper, new headlight, bodywork repairs. That would have meant a lot of damage to a garage door.'

At that moment Turner was certain of Carway's guilt, he just knew it; the furtive look in the man's eyes reminded him of a trapped animal.

Carway gained some control. 'I can't be sure, it may have been the wall . . . the house wall, I mean . . . it may have been that she hit.'

Turner refused to take his eyes off the man. 'I see, sir, so what you're telling me now is you're not quite sure what it was your late wife hit; it could have been the wall or the garage door.'

'That's right. It was nearly two years ago, for Chrissake . . . and what does it matter?'

Turner went on, 'Whichever one it was, sir, the wall or the door, there would have been a lot of damage which would have necessitated costly repairs. So, somewhere there must be a receipt.'

'Yes, yes, I suppose so,' Carway muttered.

'Perhaps you'd be so good as to look it out for me, sir . . . as soon as possible.'

Turner remembered Ashworth's assessment of Carway, that he would fall apart under pressure; it was certainly proving to be accurate.

Turner applied more. 'The money you say your late wife milked from your account . . .'

121

'I don't want to make any further comments about that.' Carway was calmer now. Turner sensed that some legal advice had been given on this point. His suspicions were confirmed by Carway's next remark.

'That's not a police matter in any case. It was a joint account and one can't steal what belongs to oneself. So, I don't see any reason to discuss that with you any further.'

'Even so, we're still very interested in it. Two hundred thousand pounds is a lot of money,' Turner persisted.

Carway was more certain of himself now. He said, 'It was money that belonged to Stella and myself. I'm sure you will appreciate that if you continue to press me about it without good reason, that could be construed as harassment.'

Turner smiled grimly. 'Very well, sir. I'd like to see the receipt for the garage door repairs . . .' He paused before adding sarcastically, 'Or the wall repairs, whatever . . . that is, if you wouldn't feel too harassed by having to produce it.'

Carway said smoothly, 'I'll check with my solicitor and take his advice.'

'Thank you. Now, I'll leave you in peace,' Turner said stiffly.

All the way to the car Turner cursed himself under his breath. He'd had the man going, but then had allowed him to regain his composure. Never mind, at the station, in an interview situation, he would have to answer the questions. This thought cheered him as he got into his car.

Later in the day, at the station, Turner relayed all of this information to Ashworth.

The chief inspector looked pensive as Turner began to tell him what he had done after leaving Carway.

'I went to the house and inspected the garage door. I couldn't see any signs of repair and it matched the others in the crescent so I reckon it's the original. I also questioned the neighbours, Jim, and none of them could remember even seeing it damaged.'

'Could any of them remember seeing the damage to Stella's vehicle?' Ashworth interjected.

Turner shook his head. 'No, they couldn't remember that either. But you were right about Carway, he'll fall apart under interrogation.'

'If we ever get a chance,' Ashworth said glumly. 'I've had that solicitor of his on the phone complaining that we've been harassing his client.'

'But that's absurd, Jim,' Turner retorted.

'I know it is, Owen. I also know that George Gallford is known in the legal profession as a brilliant criminal advocate, but to me he's just the rogue's friend, knows every dodge in the book. Sometimes I think he wrote the bloody book.'

'But he can't get Carway out of answering our questions,' Turner said heatedly.

'He can, Owen, and he will.' Ashworth looked up. 'He knows we've got no real rights to investigate the joint bank account, any more than the affair with the garage door.'

'But he's lying, Jim, I know he is,' Turner pleaded passionately.

'That's as maybe, but we can't prove it. Not yet.'

'I had him on a spot, Jim, he was floundering. Now he says that Stella either crashed into the garage door or the wall of the house, and that repair work had been carried out.'

Ashworth said wearily, 'And by the time he's consulted Gallford that will have changed to: he's a man who spends a lot of time away from home . . . his wife told him she'd crashed the car, had it and the garage door repaired while he was away . . . end of story.'

The frustration inside Turner showed on his face.

Ashworth thought deeply. Finally he said, 'No, we're not going to crack Carway during interviews. I know our presence makes him feel uncomfortable so we watch and wait. Everywhere he goes, we'll turn up.' He looked at Turner. 'He's already claiming we're ruining his life, you know. Apparently, he's broken up with his girlfriend, she couldn't take the pressure. Also, he can't stand his house any more so he's moved into a flat in Bridgenorton loaned by a friend.'

'So you're beginning to agree with me about Carway's guilt,' Turner concluded.

'No, no, no,' Ashworth said heatedly. 'But what he's conceal-
ing is preventing us from getting at the truth.'

He told Turner of his interviews with Amy and Rory James.

Turner listened attentively until he had finished, then he
said, 'What do you read into all that?'

Ashworth leaned back, put his hands behind his head. 'I'll
tell you what I think happened on 5th November 1990. Stella
Carway crashed her car and I believe Rodney Watson was
blackmailing her because of it – for whatever reason. The two
hundred thousand pounds went to Watson.'

'And you think Carway knows that?'

'I'm sure he does, and he's frightened to death we'll uncover
it because it puts him slap-bang in the middle of his wife's
murder.'

'And makes him an accessory.'

Ashworth looked puzzled.

'To whatever crime his wife had committed,' Turner
explained.

Ashworth agreed. 'Yes, but I don't feel he's thinking that far
ahead just yet. No, he's preoccupied with covering this whole
thing up. It looks bad for him, you see. Stella was being
blackmailed, she was using his money to pay the blackmailer,
so remove the victim and there's no one left to blackmail.'

'How do we set about proving any of that?'

'Well, we haven't got anything . . . we don't know anything
for sure yet, so we'd better make something happen. Now, I
want a watch kept on Steven Carway, especially at that flat in
Bridgenorton. I'd better check with Harry Dawson on that one
as it's his territory.' He scribbled a note for himself. 'Also, I've
been told – against my better judgement – that I've got to give
young Kerrie a chance out of uniform, so you can take her along
with you . . . keep an eye on her.'

Ashworth did not notice the look of apprehension on Turner's
face, he was too busy thinking this through. 'Owen, I want you
and Kerrie to work closely on this one. I appreciate that this
could put a strain on your home life . . .' He was careful to put
this delicately. '. . . because there'll be a lot of night work.'

Turner said quickly, 'That's all right, Jim. Karen's been talking about taking the kids and staying with her sister.'

'Good,' Ashworth said. 'So, from tomorrow I want you and Kerrie to keep an eye on Carway.'

Turner felt as if a great load had been lifted from his shoulders.

Later that evening, the sense of elation was still with him; even the depression he always felt on entering his temporary home did not descend.

Karen listened to his news with resigned acceptance.

'I will go and stay with Julie then,' she said, secretly hoping he would ask her not to, perhaps give some small indication that he wanted her to stay with him.

When he said nothing she fell into what Turner referred to as one of her angry sulks; it was deepened by his buoyant mood and her inability to cause any sort of argument.

11

Next morning as Ashworth opened his garage door a quote often used by his late father came into his mind: *No sky, no sun; no wind, no warmth; November*. For that was the sort of morning it was.

Thick white clouds hung heavy and motionless in the sky; not a breath of wind stirred the barren trees. A cold numbness seemed to penetrate through to the bone.

It was the fifth day of the month and Ashworth viewed his forthcoming birthday with a mixture of trepidation and anticipation. It was to be his fifty-third and the march of time worried Ashworth no less than most mortals.

But still he enjoyed his birthdays, as he did Christmas. The latter was a family time, of children and grandchildren, and bedlam. A birthday, however, was a personal thing, a time when one enjoys the full attention of one's family.

He drove towards Bridgenorton with a variety of thoughts in his mind.

Ann Thorncroft took up part of the journey. He had seen her as he passed along the high street. She must have been on her way back from the newsagent's for she was clutching two packets of cigarettes, hurrying along, no doubt intent on getting back to the salon in time to open up.

She had spotted him and that warm wide smile had covered her face. She had called something but the flow of traffic had prevented Ashworth from stopping the car, so he waved back, hoping that the warmth inside him reflected in his smile.

Was he fooling himself? Was he reading too much into the woman's friendly manner? After all, Amy had said these drama people kiss and cuddle just saying hello.

For some reason that thought depressed him so his mind chose another lane to wander along.

The case. He had to admit that this was one of the most puzzling he had ever worked on.

Turner. His face creased into a smile as he thought of his sergeant, who had yet to learn how to control his impatience. Ashworth saw him as a little terrier, forever worrying, but on this case he must be controlled.

The one thing that worried Ashworth more than anything else was that if his blackmail theory was correct – and he was certain it was – then that one missing link slipping into place would deliver Carway to Turner on a plate.

He walked into Chief Inspector Harry Dawson's office at the Bridgenorton station.

Dawson was a large man whose hair had long ago deserted him; his head glowed pink, the skin as soft as any baby's. There was an almost permanent scowl on his face, etched there by his thirty years' service in the police force.

'Jim, you old devil, you haven't changed a bit,' was his greeting.

'And you're still a liar,' Ashworth replied as he sat down.

The two men talked, asked after wives, children, grandchildren, touched briefly on how times had changed since they were coppers on the beat.

126

Finally, Dawson asked, 'Well, what can I do for you, Jim?'

'It's a courtesy call really, Harry. I want to put a couple of my people in Bridgenorton on surveillance.'

'Carway?' Dawson's scowl deepened.

Ashworth nodded.

Dawson said, 'Yes, I heard he was staying here. No doubt this is one of your "flush 'em out" pitches.'

Ashworth laughed. 'Am I that predictable?'

Dawson's attitude remained serious. 'The force is changing, Jim. Some of our methods are frowned upon now. It seems to me anyone suspected of a crime nowadays suddenly has more rights than the Royal Family.'

Ashworth looked dejected. 'Am I to take that as a no?' he asked.

Now it was Dawson's turn to laugh. 'Still come straight to the point, I see. It's not a no, just give me a good reason for your people being here.'

'I can give you that.'

'Yes, I thought you'd be able to.'

Ashworth was smiling again. 'It's not that far from the truth actually, Harry. We're getting an upturn in burglaries and we've been led to believe some of the culprits might live in Bridgenorton and – '

Dawson held up his hand and smiled. 'Leave it for the Chief, Jim. I'm only interested in covering my own backside.'

Ashworth was relieved; so many of the people he could call on for favours had retired in the last few years, replaced by computer-tapping, regulation-spouting robots. He said, 'You always did worry too much about your pension, Harry.'

'I'm seriously considering not worrying about it much longer, but starting to collect it.'

Ashworth frowned. 'Oh, come on, Harry, so many of the old guard are disappearing. It's beginning to make me feel old . . . and I definitely can't see you settling into a life of gardening and fishing.'

Dawson was resolute. 'I mean it, Jim. I just keep thinking our kind of policing has passed its sell-by date.' He sighed. 'Do you know what I'm getting now?' He pointed towards the ceiling and his superior's office above it. 'Community policing! Send our young coppers out there to have the thugs and tearaways spit at them, call them filth, pigs, and God knows what else, and our lads just have to grin and take it.'

'Times do change, Harry,' Ashworth said resignedly.

'But not for the better,' Dawson pointed out. 'Do you remember when we were on the beat? You could get away with dinging a few ears then . . . and nobody will ever convince me that it didn't straighten out a few would-be yobs in its time.'

Ashworth wholeheartedly agreed with Dawson's point of view. He knew though that in the past there had been abuses of power. He knew too that the line between enforcing the law and administering justice was a very fine one – as fine perhaps as the thin blue one that most members of society still relied upon to keep some sort of order.

He said none of these things, however, but thanked Harry Dawson for his time, said his goodbyes and departed.

Outside in his car he called Turner. He listened to the ringing tone for some time, was about to replace the receiver when the connection was made.

A breathless Turner said, 'Hello?'

'Hello, Owen, it's Jim, thought you'd deserted.'

'Sorry, Jim, I've just got back from putting Karen and the kids on the train. I'd just got out of the car when the phone started ringing . . .'

'All right,' Ashworth chuckled. 'You don't have to make a statement about it. Now, did you tell Kerrie?'

'Yes, I did. I think she was thrilled at the prospect.' He tried to sound detached.

'Of working with you? My, she must lead a sheltered life.'

'Well, I'm glad you're in a good mood, Jim,' Turner countered.

'Oh, I am, Owen, I am, because we're about to get things moving. What I want you and Kerrie to do is watch Carway's flat. I want to know who goes in and out.'

'You seem certain someone will.'

'I am, because I'm going to start putting the fear of God into

128

a few people.' He savoured the thought for a few seconds. 'I want Carway to know you're there but don't push yourselves down his throat. I've okayed it with the force this end. If anything breaks I want to know immediately.'

'All right, Jim, I'll be in touch.'

Ashworth left the car where it was and walked along the Bridgenorton high street. Like his much-loved Bridgetown it had lost none of its character; the sprawl of the developer's hand all around it had not as yet destroyed the illusion of village tranquillity.

As Ashworth walked between the stone-built structures, some of which still had roofs of thatch, he pondered how long it would be before the ominous march of bricks and mortar joined the two towns together, perhaps to be called forever more Bridgecity. He was appalled at the thought.

He stopped outside the site of an office complex still under construction. A large sign just inside the wire perimeter fence told the world that, when completed, the building would provide three hundred offices on forty-six floors. There was even an artist's impression of a skyscraper.

Ashworth went through the high wire gate, groaning as his highly polished shoes sank into the soft mud.

'Can I help you, mate?' a voice asked above the noise and general mêlée.

'I'm looking for Tony Munden,' Ashworth called back.

'He's round the back.' The man gesticulated, indicating that the back was the opposite side to the front.

Tony Munden was a wiry man, mid-thirties, with a somewhat old, weather-beaten face beneath an orange-coloured hard hat. The collar of his donkey-jacket was turned up against the bitter chill. His fingers were blue with the cold yet he was spreading mortar and laying bricks at a furious pace.

He looked up as Ashworth approached, smiled. 'Hello, Mr Ashworth. What you doing here?'

'Trying to arrest whoever it was gave planning permission for the monstrosity you're helping to build,' Ashworth replied jovially.

Tony Munden laughed. 'It might be a monstrosity to you, Mr Ashworth, but it means bread and butter to me and my family for the next twelve months, at least.'

Ashworth sobered. 'Can I have a word, Tony?'

'Course, but do you mind if I carry on working?' He peered around. 'Work's a bit thin on the ground and this lot keep their eyes on who are pulling their weight and who aren't.'

'That's fine. Do you know Rodney Watson?'

'Yeh, I know Rod.' Another brick was skilfully laid. 'Worked a lot of jobs with him. Why?'

'What's he like?' Ashworth asked, ignoring Munden's question.

Munden paused, brick in hand, thought for a moment. 'Not a bad bloke. Fond of the booze and the birds as they say. He's not on the building any more, set himself up in a garage. Mind you, he don't know as much about cars as he thinks he does. I wouldn't let him under the bonnet of mine.'

'He used to do a bit on the side, didn't he, when he worked on the building sites?' Ashworth probed.

'Yeh, that's right, in his garage, but then he got the premises and started up on his own.'

Ashworth beat his gloved hands together, trying to bring some warmth to them.

'Do you think it's possible he was saving up to start the business?'

'Saving? Rod?' Munden snorted. 'Sorry, I'm not being rude or nothing but the thought of Rod saving just creases me up. He's the sort of bloke who'd finish work on the Friday and go straight into the pub. He was always broke by Tuesday.'

Ashworth pondered. 'It would take a bit of cash to set himself up in that sort of venture. Where do you think he got it from?'

'I hadn't thought, but I suppose you're right. He's serviced a couple of the lads' cars and he's got all the equipment. But it's no good asking me where the cash came from.'

'Anything else about him, Tony?'

Munden straightened up, flexed his back a couple of times. 'Not really. Bit of a hard case, I suppose, but then working on the building you've got to be able to take care of yourself. I wouldn't think he was a head-case though.'

'Good,' Ashworth said, visibly pleased. 'What's the word around the pubs on the burglaries?'

Resuming his work, Munden looked furtive. 'All I've heard is it's a gang, working their way round the estates.' He stopped to look up at Ashworth. 'You know, it still gives me a shock to see you.'

Ashworth smiled. 'No need, Tony, all that was a long time ago. Must be fifteen years now . . . you were just a kid.'

'My mam and dad tell me you still visit them.'

'I drop in sometimes when I'm passing.'

'They're still grateful to you for straightening me out.'

Ashworth smiled. 'I helped you get a job in a good trade, that's all, you did the rest.'

Munden laughed. 'Maybe.'

'Anyway, Tony, I'd better be off. I'm perished standing here. I don't know how you can work in this cold.'

'This is easy, Mr Ashworth. It's getting out of a warm bed in the morning that's the hard part.'

They laughed, shook hands and Ashworth squelched his way back to the road.

His mind returned to community policing. He realized that over the years he had built up a small network of reliable people, some of whom could have become hardened criminals, but when offered an alternative such as a good decent life with a future, had chosen that instead.

There was a lot more to police work than hitting them over the head and locking them up . . . a hell of a lot more.

He drove back to Bridgetown. As he passed the salon he slowed, hoping to catch sight of Ann Thorncroft.

A woman was just leaving the salon, placing a pink headscarf over her newly styled hair and tying it under her chin. Ann was holding open the door.

Ashworth resisted the urge to sound his horn and drove on to Rodney Watson's garage.

*

Ashworth heard Rodney Watson before he saw him. A car was parked over the pit, its bonnet up; Watson was working on the engine, giving full vent to an out-of-key rendition of 'Achy Breaky Heart'.

When he saw Ashworth he said, 'Hello, mate,' in a rather offhand way. 'If you're after a mechanic's job you'll have to wait till I expand.'

Ashworth peered at the engine as Watson wiped his hands on a greasy piece of rag; it was debatable as to whether he was cleaning oil from his hands or simply depositing more on to them.

Noticing Ashworth's interest he said, 'The alternator's gone, but on these you have to take the bleedin' engine apart to get at it. Punters think you're robbin' them blind when they get the bill.'

Ashworth said nothing, merely continued to study the engine.

Watson's manner was uneasy. 'You're beginning to make me think you believe I've done something,' he said.

Ashworth looked at him. 'Oh, I do, Rod, I do,' he said quietly. 'Why don't you go in from underneath? From the pit?'

Watson's eyes went blank. 'Underneath? Oh yeh, I get you. Hadn't thought of that.' Then, after a pause, 'What you reckon I've done then?' He was studying Ashworth intently.

'I think you were blackmailing Stella Carway, Rod,' Ashworth said easily.

He saw the shock in Watson's eyes even though the man covered it well. With a laugh he said, 'Blackmail Stel? You're in the wrong job, mate, you should have been a comic.'

Ashworth paused for effect, then said, 'We've been talking to Steven Carway . . .'

'What's that ponce been saying?' Watson said, too quickly.

'Oh, he hasn't said anything yet, Rod, but he will.'

Watson rubbed his brow, realizing he had made a mistake. 'So, what's Stel supposed to have done that she'd want me to keep quiet about?'

Ashworth smiled, teased. 'We don't know that yet.'

Watson's reply was measured. 'So you don't know what I was blackmailing her about and you've got no proof that I was. You ain't a very good copper, are you?'

'Where did you get the money to start this place?'

'That's between me and the tax man,' Watson said stonily.

'Think on, Rod, that's a course we could well take in a murder investigation, so if you did come into a lot of money you'll have to explain where it came from.'

Watson seemed on the point of making some retort but stopped himself. He grinned, tried to regain some of his old brag and bluster. 'Look, I've got a living to earn, so why don't you go and act silly somewhere else.'

Ashworth smiled at the insult. 'Try it from underneath . . . you'll find it a lot easier. I'll see you soon, Rod.'

Ashworth walked out of the garage without looking back, pleased in the knowledge that he had thrown a pebble into the water; now to wait for the ripples to spread. If he had looked back he would have seen Watson watching his retreating figure, would have noted the worried, preoccupied look on the man's face.

Susan Ratcliffe had been in the flat for two days and only once had she ventured outside, to the corner grocer's and off-licence where she stocked up with bread, margarine, cheese, a bottle of gin and some tonic waters.

During those two days she had avidly watched every television news bulletin for information of the Stella Carway murder case. By the end of the first day the news item was given less air-time and by late evening on the second day it was not mentioned at all.

Susan knew that she would soon have to start getting on with her new life, stop existing on bread and cheese. Besides, the gin had all but gone.

Tomorrow she would open the shop below the flat before her behaviour aroused suspicion.

*

The evening was proving to be an irritating one for Turner and Kerrie. Prior to this their time together had been spent in the haven of Kerrie's flat; Turner felt ill at ease with this beautiful girl, out in the open for all to see.

At least the awkward part was behind them. Kerrie had asked, 'How long will she be away?' The enemy was always referred to as 'she'.

Would he be spending the night at the flat? The relative peace and harmony brought about by his answer of yes was short-lived for he had told her that he must return home in the morning. Under considerable pressure he admitted that 'she' would be telephoning in the mornings.

However, once the ground rules for the much-improved, if still unsatisfactory situation had been established, they began to enjoy each other's company.

Their car was parked opposite Carway's flat, the upper floor of a large terraced property in a quiet tree-lined avenue.

Carway had arrived home at eight o'clock and had made no attempt to draw the curtains. They were able, therefore, to observe him as he emptied the contents of two silver-foil containers on to a plate before consuming the meal, plate in hand, as he walked around the room.

Turner's tastebuds tingled as he watched.

The usual boredom of surveillance was relieved by the fact that they were together. Their eyes watched Carway but their thoughts and conversation were focused on the night ahead.

They planned to buy a take-away curry on the way home, and share a bottle of wine. After all, Kerrie had been quick to remind him, this would be the first time they had actually slept together.

They held hands in the darkened car and Turner wished it could always be like this. His mind refused space for the thoughts that should be worrying him, the wrecked lives that he was on the brink of creating, wreckage that could go on far beyond his own and Karen's lifetime.

The roar of a car engine shattered the peace of the quiet street. An old Cortina came into view, shuddered to a stop outside Carway's flat.

Rodney Watson climbed out. Despite the bitter coldness of the night he was dressed only in jeans and a white T-shirt. He strode up to the front steps and disappeared through the doorway.

When next they saw him he was standing inside the flat. Carway was out of sight but Watson was there for all to see, gesticulating wildly, stabbing the air with his finger as he forcefully made a point.

If Carway said anything it was in unison with Watson, for the latter continued to talk for the fifteen or so minutes he was in the flat.

Anger and tension were still in his body language as he strode back down the steps. As he opened the unlocked door to his car he spotted Turner, looked away, recognition dawned, his head swivelled back, he locked eyes with the sergeant.

Colour rose in his cheeks and for several moments he seemed unsure as to what action to take. His face contorted into an angry snarl. Turner thought he was about to cross the road and confront them. Instead he turned back towards the steps, dithered for a moment before quickly jumping into his car which then sped off.

Turner checked the windows of the flat. Carway was nowhere in sight as he picked up the car phone to dial Ashworth's home number.

The telephone had hardly rung once when Ashworth lifted the receiver. 'Yes?'

'Hello, Jim, it's Owen. Carway's had a visitor.'

'Rodney Watson.' It was a statement not a question.

'Yes, that's right, arrived at ten and he's just left. The curtains aren't drawn so we could see everything. It looked like a violent argument . . . hold on, Jim.'

Turner's voice returned a few seconds later. 'Kerrie's just corrected me. It was more like Watson laying down the law to Carway. He looked really aggressive.'

'Has Carway seen you?'

'No, I don't think so, but Watson did just as he was leaving.'

'And?'

'He looked pretty shaken up, close to panic, I'd say. I

thought he was going to come charging over to us but he drove off.'

'That's good. What I want you to do is sit tight. Are the curtains still open?'

Turner checked. 'Yes.'

'Right, I'm betting that sometime in the next half-hour Carway's going to have a phone call making him aware of your presence. After that you can both go home.'

The half-hour passed slowly. Kerrie complained that her feet were getting cold. They were becoming increasingly preoccupied with activities far more exciting than watching Steven Carway's flat.

A silence descended as the minutes ticked away, the only sound, a slight traffic hum somewhere in the distance. In the quiet of the night a toilet flushed, the sound eerily loud in the stillness.

'Let's go, it's been over half an hour,' Kerrie whispered.

'We'll give it a few more minutes,' Turner replied as he stared up at the lighted window.

Thirty-five minutes became forty, forty-five, Turner was about to give up when they both heard it . . . the ringing of a telephone.

A few seconds elapsed before Carway appeared at the window to stare into the gloom of the night. Stepping back he hurriedly pulled the curtains.

Turner started the car, pushed the gears into first and drove away.

The illuminated digits of the bedside clock said two thirty.

Moving his arm gently, Turner pulled it free from under the sleeping Kerrie. Straight away he felt his blood begin to circulate once again.

Kerrie stirred, her naked body moving slightly beneath the quilt.

Still the sweet sensation – more spiritual than physical – was within him. Surely this was how sex should be, not contrived, not entered into awkwardly or rationally, but a driving force that consumes its participants, chasing away all thought or conscious decision while the primeval fire raged inside them.

Turner desperately sought sleep for the responsibilities he held towards others still knocked at the door of his mind; so far he had managed to deny them entry but for how much longer could he do so?

12

The following morning Ashworth was put out. He tried telling himself that he was an intelligent, mature person and that he was acting like a child. It did little good. The fact still remained that today was 6th November and there had not been one solitary birthday card on the hall table. Not one.

The fact that his son and daughter had forgotten was upsetting enough, but Sarah had never, ever forgotten any one of their numerous anniversaries: their first meeting; the first time she met his parents; their marriage; even the day they planted the lilac tree – the list was endless.

Ashworth was behaving like a spoilt child. He stormed into the police station, marched straight to his office, hardly stopping to greet those he passed on the way.

There was a white envelope lying on his blotter. He sat down, picked it up, looked at it, held it up to the light, then with his paper knife he sliced it open and drew out the card that was inside.

It had a cartoon policeman on the front and the message: BE NICE TO A POLICEMAN . . . He opened the card and read: . . . ON HIS BIRTHDAY. The scrawled writing beneath said: *Have a nice birthday. Ann Thorncroft.*

Ashworth fingered the card, read the message, reread it, then picked up the telephone.

He did not get Ann straight away but someone sounding like a teenaged girl. She called Ann's name and Ashworth could hear the sound of high heels clicking on the tiled floor.

'Hello?' Ann said.

'Hello, Ann, it's Jim Ashworth. I just called to thank you for the card.'

'You're very welcome,' she said. Her voice dropped to a whisper. 'I'd sing Happy Birthday but I've got a shopful of customers.'

'That's a pity. I'd have enjoyed that,' Ashworth laughed.

'You wouldn't say that if you'd heard me sing,' Ann giggled. Changing the subject, she said, 'Have you found time to get that stuff for my wall?'

'Yes,' he lied, making a mental note to send someone out for it.

'Oh, thanks – you couldn't drop it in today, could you? The plasterer's taking the old plaster off today and putting the new on tomorrow, so I can do it tonight.'

'It will have to be early evening,' Ashworth said as he consulted his diary. 'I've got a heavy day.'

'That'll be fine. Perhaps you could stay for a birthday drink.'

Ashworth hesitated and Ann spoke again before he could reply. 'I know you won't be able to stay long. How about just after six? You'll have to put up with me smelling of setting lotion.'

'All right, just after six.'

'Good.'

'Oh, Ann . . .'

'Yes?'

'I'll look forward to it.'

'So shall I. Look, must dash . . . purple hair and all that. See you later.'

The rest of the morning was a disaster. A press conference came first. Ashworth and the Chief Constable, Ken Savage, faced a handful of reporters in one of the interview rooms.

Savage, straight-backed, thin, with receding grey hair, hooked nose, and a manner that could cause ice to form on burning coals, stood beside Ashworth as they faced the group.

The *Bridgetown Post* journalist, whose face was an acne war-zone, seemed to have a personal dislike for Ashworth. He opened with, 'Could you tell us if you've made any progress with this case? It has been – '

Ashworth cut in with the standard answer. 'We are following a number of enquiries and have eliminated a number of people from those enquiries.'

'Does that mean you know who didn't do it but have no idea who did?' the reporter quipped.

There was a ripple of laughter during which Ashworth did his best to keep his temper and voice in check. He said, 'It means it's an extremely complex case and we're making progress.'

Another reporter picked up on the theme. 'What my readers want to know is why hasn't more progress been made? They're worried that there's a murderer on the loose and you people handling the case don't seem to be taking any steps to apprehend that murderer.'

The Chief Constable intervened, his voice stiff. 'You can assure your readers that I have the fullest confidence in Chief Inspector Ashworth and the team that is working on this case. Now, gentlemen, you'll have to excuse us.'

There was a clamour of voices. Ashworth took one final question.

'When will the victim's funeral be held?'

Ashworth replied that it would take place the following day and with heavy emphasis added that the location was to be kept secret and the media were not invited.

He left the interview room with Savage. As they reached the corridor Savage said simply, 'We need some action on this, Jim.' Then he walked away.

To an observer the remark would have seemed offhand, casual even, but Ashworth, as he watched his superior's retreating back, digested the short sentence. He knew that Savage used words as if they were rationed. He also knew that the few well-chosen words that he had just received meant: I want a result on this case . . . get it yesterday!

Ashworth returned to his office and telephoned Turner, asked him to bring Steven Carway in for questioning at two p.m.

He looked at Ann Thorncroft's card which he had placed on his desk, picked it up and slid it into one of his desk drawers.

His brow was furrowed as he sat deep in thought. Self-doubt had begun to creep in. What had he really got? One dead woman. That was the only certain fact in his possession.

Say her death had been caused by someone out of his mind on drugs; a total stranger committing a truly motiveless crime.

What led him to believe that this was not so? Rory James' assumption that there had been someone else in the house on the night of the murder. A flimsy piece of evidence on which it was difficult to pin any hope in the cold light of day.

Was he simply barking up the wrong tree? He was certain Rodney Watson had been blackmailing Stella and that Steven Carway had known of this. But was that linked with the murder or just a skeleton from the past returned to cloud the issue?

After all, Stella had been promiscuous – by Ashworth's standards, very promiscuous – and even if her prime motivation had been purely sexual, surely passion and jealousy would have been mingled in there somewhere?

Was he missing the obvious in his quest for the elusive?

Throughout the interview with Stephen Carway it would be essential for him to keep in mind that the object of this exercise was to throw the fear of God into the man; it was not meant to bring instant results.

Susan Ratcliffe had risen early that morning, quite unconsciously taking pains not to be seen as she stole a glance from the window. Satisfied that there was no one watching the flat, she decided to shower, hoping that would drive away her mild headache caused by last night's gin.

The bathroom was small and without heating. Susan shivered as she slipped out of her dressing-gown. For one awful moment, as she stood in the stained bath, it seemed that the antiquated shower would not work; at first it coughed and spluttered out a slow trickle, then it vibrated and gushed out water that was gloriously hot. Her soap-covered hands brought warm relief, driving away the goose-pimples on her skin.

She dried herself in the bedroom where an ancient radiator took much of the chill out of the air, but the price paid for this luxury was a disturbing clanging sound in the pipes.

Susan studied her naked reflection in the mirror on her old-fashioned wardrobe. Her breasts were still solid, her long legs firm, but the inactivity of recent weeks was beginning to tell around her middle. The short hair – a clumsy attempt at disguise – did not suit her, she decided, placing her wet towel on the wash-stand complete with porcelain bowl.

Pulling on small white briefs she gazed around the room. Her first reaction to the flat had been one of disgust, she had considered it a tip, but that assessment had since been modified. Indeed, the antique furnishings lent it a quaintness; in the lounge the Queen Anne three-piece suite blended in well with the beamed walls and ceilings. The bedroom furniture was solid and of good quality, although a new mattress would make the bed more comfortable and perhaps ease the starkness of the plain wooden headboard. New carpets would be needed throughout as the place smelt strongly of cats. Also a modern central heating system was essential and the bathroom suite would have to be replaced; it would probably take three strong men to remove the cast-iron bath.

Hair dried and make-up applied, Susan completed the task of dressing. The waistband of her dark blue skirt felt tight around her middle; the matching blue top buttoned up to her neck to give a business-like impression.

Pausing in the lounge to pick up her heavy winter coat and handbag she then descended the spiral staircase to the shop below. Mercifully the enormity of the task before her drove away all other thoughts. The shop was chaotic; full book-shelves adorned all three walls and further books were stacked on the floor and counter. A dry musty smell prevailed and tiny specks of dust floated in the shafts of weak winter sunshine.

Letting herself out of the shop Susan walked along the cobbled street. At first she resented the quizzical glances of passers-by, they made her feel vulnerable, isolated, until she realized these people were simply being friendly and nothing more dangerous than a cheerful 'good morning' was forthcoming when she returned their gaze.

The town enchanted her. The main roads were tarmacked but many of the side streets and alleys were paved with centuries-old cobblestones. The salt blown in from the sea stung her eyes and smelt of freedom. The main street transported her back through time; although the shop interiors were ultra-modern their Victorian frontages could cause more imaginative minds to half expect crinoline-clad ladies escorted by elegantly attired gentlemen to appear.

Susan was walking down wide stone steps leading to the bank when she heard a sound that made her stomach churn, made the blood freeze in her veins. It came again.

'Susan!'

She turned. The man was hurrying down the steps. He looked straight towards her. Susan swallowed nervously but the man only pushed past her, muttering apologies as he did so. Once more he was calling her name but to the retreating back of a woman about to turn a corner at the bottom of the steps. The incident brought everything flooding back to her. Who she was. What she was doing in this place.

Susan had recovered her breath and most of her composure by the time she reached the bank but she was all too aware of the questions that remained unanswered, the countless circumstances that could bring retribution crashing down upon her. The bank manager, for instance, Mr David Darlow: had Stella conducted all of her business by mail and telephone or had she sat where Susan was sitting now, waiting to see the very same man?

This fear was quickly dispelled as the teenaged receptionist showed her into the manager's office. David Darlow rose from his red leather chair and came towards her with his hand outstretched.

'Miss Christie, it's good to be able to put a face to the name. How are you?'

His handshake was firm and Susan felt a delicious tingle pass through her body as their hands met.

'Please do take a seat.' He ushered her towards the desk and held the chair for her to sit before becoming seated himself. 'Now, let's see . . .' He opened a folder that was on the desk. 'I think you'll find everything in order.'

Susan considered the man as he spoke. He appeared incongruous in his smart business suit, starched white shirt and blue tie. His mane of brown hair which refused to be tamed by brush or comb cascaded over his forehead giving his face a boyish appeal. Sensitive brown eyes appraised her and white teeth flashed in a firm mouth as he smiled; his nose was straight and strong, as was his jawline.

'Lease paid for two years. Mrs Marsden has accepted ten thousand pounds for the stock and goodwill, and the rest of the money on account.' He looked up and smiled. 'Quite a large sum, if you don't mind me saying so, but don't worry, the bank is geared to handle accounts of this size. Maybe we could have a chat about investments sometime?'

'Yes, I'd like that. Can I draw on the account straightaway?'

'Of course. What sort of amount are you looking at?'

'Not a great deal, it's just that I need some work done at the flat . . . central heating, bathroom, carpets.' She wrinkled her nose in disgust.

Darlow laughed. 'I can believe that. Mrs Marsden kept cats; it was rumoured that she had twenty-five.'

'I believe the rumour,' Susan replied, smiling. 'I wonder if you could recommend some companies.'

'I'll do more than that, I'll arrange for people to give you quotes.' He began scribbling on his notepad. 'Central heating, bath, that's plumbing . . . and carpets. Anything else?'

'Well, I do need a new mattress for the bed.' Susan felt embarrassed talking about her bed to someone she found attractive. 'But that's silly, I shall have to look round for a shop.'

'It's not silly, bound to take you a while to find out where things are. Try Fellowes, in the main street, they stock all the leading names.'

'Thank you, Mr Darlow,' she said, still feeling foolish and finding it difficult to meet his direct gaze.

'Do you intend to keep the shop just selling second-hand books and prints?'

'No, I plan to use part of the shop for second-hand books and prints because I believe there's a good market for them, but I want to branch out and turn it into a modern bookshop.'

Darlow beamed. 'Brilliant. So many people around here complain that they have to go into Exeter to buy books. You could well corner a market.'

Susan was pleased by his praise and went on enthusiastically, 'I was also thinking of selling newspapers and magazines until I noticed there's a newsagent's just round the corner from me.'

'Again good policy. They don't exactly fall over themselves to welcome newcomers here. A stranger did settle here some hundred years ago and I believe his grandchildren are just on the verge of being accepted, but it's still touch and go.'

Susan laughed. 'You're very unusual for a bank manager, and I'm sure they're not as bad as all that.'

'No, they're not,' he said, still laughing. 'In fact they're warm friendly people. All I'm saying is, don't do anything that hints of cut-throat competition until you've integrated into the community or they're likely to freeze you out.'

'Thanks for the tip,' Susan said, suddenly at a loss for words. 'Well, I think that's all.'

'Yes, I think it is,' Darlow agreed reluctantly. 'Tell me, are you settling in okay?'

'Not very well really,' said Susan, not wanting the conversation to end. 'I don't know anyone, you see, and it all feels so strange.'

'I'm sure it must, but that should change once the shop opens and you start meeting people.'

'Yes, I suppose so.' Susan was surprised by how shy she felt with this man. She sat peering down at her hands.

Darlow said, 'Look, I hope you don't think I'm being forward . . .' Susan glanced up to see him staring down at his desk. '. . . but I wonder if you'd like to have dinner with me this evening . . . or any other evening,' he added lamely.

Susan hesitated, then said, 'That's very nice of you.'

'You'd be doing me a favour,' Darlow urged. 'I'm thirty-nine and single and in this community that raises a question mark.'

Susan found herself laughing again. 'Put that way it's hard to refuse, but I'd like it not to be formal.'

'No problem, we could nip over to Exeter for a Chinese or Indian . . .'

'Even less formal than that.'

Darlow thought for a moment. 'Well, some of the pubs serve ploughman's lunches . . .' He shrugged and grinned. 'Lunch at dinner-time . . . the West Country can be crazy. But it's good pickle, cheese, fabulous bread and real ale.'

'That sounds fine.'

'Good.' He smiled and gazed down at the folder. 'So, would it now be in order for me to call you Stella?'

'No, I'd rather you didn't,' Susan said hurriedly. 'I hate the name. Most of my friends call me Susan.' She had not planned for this, had not thought it through. How could she go through life with the image of Stella Carway's near-naked dead body springing to mind every time someone called her Stella? 'Susan's my middle name . . . Stella Susan Christie,' she explained.

'Susan sounds nice, and I'm David.'

'Hello, David,' she said, smiling.

Carway entered spot-on two p.m., followed by Turner. George Gallford was in hot pursuit as if frightened that being separated would somehow threaten his client. The young police constable sent out by Ashworth to purchase Ann Thorncroft's damp course brought up the rear, closed the door and stood beside it.

Ashworth indicated that Carway and his solicitor should sit. As they did so Turner dealt with the tape recorder.

'Thank you for coming in, Mr Carway. We'd just like to ask you a few more questions connected with your wife's death,' Ashworth said as Turner joined them.

Carway, doing his level best to sound bored, said, 'I don't have much choice in the matter. Can I have an ashtray, please?'

After a nod from Ashworth the constable fetched an ashtray from a built-in cupboard to the right of the door.

Turner spoke. 'We'd like you to tell us about the money that vanished from your current account, Mr Carway.'

The constable set the ashtray down in front of Carway, who, after lighting a cigarette, said, 'I've told you about it and as you well know it didn't vanish.'

'Tell us again,' Turner prompted.

'My wife . . .' He paused. 'My late wife and I had a joint current account. She was an extravagant person and she overspent . . . that's all.'

'How much money did she overspend?'

Carway's voice dropped to an almost inaudible whisper. 'Two hundred thousand pounds.'

'And what did your late wife spend this money on?' Each of Turner's questions seemed to be delivered with more speed than the last.

'I don't know. I've been through all this before.' Carway's nerves were beginning to fray.

'And when you discovered your late wife had overspent you were annoyed,' Turner persisted.

'Well, I wasn't very pleased.'

'Did you argue with her? Demand to know where the money had gone?'

Carway's voice rose. 'No, I didn't argue with her. I know what you're inferring but it's not true.'

'I'm not inferring anything, sir,' Turner replied. 'Just trying to establish what happened.'

Carway shot a glance at his solicitor who quickly jumped in. 'What my client meant to say was that after that instance he went to great pains to ensure that there was never again that amount of money in the account.'

'Thank you, Mr Gallford,' Turner said crisply. He then studied Carway who averted his eyes, busying himself with the stubbing out of his cigarette.

After a pause Turner said, 'Do you know a Rodney Watson, Mr Carway?'

Carway's head jerked up. 'Only very slightly.'

'Did he visit you at your flat in Bridgenorton at ten o'clock last evening?'

'That's right.' The haunted look was no longer on Carway's face.

'Would you mind telling me the purpose of that visit?' Turner asked.

Again it was Gallford who answered. 'I'm sure you know. You people had made some very serious accusations against Mr Watson – and not in an interview situation, I might add,' he said darkly. 'You also indicated to Mr Watson that my client had supplied you with information that could link him with some form of criminal activity. Naturally Mr Watson was incensed and visited my client to remonstrate with him. And I must add that my client objects to your methods which nearly led to him being seriously assaulted. He also objects to the police watching his every movement.'

'We're not,' Ashworth jumped in. 'We just happened to have a presence in Bridgenorton on another matter last night. I know there are those who hate to see policemen on the streets, but I'm sure that you, Mr Gallford, being a bastion of law and order, are not amongst their ranks.' He finished with a tight smile.

Gallford was angered. 'That's as maybe, Chief Inspector,' he spat. 'But I shall be making noises in higher places. Have you finished with my client?'

Ashworth, still smiling, replied, 'That's your privilege, and yes, we have for the moment.'

Turner crossed to the tape recorder and talked into it, giving the time the interview concluded.

Carway and Gallford stood up to leave but Ashworth remained seated. 'We'll find the link. We'll keep digging until we do.'

A pulse twitched under the pale skin of Carway's forehead, fear showed briefly in his eyes. He cast a glance at Gallford who shook his head and quickly ushered him out of the room.

Ashworth stayed in his chair, staring down at the desk, head bowed.

Turner nodded a dismissal to the young constable and stood looking at his Chief as the door closed.

'Are you all right, Jim?'

Ashworth raised his eyes. 'I'm beginning to think you're right, Owen. Maybe Carway did kill his wife.'

'I don't think there's much doubt about it,' Turner responded. 'When we find out why Stella was being blackmailed, when we can prove that, all the pieces will fit. She had no money of her own so she had to use her husband's. He may well be a wealthy man but there has to be a limit to how long he could keep that sort of payment up, so he murdered his wife. We've got everything we need, Jim, motive, opportunity . . .'

Ashworth shook his head despondently. 'No, Owen, all I've got is a higher than average mileage for Stella's car the last few months of her life, rumours, gossip, and a gut feeling so strong it hurts.'

Turner changed the subject. 'Do you want us to watch Carway tonight?'

'Yes, make it obvious as well. Pick him up outside his office and tail him. Make sure he knows you're there. I've got a feeling we're going to be called off tomorrow.'

As Ashworth drove to the Blow and Dry salon his thoughts were of gardening, fishing, and pensions. Surely, he reasoned, there must come a time when it would be wise to hand over to younger minds who could cope more easily with the pace of modern life.

He parked a few yards away from the salon door, took the tin of damp-proofing from the passenger seat and got out of the car.

Shoes clattered down the stairs almost as soon as he pushed the bell.

Ann opened the door. She smiled warmly. 'Jim. Happy birthday.'

As he followed her up the stairs he thought ruefully, Well, this is one drama person who doesn't kiss and cuddle just saying hello . . . pity.

Ann was still wearing her white work smock and did indeed smell of setting lotion.

148

'Oh, you got it,' she said, indicating the tin. 'You are a darling. Come through to the bedroom and see what he's done.'

Ashworth followed her through. The room still smelt of damp. The plaster beneath the window had been stripped off to expose the stone. Ashworth touched it, ran his hand along to feel the moisture seeping in.

'If you've got a brush I could do this in ten minutes,' he said.

Ann's face registered delight. 'Are you sure you don't mind?'

Ashworth said he did not. When she reappeared moments later with a large paint brush, she said, 'Do you mind if I take a shower? I've really had a hard day.'

Ashworth shook his head as he took off his coat and placed it on the bed. With a ten-pence piece he prised off the lid; his nostrils wrinkled against the pungent smell that rose from the can.

As the shower water began to hiss he started to paint the wall. By the time the shower was turned off and the hair-drier switched on he had completed the job.

The noise from the hair-drier ceased and Ashworth felt Ann's presence in the doorway. She was dressed in a pink bathrobe which barely reached her knees. Her newly dried hair was soft and fluffy. He noticed that she had reapplied her eye make-up.

'You're finished. Oh, great,' Ann enthused. She sniffed. 'It pongs a bit, doesn't it?'

'That'll go off in a couple of days. In fact, when it's plastered you'll hardly smell it at all.'

Ann grabbed his arm. 'Come through and have a drink, you clever man.'

In the kitchen Ann attended to the drinks while Ashworth leaned against the units watching her.

'Happy birthday,' she said, handing him scotch and ginger.

'Thank you.' They touched glasses.

Ann gazed up at him, a smile playing on her lips. She took a sip of her gin and tonic before placing the glass on the sink drainer.

Resting her hands on Ashworth's shoulders she leaned forward to kiss his cheek. 'Thank you again for the wall.' She pulled back, placed her arms around his neck then her head came forward again, her lips brushed his, causing his nerve endings to tingle and throb in a way they had not done for years.

Ann was gazing into his face. Her eyes teased, dared him to make the next move, but despite the ache in his middle this was a line Ashworth did not intend to cross.

'I think that's enough thanks . . . it was only a small piece of wall,' he joked.

'Yes, you're right.' Ann let go of him and turned away. 'It's getting silly.'

Ashworth's attempt to lighten the rebuff had only succeeded in turning an awkward situation into an embarrassing one. He finished his drink quickly. 'I'd better be going.'

'Yes, of course.' Ann gave him a weak smile.

'I'll see myself out.'

During the drive home Ashworth chastised himself. He had seen it coming and should have avoided it. There was a part of him, however, that had wanted it to happen, a part that would always regret that it had not. Now all he had done was put himself into an extremely embarrassing position.

'The weaker sex,' must be the most inapt title ever created. Ashworth decided. The fact that someone so happily married, so staid and set in his ways could still be vulnerable to the attentions of an attractive female, disturbed him enormously.

Reaching home he parked in the drive, braking sharply, gravel shooting from beneath the tyres, rear wheels skidding as he stopped. It had been many years since he had driven so badly. Suddenly he felt old, old and settled in his ways, so very settled.

If he had stopped to analyse it, he would have realized that his behaviour had been a futile attempt to turn the clock back thirty years. Impossible though, and now the only rebellion he could muster was to drive like a teenager. He stamped to the front door and entered the house.

Sarah was standing in the open doorway of the lounge,

smiling the sort of weak routine smile that one does on seeing a person one is expecting.

'Hello, darling. Good day?'

'Beautiful,' Ashworth grunted.

'Your paper's in the lounge. They've done a spread on the Carway case.' She looked at him quizzically. 'Where's your coat?'

In his mind Ashworth saw Ann Thorncroft's bed with his waxed-cotton jacket lying on it. 'I must have left it at the station,' he lied.

'Jim,' Sarah scolded as he went into the lounge. 'You'll catch cold.'

Bracing himself for the disdainful headlines, he picked up the newspaper. Beneath it were three envelopes and a small package wrapped in brightly coloured paper. A feeling of relief surged through him. When he looked at Sarah he found that she was laughing.

'I bet you thought we'd all forgotten.'

'I never gave it a thought,' he laughed.

Ashworth opened the largest envelope first, knowing that this would be from Sarah. A brown-faced Jack Russell greeted his eyes and the sight of it evoked sad memories of Jackie, their pet who had died just over four years ago.

Sarah was pouring his before-dinner drink and the soda siphon hissed as he opened the card. It read: *For my darling Jim. Every year gets better.*

She passed him the drink and, remembering that his breath would already smell of whisky, Ashworth took a sip before he kissed her thank you.

The other envelopes contained cards from his children. The one from his daughter, Samantha, was bubbly, full of life, reflecting her character perfectly. On the front was printed: YOU'RE NOT OLD AT 53 . . . Ashworth opened it up and there in large letters were the words: . . . YOU'RE POSITIVELY ANCIENT! Despite its worrying undertones it still made him laugh.

The card from his son, John, had a fishing scene on the front and a simple message inside: *Much love, dad. From John, Diana and the children.*

The brightly coloured package was a Pavarotti cassette tape, also from John. Ashworth had recently acquired a passion for Pavarotti's voice, brought about by the fact that more and more opera was creeping into the popular charts; on the occasions he listened in on the car radio he found the sounds pleasing to his ears.

Samantha had bought him a bottle of malt whisky and thirty pounds' worth of book tokens with which to satisfy his other passions.

Somehow, John's gift meant more to Ashworth than Sam's did, for as his son was a struggling writer, already living a hand-to-mouth existence, it spoke of sacrifice, whereas Sam, the wife of a successful insurance broker, could easily afford her expenditure. He would never dream, however, of voicing these thoughts to Sarah.

She had been watching his almost overjoyed reactions to everything he opened and now began to act very mysteriously, going into a childish routine of making him close his eyes and promise not to open them until she said so.

Ashworth obeyed, almost, his left eye was still slightly open and he watched her watery image leave the room.

Minutes ticked by before she returned, carrying a small brown cardboard box.

'Hold out your hand,' she ordered sternly. He did and her own hand disappeared inside the box.

Ashworth glimpsed brown and white before he fully opened his eyes and looked at the Jack Russell puppy. It was no larger than his outstretched hand on which it was resting. One ear stood erect, the other flopped. Its whole body seemed to wag in unison with its tail. Although it seemed pleased, its eyes showed fear.

Sarah watched Ashworth's face closely, studied the look of undiluted pleasure that his expression held.

'I didn't get her from a kennel,' she informed him. 'She came from a private home. They called her Charlotte.'

'This is no Charlotte,' Ashworth laughed. 'This is a Peanuts.'

Sarah tried out the name. 'Peanuts, Peanuts. Yes, she is a Peanuts.'

Ashworth placed the puppy on the carpet. Her instincts told her that she was safe and secure as she explored her new habitat.

Sarah held Ashworth's hand. 'Happy birthday, Jim.'

'Thank you, Sarah. Thank you.'

The puppy continued to explore, sniffing at Ashworth's slippers where they lay at the side of the grate, already identifying her leader's scent. She turned and looked up at this huge man, her tail a blur of movement. Her rear legs splayed out as she squatted down and they both watched as the ever-increasing puddle spread over the Wilton carpet.

13

The wind coming off the sea was a south-westerly, making the air unseasonably warm; it whipped dark angry clouds across the face of the moon, obscuring it from view for a moment until it re-emerged to bathe the heaving sea in its eerie silver light.

The heels of Susan's flat shoes dug into the soft wet sand as she walked with David, holding his hand and laughing at his latest joke.

She had realized quite early in the evening that David was not a conventional person: he had a quiet self-mocking humour that was totally disarming. Dressed now in a light grey polo-neck sweater, denim jeans and a black leather jacket, he seemed far more relaxed than he had in his office.

The small hostelry by the side of the harbour, with its blazing log fire, lobster pots and nets strewn around its walls, had brought an air of relaxation to Susan also; in there it had seemed to her that everyone knew David and countless people paused to chat with him as they consumed their delicious bread, still warm from the oven, cheese that bit the tongue, and pickle which had a sting that was masked by a veil of sweetness.

'If you want a quiet drink never become a bank manager,'

David whispered as he turned down the tenth offer of a drink for himself and his lady.

After Susan had consumed a pint of the strongest beer she had ever tasted, David suggested a walk on the beach. A feeling of peace and contentment the like of which she had never before experienced crept over her as, hand in hand, they walked backwards along the sand, admiring the brightly coloured lights adorning the front of the hostelry.

'This place is paradise,' she said, watching smoke from its chimney being buffeted and swirled away by the wind.

'Maybe we should look where we're going instead of where we've been.'

David's remark brought Susan back to earth. As they walked along the sand he told her that his father and grandfather had both been fishermen, confided that he had yearned to follow them and make the sea his livelihood but commonsense and forethought had dictated that there would come a time when the fishing industry would all but collapse so he had decided to go into banking.

As David reminisced a black depression stole over Susan. She knew that this talk about his past would invariably lead to questions about her own and she was saddened by the reality that she could not possibly form a relationship with anyone in the foreseeable future.

'And what about you, Susan Christie? Where do you come from? I mean, I know it's a place called Morton . . .'

She let go of his hand. 'I'm sorry, David, I don't want to talk about it.'

David stopped and gently caught her arm. 'What's wrong, Susan? I didn't mean anything.'

Susan placed her arms around his neck. 'I know you didn't.' She searched for words to offer as an explanation. 'It's just that there's something in my past that I need to bury before I can really start living again. Does that sound over the top?'

David held her at arm's length, his soft brown eyes studying her face. 'If that's how it is . . . no, it's not over the top,' he replied gently. 'Susan, I want to be your friend. Do you think that's possible?'

154

Susan nodded. 'Yes.'

'Good. Now, shall we head back to the car? I'll take you home.'

In David's Toyota Celica, which still had the smell of newness about it, Susan stared from the windscreen at the reflected light of the street lamp on the shiny cobblestones.

'Thank you for a lovely evening, David.'

He leant forward and kissed her lightly on the lips. A shiver ran the length of her spine.

With their lips still almost touching, David whispered, 'How about doing it again sometime?'

Susan silently reminded herself that she could not afford to become involved with anyone. 'I don't think so, no,' she replied.

'Oh.'

Susan looked at David and saw the sadness in his eyes.

'I don't mean that how it sounds,' she relented. 'I've enjoyed your company but I've so much work to do with the shop.'

Again their lips met but this time there was more fire, their arms became entangled in embrace. A fluttering in the middle of Susan's body and the moistness there told that her instincts and emotions would soon be in conflict.

When the kiss ended she reigned in her feelings and said lightly, 'Now if you really were my friend you'd offer to help with the shop, or maybe . . .' She stabbed him playfully in the chest. '. . . you just want to be seen about with me to prove to people you're not a raving poofter.'

'Ah, you've found me out,' he laughed. 'Did you mean that about helping you with the shop? I'd enjoy that.'

'So would I. Shall we say seven o'clock tomorrow evening?' David nodded. 'I won't ask you in tonight . . .'

'Because of the smell of cat's pee, I know.'

'Not because of the smell of cat's pee, you bloody fool,' Susan laughed. 'I've got an early start in the morning.' She touched his hand. 'I'll look forward to tomorrow.'

'I will too.'

Susan climbed the spiral staircase to the flat, poured herself a liberal gin and tonic and switched on the portable television for 'News at Ten'. Although the half-hour report made no reference

155

to the Stella Carway case or, more importantly, to herself, her feeling of trepidation continued. She knew that sometimes the police held information back. In her imagination she saw her photograph flashing on to the screen, heard the announcer reporting: 'This is Susan Ratcliffe who police believe may be able to help with their enquiries into the murder of Stella Carway.'

The cemetery was bathed in the soft glow of a hazy sun and although no rain had fallen for two days the grass still squelched underfoot.

Ashworth picked his way through the elaborate Victorian gravestones, vault-like and decorated with angels on winged horses, no doubt intended to propel the spirits of the deceased to the afterlife.

He crossed the path, gravel crunching beneath his shoes, to the more modern part of the cemetery with its smaller, less fussy headstones.

He kept a discreet distance behind the funeral procession, not wanting to look part of it but at the same time loath to arrive at the small chapel after the service had begun.

Steven Carway walked with Ann Thorncroft behind the coffin. The sight of the latter caused Ashworth to anticipate the embarrassment that would surround their meeting. There were three others whom Ashworth could not identify; the rest of the party was made up of black-suited professional mourners.

Ashworth quickened his pace as the coffin disappeared through the metal-studded gates of the chapel. By the time the last of the mourners had passed through he was about forty yards away. He passed the hearse where the driver and his young assistant were already lighting cigarettes and making small talk.

Slipping quietly through the door Ashworth settled himself at the back of the chapel. Ten pews in front sat Steven Carway and Ann. The door of the chapel closed slowly, the latch clicking noisily into place causing the mourners to turn.

If there had been any colour in Carway's face Ashworth felt

certain it would have drained away; as it was his eyes seemed to become more haunted and harrowed in the white mask that was his face. He turned quickly back before any eye contact could be made.

Ann smiled tightly at Ashworth while the other mourners, professional or otherwise, regarded him with varying degrees of indifference and idle curiosity.

Ashworth felt, as he always did in a holy building, a feeling of awe mingled with an air of foreboding, perhaps because holy ground was the closest link we have with whatever we hope lies beyond this mortal existence.

The vicar, because of the circumstances of Stella's death and the low attendance at the funeral, had suggested that the service should be kept short. To his relief – he had a christening in little more than an hour – his advice had been accepted and his professional manner allowed him to hurry through the service without appearing to do so.

After two hymns he said a few words about the deceased, asked that her soul be granted peace.

'And let us not forget those who are left behind,' his voice boomed out. 'Merciful Lord, please allow them to pick up the pieces . . .'

'Amen to that,' Ashworth said silently as the vicar concluded.

As soon as the service had ended Ashworth slipped out to stand discreetly to one side beyond a line of conifers as the coffin was carried out of the chapel. No one looked in his direction as the party proceeded to the grave.

Ashworth watched as the coffin disappeared into the ground. Steven Carway, head bowed, picked up a handful of earth and half-heartedly tossed it into the grave. Ann followed his example and then the group began to break up.

Already the two grave-diggers, eager to become grave-fillers, lurked in the distance.

Ann, a graceful figure in a full-length black coat, walked to where Ashworth was standing. As she neared he noted a redness around her eyes; it marred her good looks.

'Jim.' She smiled but there was no warmth in it. 'I thought I'd better apologize for last night.'

Ashworth was uneasy. 'No need for apologies, and if there were I should be the one making them.'

Ann stopped in front of him, glad that the first disconcerting encounter was here. 'I was a little shocked,' she said. 'I've begun to wonder about my deodorant . . .' There was some warmth in her smile this time.

'I was . . . very flattered.' Ashworth thought how corny this sounded. 'But I do have responsibilities.' Now he felt about a hundred and three.

'Your wife? That's nice,' she said, without any real feeling. 'I had noticed that she's booked in for a wash and set . . .' Her eyes danced with devilment. 'But don't worry, I won't mention the little job you did on my bedroom wall. By the way, you left your coat at my place.'

'Yes, I know, I'll come round to pick it up.' He paused. 'Where's Carway?'

'He's wandered off,' Ann replied, staring across to the far perimeter of the cemetery. 'Leave him alone, Jim, at least for today,' she implored. When there was no response, she said, 'Tonight?'

'Tonight?'

'To pick up your coat.'

'Oh, yes, if that's convenient for you.'

'It'll be fine. About six. See you.' She made an attempt at her usual bubbly cheerfulness but fell short of it.

As Ashworth watched her depart he briefly wondered what might have been.

The two men were already filling in the grave as Ashworth went in search of Carway; even at a distance of some hundred yards he could hear the heavy sound of hard earth hitting wood. In the midst of life, he thought.

He found Carway at the very rear of the cemetery which overlooked farm land, land that would soon have to be purchased by the local council to be incorporated into the almost full cemetery.

Carway was in an area behind two large sheds where the workmen kept their equipment. He was leaning on the stone wall which marked the boundary.

He looked up as Ashworth's footsteps sounded on the tarmac but refused to meet his eyes. 'Chief Inspector, I'm beginning to think of you as the proverbial bad penny.'

When he received no reply he turned to face Ashworth who was shocked by his appearance; dark smudges were beneath his eyes, his face was drawn and haggard. He put a cigarette to his lips with quick jerky movements. The fingers holding that cigarette were badly stained.

Carway said, 'Your people were watching me again last night. I'm going to have it stopped, you know.'

'It will be stopped,' Ashworth replied softly. He was beginning to think that he had misjudged Carway for there was no doubt that the man was grieving. Perhaps seeing someone who had been part of his life for so long – good or bad – encased in a wooden box and committed to the earth had washed away the heady almost light feeling of shock and allowed hard reality to flood in. The humanitarian inside Ashworth wanted to leave the man alone but the policeman wanted to hear the self-justification that was sure to follow.

'It wasn't always bad, you know.' Carway was not really talking to Ashworth, his eyes were focused on the bare branches of an oak in the adjacent field. 'We did have two really happy years.'

He dropped the cigarette, crushed it beneath his shoe and almost immediately lit another. 'Why do men think with their balls?'

This question was directed at Ashworth who merely shrugged, knowing that whatever Carway had to reveal would be arrived at by a roundabout route.

Again he returned to his own private world. 'Sometimes I wish women didn't fancy me at all. They look at you, make it plain that they're available . . . but you have to know, you see, you have to know and there's only one way to find out.' He sighed heavily. 'The funny part is, I don't really enjoy it. It's no more than an ego thing with me . . . notches on a gun.'

Suddenly he gazed earnestly at Ashworth. 'Do you think we become better people as we get older?'

'If we learn by our mistakes, yes.'

'That's what I've been trying to do,' Carway said intently. 'That's why I use call girls . . . nobody gets hurt.' Wistfully he said, 'Two happy years, and do you know what happened?' He did not pause. 'It was at an office party. I'd had a few drinks and this girl made all the running. Anyway, after that I had to know if it was just the booze. It wasn't and I kept going back to her, just like a child who can't leave sweets alone . . . until Stella found out.

'God, the rows and scenes we had. I'd wake up in the middle of the night to find her crying.'

Again he trod the cigarette into the tarmac, swallowed, licked his dry lips as if trying to free his mouth of the foul taste.

'Stella even convinced herself that it was all her fault, that it was something lacking in her that made me go elsewhere.

'We did try to patch it up . . . I really did try, but it couldn't work after that. Every time I was late home or if I was seen with a woman the rows would start again. No marriage can survive that.'

Just as the floodgates of regret began to close Ashworth jumped in. 'We'll find out what it is you're hiding, Steven,' he said gently.

Carway looked at him, gave a humourless laugh. 'Yes, I think you will.'

'Then why not tell me?'

Carway was now beginning to take charge of his battered emotions. 'All right, Chief Inspector,' he said, almost cheerfully, 'while there's no tape recorder, no one taking statements, I'll tell you this much: if you unearth certain facts I just might serve life for my wife's murder.' His mouth broke into a smile but his eyes showed acute pain.

Ashworth said, 'If that's the case you will because, believe me, I shall unearth them.'

Carway sneered. 'Ah, there's always a chance that you won't.'

'A remote one,' Ashworth countered.

'In my position a remote chance is better than none at all.'

Carway walked away. Ashworth watched him go. He looked a pathetic figure as he walked the long winding gravel path.

After arriving back from Stella's funeral, the first thing Ann did was rush into the bathroom to check on her make-up. She winced at her reflection with its smeared eye-shadow and mascara.

It was four thirty. The salon was closed for the day so she took a bath, washed her hair, dressed in a white blouse and black skirt which finished an enticing couple of inches above her knees and sat watching the clock, waiting for Ashworth.

Six o'clock came and went; six thirty did the same. When the door bell rang at five minutes to seven it startled her. Rather too quickly she opened the door to find a tall, good-looking young man smiling at her. He flashed something that resembled a wallet.

'Detective Sergeant Turner, miss. Chief Inspector Ashworth asked me to call and collect his coat.'

'Oh, I was expecting Jim to call.'

'He got tied up and asked me to collect it,' Turner replied. He had wondered why Ashworth's coat should be at this woman's flat and now the intimacy of first-name terms made him wonder still more.

'You'd better come up then.'

Ann slowly climbed the stairs and after closing the door Turner followed.

'I had a job to find you,' he said as they entered the flat. 'Phyllis Sharman gave me your previous address.'

'Ah, Joan Collins' mother,' Ann replied in a good-natured bitchy tone. 'I bet she told you I worked at the hair salon as well.'

'Yes, I think she did.'

'I did until about six months ago.' She went to collect Ashworth's coat from the bedroom, telling Turner in a loud voice as she went, 'I did, but I had a chance to buy the place and jumped at it.'

161

She came back with the coat and handed it to Turner. 'Dear old Phyllis knows that but she hates to see people getting on.'

He took out his notebook. 'I'll just take a note of your new address in case I need to speak to you again.'

'I was expecting Jim. Did he send a message?'

Turner made no reply. He was staring at a page in his notebook, a page containing the address for Rodney Watson which Turner had taken from Phyllis Sharman's address book; it did not match the one he had now. A deep flush crept into his cheeks.

Ann gave a nervous laugh. 'Are you all right? I only asked if Jim had sent a message.'

The full implications of what he had discovered finally hit Turner. He said hurriedly, 'No, no, there's no message.'

He excused himself and left the flat in great haste.

At the traffic lights Turner steered the Sierra into the outside lane that was for turning right. He cursed; he needed to go straight ahead. He would just have to risk the wrath of his fellow drivers when the time came for him to cut in front of them.

He was not disappointed; as the lights turned to green and his foot stabbed down on the accelerator, a car horn and a shout of 'Bloody fool' cut through the night air as he shot forward and steered to the left.

His mind was elsewhere, worrying about the mistake that had just come to light. Was it totally his fault or was Jim Ashworth partly responsible for it? And more importantly, would the mistake have any bearing on the case?

These thoughts chased from his mind his tangled domestic life. Whether this was a blessing or not only the next few days would reveal, for the storm that had been brewing in the skies around Eros was now threatening to break.

Sixty miles away, in the industrial town of Rothcombe, Karen Turner sat in the spotlessly clean kitchen of her sister, Julie.

162

The house was a neat semi-detached, blessed with nice quiet neighbours. Julie was two years older than Karen, married to Tony who worked in a car component factory.

By and large they were an unimaginative couple, a fact reflected in the MFI kitchen, the MFI fitted bedrooms, the plastic ceiling beams in the hall and lounge. But although they lacked imagination they were abundantly happy.

Julie was listening attentively to Karen's worries as they sat drinking coffee at MFI's best deluxe breakfast bar. From the lounge she could hear the loud roar of a crowd, her husband making remarks about a blind referee, and concluded that his team had conceded a goal.

'I know he's having an affair . . . I just know it,' Karen said morosely.

'You know no such thing,' Julie, ever the practical one, replied.

'What else can it be? I ring him every morning and he says he's just got in and he's going to bed, but if I ring back later he doesn't answer the phone.'

Julie gathered up the coffee mugs and began to wash them under the latest design in mixer-taps. 'There's probably a very simple explanation for all this,' she urged.

She was however having grave doubts about her brother-in-law's behaviour. Being an avid reader of romantic fiction and loving such articles as 'Signs to look for if your partner is having an affair', she saw herself as an authority on the subject.

Karen was saying, 'Name one.'

Julie dried the mugs on a tea towel which looked new. 'Simple. He's been working all night and he crashes out. He doesn't hear the phone.'

'Impossible. There's a phone beside the bed and anyway Owen's a light sleeper.'

Although Julie was concerned about Turner's alleged activities she, like any other budding agony aunt, knew that most affairs are short-lived, the novelty losing its appeal within a few weeks, and she saw it as her duty to guide her sister along a course which would cause her marriage the least harm.

Sitting at the breakfast bar again she said, 'You'll be all right,

Karen, when you get your house. It'll all look different then.'
She cast around for some crumb of comfort; the best she could
come up with was, 'When you buy your house I'll come and
stay . . . we can go to MFI and I'll help you choose your
furniture.'

'I want to go back,' Karen stated resolutely.

'What, tonight? But it's almost seven o'clock.'

'There's a train at seven fifteen. If Tony runs me to the station
I can make it.'

'But what about the kids? They're in bed . . .'

'Let me leave them with you overnight,' Karen implored. 'I
must know what's happening. Please?'

Much against her better judgement – some things are best left
alone – Julie agreed.

She asked Tony if he would mind taking Karen to the station,
and although the second half of the match had just started he
cheerfully agreed.

Susan sat on the bottom step of the spiral staircase, sipping
coffee, watching David taking books from the top shelves and
piling them on the floor, occasionally coughing as the disturbed
dust irritated his throat.

He had discarded his heavy sweater and the body beneath
his tight blue sweatshirt looked fit and athletic. The more Susan
attempted to divert her eyes from the bulge in his faded jeans
the more they seemed drawn to it. She told herself that she had
dressed for comfort but this was a lie, she had dressed for
David; the line of her small panties was clearly visible beneath
her tight jeans and her firm breasts, free from the restrictions of
a bra, bounced enticingly under her blue-and-white check
blouse.

She hoped David would not sense the turmoil taking place
within her. In all of her thirty-six years she had only been to
bed with three men. The low figure was entirely due to her lack
of desire, not lack of opportunity; this is not to say that strong
fires of need did not burn within Susan for they certainly did,

164

but past experience had taught her that sex was likely to add to the gnawing want inside her rather than alleviate it.

Five years ago she had given up her half-hearted search for sexual satisfaction and concentrated on making something of her life.

Her eyes wandered around the shop; now, at long last, she had something on which to build and she did not need to complicate it with an unsatisfactory relationship.

'Your coffee will be cold,' Susan called softly.

David looked around, his face streaked with dirt, 'Some of this dust must be antique,' he laughed. Picking up his coffee mug he squatted on the floor in front of Susan and gazed up into her face. 'It'll soon come right,' he said reassuringly.

'If you say so.'

'Don't ever try to tell lies, Susan . . .' He smiled as he sipped his coffee. 'Your face just won't let you. At the moment it's saying: This come right? There's more chance of winning the pools.'

Susan giggled. 'That's just what I was thinking. I shall have to watch you.'

Glancing at the mountain of books he said, 'It's not that bad. As you've said, you want to sell new literature, novels, text-books, so that will take up ninety per cent of your trade. If you want my opinion, your second-hand books and prints are stock of a specialized nature and therefore should be at the rear of the shop.'

'What do I do with this lot, then? Oh, I know, a sale,' she said brightly. 'An opening sale. Say . . . fifty per cent off everything.'

'Yes,' David said doubtfully. 'But somehow I can't see the good people of Barcliff turning out in droves for a second-hand book sale. I'd say your best bet would be to get a dealer in. I do know one actually. I could sound him out for you.'

'You seem to know everyone.'

'Part of being a banker. He's all right, he won't try to screw you.'

'I probably wouldn't let him,' Susan chuckled, wondering

165

why she was steering the conversation towards sexual matters rather than away from them.

David laughed. 'Bad choice of words. What I meant to say was he's as honest as a very short day. He'll try to knock the price every which way but he won't say something's only worth a few pounds if it's really valuable.'

Susan was interested. 'When can you get him here?'

'Ah, there's a catch – everything would have to be indexed, either by title or author.'

'Index this lot?' Susan said hopelessly.

'It's not that difficult, Susan. If you work on it during the day and I help you in the evenings, it could take what . . . a month? And I'd calculate that it'll take that time to get new stock delivered, get the shop fitted out . . .'

'You are clever.'

'Yes, I know,' he replied immodestly. 'So, have I earned a shower?'

David showered first. Susan was in the bedroom when he walked in wearing just his jeans and with his hair dripping wet. 'Jesus, it's cold in here,' he said as he picked up a towel and vigorously began to dry his hair.

'I've got the heating on, you'll soon warm up.'

Susan noticed his deep full chest, wide shoulders, flat stomach, before she excused herself and went into the bathroom.

All the time she was under the shower Susan wanted David to be just where she had left him. In the bedroom; she wanted it to be easy, without embarrassment. She took off her shower-cap and dried herself, then reapplied make-up as best she could to her distorted image in the cracked mirror.

She put on her blouse and her prettiest panties, then picked up her jeans and left the bathroom.

After hesitating for a few seconds on the small cold landing she went into the bedroom. David was trying to get some warmth from the radiator which was making a strange gurgling sound. His hungry eyes went to her long shapely legs and the tiny white briefs which did little to conceal her thick pubic hair.

'I thought you'd be in the lounge, David,' she lied. There was a tremor in her voice.

David came towards her, still naked apart from his jeans. 'Susan, this is awkward, I don't know if I'm putting the correct interpretation on the signals I'm getting from you, and it's not a thing we can sit down and discuss rationally . . .'

He was by her side, Susan could hear and feel his breathing, could smell his male scent. As she gazed deeply into his eyes she unbuttoned her blouse but did not let it fall open immediately. David was staring approvingly at her cleavage. Tiny pulses beat all over her body and her legs felt weak as she opened her blouse in a token of surrender.

Susan was lost in a sea of pleasure, her head tossed from side to side on the pillow, incoherent words of joy tumbled from her lips. Their naked bodies touching, merging, joining in sensual delight drove all else away. The delicious sensations pulsating from the centre of her body were becoming hard to bear. A warm feeling began, built and subsided, climbed again and spilt over, bathing her in a spreading glow of pleasure.

'I'm coming, David. I'm coming. It's beautiful,' she panted, moving her body in time with his. She heard him groan, felt the urgency in his movement, then his body quivered and trembled as he ceased to push.

14

Ashworth had just finished reading *House Training Your Puppy*. Sarah had borrowed it from the library. They were sitting in the lounge watching the ball of brown and white energy.

Their carpet had suffered a series of assaults, indeed, Peanuts had performed every bodily function imaginable, at regular intervals.

With a sigh Ashworth fetched the lead from the sideboard, clipped it to the puppy's collar and dragged the reluctant

167

creature towards the back door in order to spend yet another quarter of an hour in the freezing cold as he willed the dog to do something.

The fifteen minutes became twenty, during which time the puppy managed to dig up one corner of the lawn, rolled about in the saturated earth to become a wringing-wet mass of mud, but at no time did she make any attempt to avail herself of the toilet facilities the garden was meant to provide.

A disgruntled Ashworth took her back into the house, dried her in the kitchen with the new towel with DOG embroidered on it.

Once back on the floor she scampered, slipping and sliding, back to the lounge. Ashworth got there just in time to hear Sarah's cry of, 'Oh no, not again!'

Peanuts had adopted her now familiar position, rear quarters pressed firmly into the carpet. Somehow she still managed to wag her tail as she sat in the spreading patch of urine.

Ashworth moved sharply, bringing the palm of his hand heavily down on to the puppy's small black nose. Peanuts yelped in protest, abandoned what she was doing – or rather, she postponed it temporarily – and ran for cover behind the armchair, urine shooting from her in short bursts as she ran.

'You hit her too hard, Jim,' Sarah protested.

'I did it just how the book says, Sarah. You have to let them know who's boss,' Ashworth replied defensively.

Having reached the sanctuary of the armchair the puppy seemed reluctant to stay there. Her head kept popping out, cocked to one side. She whimpered pathetically. Her eyes were frightened, showing the puzzlement that she felt. What could she have possibly done to attract such a violent reaction?

The front door bell rang.

Feeling very guilty now, Ashworth pointed to the puddle and said, 'Naughty girl,' in a gruff tone before stamping off to the door.

Turner rang the bell again. When Ashworth opened it and saw Turner's state he said, 'Owen, whatever's the matter?'

'Jim, I've made a cock-up.'

As Sarah came into the hall the men were climbing the stairs to the study. It was not long before she heard raised voices. Firstly that of her husband whose temper, once unleashed, was legendary. But then Turner's voice reached her; he at least seemed to be holding his own.

Karen dialled the number and waited. She was standing in the hall of their rented house; she steadfastly refused to call it home. As ever, the steady drone of their neighbour's television was in the background. The house felt cold, unlived in.

'Come on,' she muttered impatiently.

This was her last hope. Her husband was not in the house, no one at the station had seen him since late afternoon and as far as they knew he was not on surveillance.

The receiver at the other end was lifted. A familiar and friendly voice said, 'Yes?'

'Hello, Sarah, it's Karen.'

'Hello, dear, where are you phoning from?'

'I'm at the house,' Karen said quickly, eager to ask the question, 'Do you know where Owen is?' A dread that her suspicions were about to be confirmed made the words stick in her throat.

'Yes, dear, he's with Jim at the moment.'

Karen's knees went weak as Sarah said, 'They're having some sort of conference. Shall I get him to call you back?'

'Please. I was afraid he was on surveillance. I thought that's what he told me anyway but I couldn't remember.' She was rambling, she hoped Sarah would not pick up the probing edge in her voice.

Sarah did though and her heart went out to the girl. She kept her voice conversational. 'Not tonight, dear, but he was earlier in the week.'

'Thanks, Sarah. Sorry to bother you.'

'No bother, dear. I'll get him to phone. Bye.'

Sarah put down the receiver, stood staring at it for minutes, pity flooding through her.

It was almost an hour before Ashworth and Turner emerged from the study. During that hour Sarah had had to mop up two more puddles.

Sarah informed Turner of Karen's call and followed Ashworth into the lounge, leaving him alone with the telephone.

When he had finished he went in to apologize to Sarah for interrupting their evening and was about to leave when Peanuts broke cover, gave Ashworth a wide berth and, with body wagging, welcomed Turner.

At any other time Turner would have been enchanted but tonight the best he could manage was a couple of pats on the puppy's head.

Ashworth showed him out. 'Well, Owen,' he said, 'if the outcome of this is what we think it is, you might just prove your case. Bring Carway in first thing in the morning.'

Sarah heard the door close and a few minutes later found Ashworth still staring at it.

'What's the matter, dear? Problems?'

'I don't know what's wrong with Owen of late. He failed to spot that one of our chief suspects had changed addresses in the last couple of years. It could make a big difference to our enquiries.' He huffed. 'Everybody's in such a hurry they don't stop to check things properly. I'm beginning to think it's time I stood down.'

Sarah pooh-poohed the idea. 'Come through and have a drink,' she coaxed. Then she paused. 'Oh, do you think you should take the dog in the garden again before we settle?'

Ashworth's expression indicated that it was not a chore he was approaching with relish.

Turner sat in the car for a few minutes. Karen was checking up on him, he knew it. The thought angered him. She had left the kids at her sister's and come back to spy on him.

But for the chain of events that evening it would have worked. After collecting Ashworth's coat he would have gone to Kerrie's flat but after his discovery he came straight to

170

Ashworth's house. If Karen hadn't phoned him he would, at this very moment, be heading for Kerrie . . . Kerrie's bed.

These thoughts brought on a wave of nausea, bile rose in his throat, his heart beat rapidly.

He must phone Kerrie, break the unpleasant news. Better find a call box, car phones are too easily intercepted.

He started the engine. For Turner the world was beginning to seem a very small place.

At eight o'clock the next morning Turner, in a foul mood, was driving to Bridgenorton. Kerrie was sulking in the passenger seat.

They had said their good mornings ten minutes earlier and neither had made an utterance since, both no doubt feeling that the blazing row they had had over the telephone the previous evening left little to be said between them.

Turner felt doubly aggrieved: all Kerrie had to complain about was a night spent alone; he had Karen to contend with.

The searching questions which, when answered, only heightened her suspicions had in turn led to a sullen silence that prevailed throughout the sleepless night. Karen tossed and turned, contemplating the ceiling, scenario after scenario going through her mind.

Carway opened his front door. He was dressed in a dark blue bathrobe. In his hand was a battery shaver, switched on and buzzing.

Turner said, 'Steven Carway?'

Carway's annoyance was obvious. 'You know damn well I am,' he retorted. 'What do you want?'

'We'd like you to accompany us to the station to assist in our enquiries, sir,' Turner said politely, although on this particular morning he felt anything but polite.

'I want my solicitor present,' Carway stated, his voice rising.

'You can phone him from here or at the station. Now might I suggest that we step inside, sir, and wait for you to get dressed?'

Carway simply turned and walked into the flat leaving them to follow.

171

The interior could at one time have been described as luxurious, but now it was badly in need of a clean. Empty take-away food containers and brown carrier bags littered the coffee table. Ashtrays, full to overflowing, were dotted about the deep-pile red carpet; the light pastel walls were beginning to show hints of future nicotine stains. A half-empty bottle of whisky and an overturned glass were on the floor by the settee.

'Not a happy person, I'd say,' said Turner, trying to make conversation.

'Tell me about it,' Kerrie snapped back.

They exchanged no further words but moved about the flat, keeping Carway in earshot.

When he finally emerged from the bedroom he was dressed in a light grey suit, white shirt and blue tie.

Sullenly, almost with an air of defeat, he walked in front of them to the car, climbed into the back seat, sat staring out of the side window as Kerrie climbed in beside him.

Carway had been in the interview room for two hours.

On his arrival at the station he had tried to telephone his solicitor only to be told that Gallford was playing golf all morning; he was advised to say nothing until Gallford was available.

At first Carway had been angry. Had Ashworth planned this? Picked a time when Gallford would be tied up? Brought him in, hoping he could be tricked into making a mistake?

Well, he wouldn't fall for it. He would simply wait for Gallford who would have him out of here within the hour.

Carway cursed the scotch he had consumed before the funeral and during it, the nips taken from the hip flask whenever the opportunity arose. It had done its job well in as much as it had built a numbing wall between himself and reality . . . but it had loosened his tongue.

Had he really been fool enough to admit there was evidence to convict him if only the police could find it?

That's what this was all about. That's why they had brought him in. They were hoping to wheedle something out of him.

172

After all, if they hadn't unearthed anything by yesterday, how could they have done so since? And if they had, why hadn't they arrested him?

The thoughts cheered him, made him feel better, and under the watchful eye of the constable at the door he paced the small room.

But it was not long before doubts began to creep back into his mind. Hadn't he read somewhere that the police deliberately keep suspects waiting if they can, just to unnerve them?

He returned to the table, took a cigarette and lit it, noting his shaking hand. He wondered, as he had done many times over the past few weeks, how much the human mind can take before it shatters.

In one way he would welcome it; insanity would bring a cosy room in a mental home, almost a relief compared to the rigours of prison life.

God, he'd already started to accept that he was guilty, that they had some damning evidence with which to convict him.

The door opened. It startled him out of his reverie. The young one, Turner, came in first. Carway did not like him; too terse. His words were polite but his tone rarely was. He was carrying tea in two plastic cups. Ashworth was behind him, carrying a third.

'Sit down, Steven,' Ashworth said in that quiet way of his.

Carway sat in the hard wooden chair. The detectives sat opposite under the harsh light of the fluorescent strip; it showed up every blemish, every tiny line on their faces.

Its fierce light made Carway feel vulnerable; he could imagine their prying eyes penetrating through to his mind, reading the thoughts there.

He averted his eyes, stared down at the cup that had been placed in front of him, studied the tiny-bubbled surface of the tea. 'I'm not going to say anything,' he stated flatly.

'There's no need to, Steven.' That was the calm reassuring voice of Ashworth.

With his carefully chosen words delivered on a knife-edge, Turner said, 'But do you mind if we talk to you? Would you object to that?'

Carway knew that he was shaking his head.

Turner produced a map of the Bridgetown area. Picking up Carway's cigarettes, lighter, cup, and moving them out of the way he unfurled the map on the table.

Carway stared down at it; he could feel Turner's eyes boring into the top of his skull.

'You see, sir, we know,' Turner announced softly, 'and you'll note that I say know as opposed to suspect, that something happened on the night of 5th November 1990 that led to your late wife being blackmailed. We also know the identity of the blackmailer . . . one Rodney Watson.'

Carway kept looking down, afraid to lift his head in case they read something into his expression.

Turner continued. 'But the problem we had, sir, was the fact that we could find no reported incident that night that would warrant the attention of a blackmailer. We know your late wife attended the drama group that evening . . .'

Turner's thumb came into Carway's line of vision, pinpointing the road where the drama productions took place.

'We also know that Stella and other members of the group went to a pub for a drink . . . here.'

Carway watched the thumb draw an invisible line on the map.

'Then she gave Rodney Watson a lift home. Do you know where he lives, sir?'

Carway shook his head. He could feel his legs trembling beneath the table.

'His premises are here and he lives three doors away from them . . . here. So, that left us with a big problem. You see, the only serious road accident recorded that night occurred on the other side of Bridgenorton . . . here. A hit and run. A girl was killed. So, we looked into it and do you know what we found? We discovered that at the time of the incident Rodney Watson lived on the other side of Bridgenorton, near to where the incident occurred. He moved to his present address some months ago.'

Carway felt the tremor in his legs become more violent; one

of his knees knocked against the table leg, it made a scraping sound on the floor.

He saw Ashworth's hand touch Turner's sleeve just before he said, 'Do you want to tell us about it, Steven?'

Carway looked up, glanced from one to the other. He felt trapped; something cold gripped his middle. He blurted out, 'Stella just didn't see her. There wasn't a light on the bike . . .'

'Steady, Steven, just tell us in your own time.' Ashworth's voice soothed him.

'The first thing I knew about it was when Stella arrived home just after midnight. She came in with Watson. I didn't know him. She looked as if she'd seen a ghost. She told me she'd knocked a girl off her bike and that they thought she was dead. But she said it would be all right because Watson could repair the car and no one would ever know.'

'Why did you go along with that? Why didn't you report it?' Ashworth probed.

For some reason Carway was feeling better now; telling them was like lifting some great burden from his shoulders. 'I don't know. It was a shock. I just went along with it. I suppose it seemed the easiest way out of a mess.'

Turner, his voice terse, said, 'So Watson repaired the car and then began to blackmail your wife?'

Carway nodded. 'Yes, but it wasn't quite as straightforward as that. We heard nothing from him for about six months, then he asked if he could come round one evening. He said he was thinking about starting a business and he wanted my advice. He made me look a real fool, let me spend an hour explaining things like low-interest loans. Then he said it wasn't a low-interest loan he wanted, it was a no-repayment one. It took me a few minutes to realize what he meant. It dawned when he said he'd done us a favour and now he was calling it in.'

Moisture glistened on Carway's upper lip despite the coldness of the room. He began to feel an almost euphoric enjoyment in unburdening himself.

'So you started paying the blackmail money,' Ashworth prompted.

'Well, neither of us saw it as blackmail. We thought he just wanted ten thousand pounds to set up his business and that would be it.'

'But he kept coming back.'

'Yes, although I never saw him again. He kept asking Stella for the money.'

'Until when? At what point did you decide to stop paying?'

With some relief Carway sensed that Ashworth was on his side. He said, 'When Stella and I decided to divorce.'

Ashworth sighed. 'You realize this looks bad for you, Steven? A lot of people would accept that if your wife was dead the blackmailer would be redundant.'

'Yes, I know that, just as I knew that would be the interpretation you'd put on it.'

'Then help me to help you.'

Carway looked wary. 'What do you want to know?'

'Steven, you're an intelligent man,' Ashworth said with exasperation. 'Why didn't you just tell Watson to go away? After all, he was an accessory to the crime. What could he have done?'

Carway gave a bitter laugh. 'Stella always said I was a snob and I suppose she was right in a way. I tend to think that anyone who doesn't have a posh accent is thick. But Watson's all there, believe me. He'd already worked that one out. He wasn't going to you people, he was going to make an anonymous phone call to the girl's parents. It nearly sent Stella out of her mind.'

Ashworth and Turner exchanged a glance. Without saying anything Turner left the room.

Ashworth went on, 'How did he intend getting round the fact that he was in the car?'

'Easy, he was going to claim that Stella had dropped him off in the centre of Bridgenorton and then she'd carried on to pick up the ring road.'

'And I suppose he'd have friends willing to back him up,' Ashworth ventured.

Carway shrugged.

176

After a moment, Ashworth said, 'Why didn't she use the ring road to take Watson home, do you think?'

Carway tried a smile. 'Chief Inspector, she wasn't giving Watson a lift for the company. Dark country lanes . . . car with a back seat. Do you get the picture?'

'I see, and did the sex thing carry on after the hit and run?'

'Yes, that was one of the things that annoyed Stella, her body had become part of the package deal for repaying the favour.'

Ashworth seized on this. 'Say Watson had been at your house, wanted to take a bath before having sex with Stella . . . would she have refused?'

'I doubt it. She was terrified of him.'

Ashworth leaned forward. 'Now, I want you to think carefully, Steven. Did Stella appear to be happier for the last two months of her life?'

Without hesitation Carway said, 'Markedly so, yes.'

'Didn't that strike you as strange?'

'Not really. She'd told Watson there was no more money so that was it. He made a lot of noisy threats but as the days went on and he didn't do anything we assumed that she'd called his bluff.'

'So Stella was out of his clutches.'

'No, I don't think so. I think he realized that the goose which laid the golden egg was dead but he was still quite happy to pick up small amounts of money from her . . . and, of course, sex.'

Ashworth pondered for a moment. 'So he could well have been at your house on the night of the murder?'

'I don't see why not.'

Ashworth allowed this to mull around in his mind. The pieces were beginning to fit into place. But were all the pieces in the box?

Carway said, 'Are you going to charge me, Chief Inspector?'

'Not as yet, Steven, no, but you'll be asked to stay here for a while and help us with our enquiries.' He leaned forward confidentially. 'Now, this hasn't been an official interview, it's not on tape or written down. Do you understand me?'

Carway nodded.

'Right, you get your solicitor to help you. Put the facts, such as they are, in the best possible light for yourself.'

The gratitude almost shone from Carway's face. 'Why are you doing this for me?'

'One reason and one reason alone . . . I don't think you killed your wife.'

Carway said, 'There's one other thing.'

'Yes?'

'I'm nearly out of cigarettes. Will I be allowed to get some more?'

'Of course, I'll send someone in. Tell him what you want and he'll see to it.'

Without another word Ashworth rose and left the room, nodding to the constable as he passed.

Ashworth lengthened his stride as he walked along the corridor. Things had started to move from the time he had ordered surveillance on Carway and now the roller-coaster was gathering speed.

Turner was in the office, diligently studying a file. As Ashworth entered he said, 'I've found what we wanted, Jim.'

Ashworth sat behind his desk, took in the view of the town through the glass wall as Turner continued.

'The victim of the hit and run was a fourteen-year-old girl. Kathy Carter. Died instantly. Head injuries and internal damage.' He was hurrying through the papers that were not relevant. 'Ah, this is interesting, at the inquest the girl's father, John Carter, broke down and swore he'd kill whoever had done this to his daughter.'

'Who can blame him for that?' Ashworth interjected.

Turner went on. 'His troubles had hardly begun though. His wife never recovered from the daughter's death and spent some time in a psychiatric hospital. The day after she was released . . . let's see . . . twelve months ago, she committed suicide. Plastic bag over her head. Her husband found her. At the inquest he again threatened to kill the person who had wrecked

178

his life. His exact words were: "I'll choke the life out of him."
He's spent some time as an outpatient at the psychiatric
hospital.'

'When was that?'

Turner checked the file. 'The same time as his wife.'

'Was he known to us?'

'No, Jim, the family was perfectly respectable. Kathy was
their only child. The local press . . .' Turner sneered. '. . . did a
piece on him after his wife's death: How many more lives will
be ruined before police crack down on hit and runs? That type
of thing.

'John Carter was a factory foreman apparently, good standard
of living, happy marriage. The only hint of any violence in his
background is the fact that he was once an amateur boxer.'

Ashworth studied the spire of Bridgetown's ancient church.
After a moment he said, 'So, what we're looking at is, when
Steven Carway stopped paying the money, Rodney Watson
could have carried out his threat, phoned John Carter and
passed on Stella's name.'

He swivelled his chair round to face Turner, who said, 'It fits,
Jim. It could have tipped the balance of the man's mind . . .
and it does fit in with the Christmas bow angle.'

Ashworth frowned. 'How's that?'

'Well, if you lose a child when would the memory be most
painful? Birthdays? Christmas?'

'Yes,' Ashworth mused. 'Owen, there's something else I
want you to check out . . .'

'Done it, Jim. Rodney Watson's stay in hospital on the night
of the murder doesn't hold up.'

Ashworth smiled. 'He wasn't there?'

'He was there all right, the surgeon was going to look at his
foot the next day, but that night he was in the convalescent
wing. He could come and go as he pleased.'

Ashworth stretched out in the chair. 'Good. So, he could
easily have gone to Stella, demanded money, then turned ugly
when none was forthcoming.'

'Not only likely but highly probable, I'd say,' Turner agreed.

Ashworth said, 'Well done, Owen, fine job.' Then his face

clouded and after a short hesitation he said, 'Which brings me back to last night really, and while I accept that the foul-up over Watson's address was partly my responsibility insomuch as I superimposed myself on you by taking the address from the service receipts rather than allowing you to follow through your line of enquiry . . .'

Turner tried to interrupt but Ashworth silenced him. 'No, Owen, this has been a long time coming and it needs to be said. I did superimpose, I admit that, but if you'd been working at maximum efficiency you would never have allowed me to.'

Turner was standing by his desk, slowly clenching and unclenching his left hand; some colour had crept to his cheeks. 'Any more complaints while we're on the subject?' he asked tartly.

Ashworth held his gaze. 'Since you ask, yes. I didn't like the way you handled Carway just now. There was something almost brutal about it.'

Turner's temper finally frayed. 'I resent that, sir,' he threw back.

Ashworth noted that he was 'sir' again. He said, 'It was brutal, Owen. You were enjoying watching the man squirm.'

'I'm quite willing to let a disciplinary committee examine my conduct and the standard of my work.'

Ashworth's fist hit the desk-top. 'Don't be so bloody silly, I'm not talking about disciplinary committees, I'm talking about our working relationship.' He took a deep breath. 'What I'm saying is, I think there's something wrong in your personal life and I . . . Sarah and I would be happy to help in any way we can.'

Turner said stiffly, 'I do have a few problems at the moment, sir, which I'm endeavouring to sort out. Now you've brought this to my attention I shall make every effort to see that it doesn't interfere with my work. Now, which line of enquiry would you like me to follow?'

Ashworth felt as if he were banging his head against the one thing he didn't have in the office . . . a brick wall. He said, 'You take Watson. Carter will need a delicate touch so you'd better

180

leave him to me.' He regretted the words as soon as they were uttered.

He sat back, muttering, 'Damn', under his breath as the door slammed on Turner's hostile exit.

'Pull over, Owen,' Kerrie pleaded. 'We have to talk.'

The argument with Ashworth was still uppermost in Turner's mind so he replied, 'We're working, Kerrie, we'll talk later.'

'When? How?' she flared back. 'She's home. You'll be running back to her tonight.'

Reluctantly Turner steered the car into a lay-by which was no more than a strip of concrete just wide enough for a car.

They were on their way to bring Rodney Watson in and this was the quietest stretch of road that they had encountered *en route*.

Turner was beginning to feel that he had entered into some form of double marriage – whichever way he turned there was a woman reminding him of his shortcomings.

As is so often the case in these situations, the overwhelming need to talk seems to vanish as soon as the opportunity presents itself. The ominous signs that a decision must be taken, one way or the other, undoubtedly cause the participants to hold back.

Kerrie was staring blankly out of the window; Turner, his face grim, looked straight ahead.

The minutes ticked away before Kerrie said sullenly, 'I can't go back to how it was.'

'Just give me time to sort it out,' Turner pleaded.

Kerrie was determined. 'No more time, Owen. It's here and now . . . her or me.'

Now afraid that she had put her case too bluntly, she began to list the reasons why he should choose her.

'We're good in bed, Owen, you know we are, and we're good out of it. We're in the same job. And you say you'd rather be with me . . .'

'You know I would,' Turner quickly agreed.

181

'Then tell her,' Kerrie said stridently. 'Tell her. Get it over with. It's not as if we're the only people this has happened to.' She looked at him then, her large dark eyes shining with unshed tears. 'Owen, I'm not willing to go on just being someone who lets you have a bit of fun in bed.'

Turner rounded on her. 'Is that how you see it? Just letting me have a bit of fun?'

Kerrie backed down a little. 'You know it's not, it's better with you than it's ever been with anyone else.'

That statement hurt; thoughts of her past lovers tormented him. He stared hard at her as his divided loyalties pulled him in conflicting directions.

Was he in love with her? Did he know what love was? Or was it simply lust? Turner pushed the thoughts from his mind for to allow them entry would be admitting the fact that he was using another person for his own sexual gratification and that was unacceptable to him.

As he watched Kerrie the familiar warm feeling swept over him. They were good in bed, it was true. Verbally she was so explicit; that was new to him as were so many of the things they did together, things that he believed women rarely did outside of books and films. The thought of Kerrie doing them with someone else filled him with an insane jealousy.

Kerrie said sulkily, 'I can't waste my whole life, Owen.'

Suddenly it was clear to Turner. 'I'll leave her,' he declared.

'When?' A tear spilled over on to Kerrie's cheek.

'Tonight,' he replied jubilantly. 'I'll tell her tonight, then I'll come round to the flat.'

So his decision was made and without checking for cars or pedestrians they kissed openly and unashamedly.

15

Rodney Watson looked up as Turner and Kerrie entered the garage. Picking up a piece of oily rag he stepped back from the vehicle on which he was working and casually wiped his hands, saying, 'Well, if it's not PC Plod. Who've you brought with you this time?'

'This is Detective Constable Stacey,' Turner replied curtly.

'Hello, darling,' Watson said with a sneer. 'How'd you fancy coming round and studying my bedroom ceiling for a couple of hours sometime?'

Turner tried to keep his voice pleasant. 'Mr Watson, I wonder if you'd mind accompanying us to the station. There are a few questions we'd like to ask you.'

Watson smirked. 'You must be joking, mate, I've got work to do. Ask your questions here.'

Trying to keep his patience, Turner said, 'I'll ask you once again, Mr Watson, will you please come to the station with us?'

'And I'll tell you once again . . . naff off.' Watson laughed.

Kerrie stepped in, hoping to defuse what was fast becoming an ugly situation. She said nicely, 'We have some very important questions we need to ask you, Mr Watson, and here is not the place.'

Watson leered at her. 'Now, I like the way you ask, darling. Better than this pompous prat.' He glared at Turner. 'Now, what do you want to know?'

Turner's voice stayed very even, only his phrasing changed. 'We want to talk to you about a hit and run accident, extortion . . . oh, and a little matter of murder. Now, I'm asking you for the last time, come with us please or I'll arrest you.'

Watson threw down the rag. 'You arrest me, you prat? I'd have you for breakfast before my three Weetabix.'

Turner took one step towards him and the world went black. A blow caught him on the nose and in his right eye, knocking him backwards. He toppled over a car jack; the world reeled as his head cracked on the concrete floor.

He must have lost his senses for a few moments for when he opened his eyes Kerrie was on her knees, doubled over, her face a deathly white as she clutched at her stomach.

Watson's car could be heard moving off at a dangerously fast pace.

Turner struggled to his feet, staggered, regained his balance.

There was blood on his suit, he could feel it running down his face.

By the time he reached Kerrie his legs felt stronger. 'You all right?' he asked.

'Yes.' She smiled bravely. 'I feel as if I've been kicked by a horse. God, look at your face.'

Turner tried a feeble joke. 'You'll get used to it as the years go by.'

In spite of her pain Karen gave it more laughter than it deserved because he was referring to their future together.

Turner took the walkie-talkie from his pocket, pressed the switch, nothing happened. 'Blast these things,' he said as he wove an erratic path outside.

He made the call, gave Watson's name, car registration number, informed control that they were injured but capable of returning to the station.

A small crowd had gathered by the time he finished: housewives, workmen, unemployed youths; all speculating as to what had happened, none of them offering assistance.

On arrival at the station both were sent to the hospital. Turner needed three stitches over his eye. Kerrie underwent an extensive examination to determine whether anything was broken; luckily nothing was, although she had suffered bruising to the rib-cage and abdomen.

By the time they got back to the station it was past midday. Ashworth was sitting in his office, staring down at his blotter. He glanced up as they came in.

'Are you two all right?' There was genuine concern in his voice.

'We're both okay, sir,' Kerrie said with a cheerfulness she did not feel.

Turner ignored the question and asked one of his own. 'Is Watson in custody yet?'

'Yes, he's downstairs in the cells,' Ashworth confirmed. 'He was caught after a car-chase; it ended when he hit a tree. Still took five officers to bring him in.'

Turner fingered the stitches above his eye, his rapidly swelling nose, and said, 'I can believe that. What's the news on John Carter?'

'Bad,' Ashworth replied morosely. 'John Carter's where he's been since two weeks after his wife's suicide . . . in a secure mental institution, either under restraint or heavily sedated. Odd, what takes just seconds to happen can ruin so many lives.'

'Perhaps it's not wise to get too involved, sir,' Kerrie said gently.

Ashworth looked up, smiled. 'You two look like you've tangled with Frank Bruno. Why don't you take the rest of the day off?'

'No, thank you, sir.' Turner still felt frosty towards his superior but was beginning to thaw. He exchanged a glance with Kerrie. 'We'd like to interview Watson.'

Ashworth gave him a sharp look.

Turner said quickly, 'It's not personal, sir, we just want to see the line of inquiry through.'

Ashworth conceded. 'All right, go and get him out of the cells.'

They went to leave; as Kerrie's footsteps echoed down the corridor Turner stayed in the doorway. He appeared to be embarrassed. 'Sir . . . Jim, I'm sorry about earlier on. I had no right – '

Ashworth stopped him. 'I should be the one to apologize. I was meddling and I shouldn't have questioned your efficiency. You're the best detective sergeant I've come across.'

Turner became awkward at the praise. 'Thank you. You were right, you know, I do have personal problems but they'll be over in the next few days.'

'Good. Oh, and Owen, have plenty of back-up outside the interview room.'

'Okay, Jim.'

'And don't forget to duck this time.'

Turner laughed then immediately cringed at the pain it produced.

Ashworth felt better for having made up with his sergeant

but gloom still surrounded him. The roller-coaster was beginning to slow.

Watson? He shook his head; true, he had demonstrated he would use force as a first resort but, no, Ashworth could not cast him in the role of murderer.

Over the weeks he had built up a clear picture of the killer; all it lacked was a face. He was cool, calculating, strong-nerved. Ashworth had the idea that this crime had been a spur of the moment thing, carried out in a fit of passion or rage; it had not been planned. Its perpetrator had left no clues so all they had been able to do was flounder about in the tangled life of the victim.

Why did he always think of the killer as a male? Wasn't it quite possible for a female to have carried out the crime? After all, the blow to the head would have rendered Stella Carway almost unconscious. Ashworth shook his head wearily.

Turner in no way thought of himself as a physical or moral coward but there was fear in his stomach as he entered the interview room, closely followed by Kerrie.

Watson was sitting at the table which was dwarfed by his massive frame, his enormous forearms rested on its top. A sneer played around his lips as he noticed Turner's eye which was already beginning to tinge purple, blue, around the stitches.

'Well, if it ain't hard case,' Watson commented arrogantly.

Turner took his time, knowing he must stamp his authority and superior intellect upon this situation. He glanced at the uniformed police constable standing by the door before sitting down, elbows on the table.

After a few moments he leant forward and rested his chin on his clenched fists. 'Wait until the return, Rod,' he said lightly.

'Can't see a ponce like you doing any better then.'

'Can't you, Rod?' Turner gave a humourless smile. 'I'd say you'd be way past your best by then. Fifteen years in prison ages you . . . the lack of exercise, I suppose. Does something to the head as well . . . the brain. A lot of people become institutionalized, can't cope with the outside.'

Watson rose, gripped the edge of the table and pushed his face close to Turner's, a snarl contorted his lips. 'Piss off,' he hissed.

Turner held up his hand to stop the uniformed officer coming forward. When he spoke the calmness of his tone did not reflect the nervousness he felt inside. 'I can't do that, Rod, now sit down.'

Watson ignored the request and remained standing, his face a foot away from Turner's.

'You disappoint me, Rod, I thought you were intelligent. This isn't something you can punch your way out of . . .' Turner's tone was now persuasive. 'You tried that at the garage and now you're here, in even more trouble than before. However many people you beat up, Rod, the questions are still there and we're going to keep asking them until we get answers. Now, sit down.' Turner's last directive sounded offhand, dismissive.

For a few seconds it was touch and go. Watson's eyes were wild as all that Turner had said went around inside his brain. Then something seemed to go out of him. As he slumped back into the chair, he muttered, 'You can't put me away for fifteen years.'

'Can't we, Rod?' Turner was now brisk; there was a sharp sting to the edge of his words. 'Hit and run, the death of a child; these are emotive subjects . . . and that charge could be the least of your problems.'

'I wasn't even driving the car,' Watson blurted out.

Turner heard the click as the tape recorder was turned on, followed by Kerrie's voice giving the time, the date, and the name of the person being interviewed.

'Yes, we know Stella Carway was the driver.'

'She didn't stand a chance, nobody would have. One second the kid wasn't there, the next she was under the wheels,' Watson stammered.

'Okay, Rod, keep calm.'

'But there were no lights on the bike . . . and the kid was wearing dark clothes.'

187

'So after the accident you panicked.'

Watson nodded slowly. 'Yes, Stella was out of her head, she threw up in the car.'

'So in that panic you decided to drive on and repair the car.'

'Yes, but I checked on the kid first . . .' Watson buried his face in his hands. 'God, that sight'll haunt me for the rest of my life. She was all mangled up.'

The show of grief had little effect on Turner who assumed it was feigned. He said, 'And six months later you decided to capitalize on it . . . make some money.'

Watson pondered the implications of this, how it would look in court. 'No,' he said finally. 'It wasn't how you're saying. Stel gave me the money to set myself up in business.'

Turner sucked in breath and shook his head. 'Won't do, Rod. You went to see Steven Carway and demanded ten thousand pounds.'

Watson mulled this over; like most criminals, once cornered he could see little point in continuing with the charade. 'Okay, I had the ten grand. I didn't see why I shouldn't get something. That kid'll be on my conscience for the rest of my life.'

'You had ten thousand the first time?'

'That's all I had.'

'Steven Carway says you had two hundred thousand.'

'Then he's a liar.'

'Think about it, Rod – the more you help us the more we can help you.'

'That's all I had, for Chrissake. You can check . . . the business, my house, it's all on mortgage . . . I used the ten grand for deposit.'

'We will check it, you can count on that,' Turner said lightly. 'Okay then, you say you never asked Stella for more money?'

'Yes, I asked,' Watson said resignedly. 'But I didn't get any. What's the point, you're gonna find out in any case. That's what all the rows were about. I wanted more money, she said her old man wouldn't pay any more.'

At this point Turner changed course. 'Did you use the hit and run to force Stella into having sex with you?'

Watson's eyes widened in surprise as he laughed. 'Force Stel to have sex? You had to force her to stop, mate, she was like a bitch on heat.'

Turner was silent for a moment, then he said, 'Do you think one of Stella's lovers killed her, Rod?'

The question took Watson off-guard. 'Well, I suppose it's possible. She often said her life was just one lie after another. That's why we got on so well, you see – and we did, whatever people tell you about the rows we had – 'cause I didn't care what she was doing when she wasn't with me as long as I was getting my share.'

'Did she mention any names? The people she'd lied to, I mean?'

'Yes, the gardener bloke, Fanny Faulkner . . . she used to tell them what they wanted to hear, like they were the only ones getting there. And her old man . . .' He pointed a finger at Turner. 'Because whatever he says he used to keep pretty close tabs on her, like he didn't want it getting round that his wife would do a quick turn for anybody she fancied. He used to have the house watched, things like that.'

'Anyone else?'

Watson hesitated.

'Come on, Rod, tell me.'

'Look, I can't vouch for this being true . . .' he said hesitantly, 'but Stel told me she was trying a bit of the other, mind you, she was pissed out of her skull at the time.'

'A bit of the other,' Turner repeated.

Watson spelt it out for him. 'Yes, like in lesbian.'

'Are you telling me Stella became a lesbian?' Turner said incredulously.

'No, I'm saying she tried it.'

'Do you know who this woman was?'

'No, Stel never said and I wasn't interested. Like I say, there was a lot of booze doing a lot of talking.'

'And was she converted by this female lover?'

Watson shrugged. 'I don't know about converted but she liked it well enough.'

189

'It must have seemed like some sort of solution. None of her male friends or even her husband could object to her having a female friend,' Turner surmised.

'No, I don't think so. I remember her saying this woman used to climb out of her tree if Stel went anywhere near another woman, let alone a man. She said she'd be glad to get away from it all.'

'And what did you take that to mean?'

'Dunno. Like I said, I wasn't that interested.'

'Thanks, Rod.' Turner stood up. 'That'll be all for the moment.'

Watson stared up at him. 'What happens now?'

'We'll have to sort out what we're going to charge you with but it shouldn't be as bad as I first thought.'

'Give me some idea.'

Turner sighed. 'Well, you're an accessory to the hit and run, you helped to conceal the crime . . . the blackmail charge will depend on what Steven Carway says.'

Turner left the interview room with Kerrie. Outside Kerrie said, 'That was really hairy in there for a time. I thought he'd go berserk.' She touched Turner's arm. 'You were magnificent.'

'I've watched all Clint Eastwood's films,' he joked.

They started walking back to the office.

'Do you believe the lesbian bit?' Kerrie asked.

'Possible. After all, Stella must have been through all the men in Bridgetown and surrounding areas, so what's more logical than starting on the women?' Turner quipped.

'I'll be interested to hear what our strait-laced chief inspector makes of all this,' Kerrie said mischievously.

Turner chuckled. 'He'll probably have us out on the streets asking women passers-by if they're lesbians and the ones that say yes will have to be brought in for questioning.'

'Come on, he's not that bad,' Kerrie laughed.

'I'm not saying he is, Kerrie, but he's definitely that meticulous, and whisper has it, this case is taking too long.' He pointed towards the ceiling. 'Anyway, I'll leave you to tell the old man what's happened. I'll attend to Steven Carway.'

'Owen, I can't tell Ashworth about lesbians, I'll die of embarrassment,' Kerrie whispered urgently.

Turner stared down at her with mock amazement on his face. 'You? The things you do in bed . . . head under the quilt? Yes?'

'Shut up,' she giggled. 'Someone might hear you.'

Kerrie told Ashworth about the Watson interview. He listened intently and then fell silent. A combination of things made Kerrie feel very ill at ease in his presence; uppermost was the fact that she knew he had opposed her appointment to the CID, opposed it to the point where it had been forced upon him; also, she found him difficult to get along with, a loner unwilling to share totally, even with the closest of colleagues. All in all she found him to be a sexist.

'Kerrie?'

Surprised, she looked up. 'Yes, sir?'

'Does this lesbian thing have a ring of truth about it?'

'Do I think Stella Carway could have had an affair with a woman, you mean?'

He gave a curt nod.

In spite of herself she was pleased he had asked for her opinion. 'Yes, I think so. Stella was, by any standards, a swinger. And of course there's nothing particularly new about that sort of thing; in the Middle Ages men had boys, women had women . . .' She found that Ashworth was watching her with interest, felt her face colouring under his stare. 'I studied history at school,' she said lamely. 'I don't quite know when it was we started labelling people homosexual but I do know that all through history a certain percentage of people have alternated between the sexes. And they do say it's in all of us, sir, to a greater or lesser extent.'

'Do they now? Well, I'm glad it hasn't surfaced in me,' Ashworth said gruffly and went back to studying the map on his desk.

Kerrie sat at Turner's desk, sullenly studying the top of Ashworth's bent head. He had this knack of making her feel foolish, would ask her some patronizing little question for no other reason than he felt he had to involve her.

She wanted to scream at him: Talk to me . . . discuss it. Don't wait for Owen to come back . . . I'm a detective too; I know I haven't got a pair of balls dangling between my legs but that doesn't mean I'm only capable of cooking, washing and giving birth!

Her irritation grew when, as soon as Turner entered the office, Ashworth said, 'Right, Owen, what have we got? Let's get this thing moving.'

Turner's injured face was beginning to show signs of strain brought about no doubt by the dread of the evening which lay ahead. He said now, 'Not much. I've interviewed Carway again and even with his solicitor present he's still dug his own grave. We've got to charge him, Jim.'

'The missing money, what did he say about that?'

'He's sticking to his story.' Turner glanced at Kerrie as he perched himself on the edge of Ashworth's desk. 'He personally gave Watson ten thousand, the rest he gave to Stella to pass on.'

'So . . .' Ashworth said thoughtfully, 'Stella salted away one hundred and ninety thousand pounds.'

'If we believe Watson's story.'

'Of course we do,' Ashworth replied sharply. 'The man's not bright enough to take out a mortgage just to cover his trail. If he'd got the money he'd have spent it.'

'That only strengthens our case against Carway then,' Turner pointed out. 'If he found out his wife had been duping him about the money.'

'We don't know that's what happened,' Ashworth growled.

'Short of a confession we'll never know exactly what happened, Jim,' Turner said diplomatically. 'All we can do is put forward a case and hope it stands up in front of a jury.' He realized then that he did not have Ashworth's attention. 'Do we charge Carway?'

'No, hold him,' Ashworth replied absent-mindedly, 'but don't charge him. There's this lesbian thing to look at.'

'What lesbian thing?' A note of exasperation had crept into Turner's usually placid tone. 'We don't know there was a woman let alone who she is.'

'There's Susan Ratcliffe.'

'Jim, you've eliminated the woman . . . there's not one thing to link her with Stella Carway.'

Ashworth silently regretted going underground about the Ratcliffe woman; if he had been open about it instead of getting Mike and one of his officers on to it unofficially, it would be plain to Turner that she had intended to vanish.

Ashworth went on, 'There are others in the frame. Ann Thorncroft for one, she and Stella were very good friends and don't forget she bought the hairdressing salon recently.'

'We can't investigate everyone who has started a business in the last eighteen months.' Turner sounded incredulous.

'I'm not saying we can.' Ashworth stood up and crossed to the coat-stand. 'What I am saying is, a large sum of money is missing and that's tied up in this murder somehow, so we investigate it.'

He put on his waxed-cotton jacket and left the office without another word.

The door had hardly closed behind him before Kerrie blurted out, 'He's impossible, Owen, bloody impossible!'

Turner watched the door, half expecting Ashworth to hear the outburst and reappear. 'Calm down, Kerrie,' he urged.

'I will not calm down. I'm pissed off with him. Have you noticed how he's always right? It doesn't matter what we think.'

'Come on, you're exaggerating – '

'No, I'm not. Did you see him then? He didn't look or speak to me once, it was as if I wasn't here.'

'Kerrie – '

'Kerrie nothing, he's a sexist, Owen. He didn't want me here and he's made it very plain that I'm not welcome.'

'It's not personal,' Turner said in an effort to mollify the situation. 'He doesn't want women in CID because he doesn't believe they should be in the firing line when people like Watson cut up rough. He only wants to protect you.'

'Yes, he wants to protect me because he doesn't think I'm capable of doing the job as well as a man could do it . . . and that's sexist,' Kerrie said with a huff.

Turner pushed himself off the desk and went to her. 'I don't know if it's escaped your memory but tonight I'm going to tell Karen I'm leaving her and I think that's far more important than Jim Ashworth's idiosyncrasies.'

As Kerrie exhaled the anger left her body with the breath. 'Yes, I know, the stress that's causing is probably affecting my sense of proportion.'

Kerrie left the station at six but Turner remained in its sanctuary for as long as he possibly could, not relishing what the night ahead held.

He fetched himself a cup of coffee from the vending machine at seven o'clock, took two painkillers to ease the dull throbbing ache in his head; they helped, but his eye and nose still hurt.

At seven fifteen he realized he could postpone it no longer and left the station.

As he walked across the car-park light snow began to fall; already a dusty powdering lay on the ground and decorated the parked vehicles.

Turner drove slowly, a reluctance to reach his destination prompting his caution rather than the need for care. He reached the house without mishap, parking on the road rather than in the drive, reaffirming his resolution not to stay.

A chink of light escaped from between the curtains. Walking down the drive he took a deep breath, bracing himself for the storm that was about to erupt.

Pushing open the door he noticed that there was no noise inside the house, even next-door's television was silent (it must have broken down, surely).

Karen was not in the lounge; the room was cold, no warm glow came from the coal-effect gas fire. He returned to the darkened hall, called to Karen from the bottom of the stairs. The eerie silence remained.

He opened the kitchen door, the light was on and in the

194

centre of the table, propped up against a vase of dried flowers, was a long white envelope.

'She's left me. Thank God, she's left me,' he said aloud as he picked up the envelope and tore it open.

Sarah Ashworth knew her husband was troubled. He picked his way through dinner with hardly a word spoken. She left him alone, knowing full well that he would discuss whatever it was with her in his own time.

She did regret telephoning the station that morning to report a big improvement in Peanuts' toilet training since the slap on the nose the previous evening; three times Sarah had taken her into the garden and three times the puppy had obliged her by relieving itself. But mostly she regretted ringing in the afternoon to tell him there had been a reversal and Peanuts now seemed to be favouring the kitchen floor. When would she ever learn to stop behaving like a newly-wed and leave him in peace when he was busy?

As she cleared away the dishes Ashworth went through to the hall and came back with his coat on.

'Where are you going, dear?' she asked.

'I'm going to take Peanuts into the garden and stay out there till she does it, then praise her.'

He was now trying to catch the dog to put the lead on. Peanuts, loving the fun of the chase, bounded through into the lounge to be finally pinned down by the settee.

Ashworth's face was dark when he entered the kitchen with the now safely harnessed dog.

Sarah looked up from the sink. 'I think the slap on the nose worked. I really do think that's worth persevering with.'

'I didn't like it,' Ashworth said roughly as he opened the back door.

Sarah said helpfully, 'It says in the book that it helps if you say "busy". The puppy begins to recognize what you want it to do.'

Ashworth turned. 'Busy,' he said flatly.

'Yes, over and over again . . . busy, busy, busy.'

Sarah watched from the kitchen window as Ashworth walked about, leaving footprints in the snow. She could see his moving lips, watched the dog, head cocked to one side as if trying to discover exactly what was required of her.

After some fifteen minutes – and probably out of necessity rather than a desire to please – she stooped down.

Sarah watched the man – who, in his time, had put the fear of death into criminal and policeman alike – pat the dog, saying, 'Good girl. Jolly good girl.'

And as she watched she felt a surge of love so strong it misted her eyes.

Turner drove with care for it was needed now; the snow had begun to fall quite heavily. The windscreen wipers on maximum speed were just about keeping the screen clear.

Several times during the journey he had touched the brakes only to have the rear wheels slip and slide, so now, as he reached his destination, he used the gears to bring the car to a halt.

His feet crunched in the virgin snow as he walked up the wide steps, through the double doors into the warmth beyond.

The surrounding smell assaulted his nostrils. Turner, like most people, hated hospitals; sickness reminded him of man's vulnerability.

He asked directions at the reception desk and took the lift up to Lancaster ward. Karen was at the bedside; she looked haggard, dark hollows were beneath her eyes.

As soon as she saw Turner she snapped, 'Why have you taken so long to get here?' There was bitter recrimination in her voice.

'How is he?' Turner stared down at his six-year-old son, Matthew, whose pale face poked out above the sheets.

'Keep your voice down, he's asleep,' Karen said, making no effort to lower her own tone. 'Where have you been?' she demanded.

'For God's sake, Karen, I read your note and came straight

here. It's a sixty-mile drive and there's three inches of snow,' he hissed back.

'I left messages for you at the station. Why didn't you ring?'

'I didn't get the messages. I was interviewing all afternoon.'

'That's all you think about . . . your bloody work.'

Their dispute had reached the ears of the night sister. The sight of Turner's battered face made her hesitate before intervening but when it became apparent that the argument was getting out of hand she was forced to take action.

As she approached the bed she said in a hushed tone which she hoped they would copy, 'You must be Mr Turner. I'm glad you're here. This has put a terrible strain on your wife.'

'How is my son, Sister?' Turner asked shortly.

She was surprised that he was so well-spoken. She said, 'He's quite all right, Mr Turner. It's just a chest infection, no more. Your sister-in-law's action was quite understandable under the circumstances, what with you and your wife being away, but it was a slight over-reaction. We'll keep Matthew in overnight just to be on the safe side but a course of antibiotics should clear it up.'

Satisfied that she had defused the situation she smiled brightly, saying, 'Now that you're here, perhaps Mrs Turner would like to go and have a snack in the canteen.'

Karen shot Turner a glance loaded with hostility before she flounced off towards the door.

Turner sat beside the bed. Yes, sister Julie would over-react, she'd do it deliberately and with more than a small helping of malice; any chance of disrupting an already shaky relationship would be seized upon with glee.

Karen's family, from her parents downwards, had never taken to Turner. He had tried, tried damned hard, until it became apparent that the fault did not lie with him.

Karen's family were caught up in a time-warp of dogma. To them ordinary people did not aspire to become top policemen, set up in business, do anything to improve their lot; ordinary people worked in factories – although it was quite acceptable for the more intelligent to have office jobs.

197

None of Karen's family enjoyed their work. They sacrificed a third of their lives so that they could have nice homes – be the envy of their neighbours – and spent fifty weeks of the year planning two precious weeks away. At one time top of the list had been Blackpool but they had now updated this to somewhere which came under the vague heading of 'abroad'.

Turner had often wondered if Karen's motive for marrying him had been to escape the life that had been imposed upon her; if indeed that had been the case she had very quickly decided that she did not enjoy the freedom outside the restriction and soon hankered to return to it.

His son turned in his sleep; a chesty wheeze escaped his lips. Turner knew that his son and four-year-old daughter, Jo, were the fragile thread that was holding him and Karen together; earlier in the evening he had been willing to break that thread.

The note about Matthew had shattered him, almost driven all other thoughts from his mind. But still he had considered Kerrie.

When she picked up the telephone he had expected a tirade of abuse but it had not been like that. True, she had cried, begged him to go on seeing her whenever he could, had fervently asked his forgiveness for her pushy attitude. She also told him that if he finished with her completely she would stop taking the pill, a statement Turner took to mean that if he couldn't have him she would have no one.

When Karen shouldered her way back through the door, the storm-warning still on her face, Turner took a decision: he would have some happiness, Kerrie would have some happiness . . . Karen would have to seek her own peace.

She approached the bed. 'We have to talk,' she stated flatly, making no mention of his injured face.

He offered up a silent prayer – God, give me the strength – as he said, 'Where?'

Not wanting to attract the attention of the sister Karen spoke in a whisper. 'There's a day room.'

She marched off. Turner, after glancing at his sleeping son, followed.

The day room turned out to be an area outside the ward;

around its three sides it had rows of seating fixed to the walls. The area and the corridor were bathed in the soft glow of the hospital night light. Beyond the window was the Christmas card scene of the car-park.

Their separation had not dulled Karen's determination to pick a fight. She rounded on him as soon as he entered the area. 'We have to sort our marriage out,' she said fiercely.

Turner sat down. 'How do you suggest we do that?' he asked wearily.

'It's your job, that's what causes all the trouble. I never know where you are, who you're with – '

'Karen, don't be so bloody silly, we're talking about my career, our livelihood – '

'Our livelihood,' she scoffed. 'I want a life, Owen, a husband who goes out at eight in the morning and comes back at six.'

She went and sat at the other side of the room, a good five yards from him as if to emphasize the gulf between them. She sneered. 'I can smell her on you, you know. I can smell her perfume on your clothes now. I smell her on you sometimes when you come to bed . . . I don't mean her perfume either, I can smell when you've been up her.'

Turner had often wondered what he would do when this moment came, whether he would admit or deny the accusations; he did neither, just sat staring at her.

Triumphantly she said, 'Well, you haven't had it all your own way in that department . . .'

There was a look of pure hatred on her face and he realized that over the years they had grown to despise each other. It had been disguised as they made some sort of effort to live together but of late if had been forcing its way closer to the surface and now it had broken free.

'Since I've been here . . .' Karen was saying callously. 'It's someone who works with Julie's husband.'

Family members who were not blood relatives were always referred to by their relationships, never their names.

'Have you been to bed with him?' Turner did not really know why he had asked this – he certainly did not care – but it was all he could think of to say.

199

Karen went and stood by the window, looked out into the dark, made lighter by the snow, not seeing the beauty before her eyes.

She said, 'Oh, this is the male pride bit . . . if I haven't been to bed with him I suppose you'll suggest we try again . . .' She turned to him. 'But if I've let him screw me, that's it.'

Turner tried to interrupt but Karen would not allow it; the stored-up hate and resentment flowed from her. 'Well, I did . . . and enjoyed it.' She paused to see if this had wounded him. 'It was nice to be with someone who wanted to do it. I don't know where in the wedding ceremony it says: I promise to climb on top of this woman three times a week . . . but that's how it's seemed to me these last few years, and the last couple of months you've even forgotten to do that.'

Turner's mind was desperately trying to absorb this – his marriage was over, ended by mutual consent. Thank God. He felt a wild sense of excitement before his mind focused on the one area that involved heart-break. He said, 'What about the kids?'

'You'll never get your hands on them,' Karen spat.

'Karen, don't be silly, you know I'll get access to them.'

'Over my dead body.'

The night sister came storming along the corridor. 'I must ask you to stop this noise. I have a ward full of sick children.' Her face was flushed with annoyance.

Karen almost shouted, 'Just get him away. I don't want him anywhere near my son.'

'Control yourself, Mrs Turner,' the sister barked. 'And Mr Turner, I must request that you leave the hospital. Mrs Turner can stay because of the sick child but she must moderate her behaviour.' Her baleful glare told that she would not tolerate further nonsense.

Turner backed away, tried to speak but his words lay impotent in his throat. Sharply he turned and went to the lift, contemplating a sixty-mile drive through atrocious conditions to where happiness waited.

*

Such was Turner's mood the next morning that a visit to the council's refuse tip could have brought him pleasure, so the virgin snow of the Christmas card Bridgetown that met his eyes as he drove to work afforded him inspiration aplenty.

He had left early to avoid the snowy chaos which would ensue as the roads rapidly filled with traffic. A frail sun peeped over the horizon, bathing the white fields in its pale glow.

Turner's mood was good; the euphoria of freedom had not yet become clouded by the enormity of the problems that would arise out of his separation from Karen and the children.

Neither he nor Kerrie had slept more than a few hours for the security and sense of permanence which had come into their relationship had manifested itself in the form of heightened sexual appetite. Even the discernible discomfort Turner was experiencing due to this excess of indulgence had done nothing to dampen his ardour.

Although Kerrie, watching him dress as she remained in bed, had said, 'Just tell them I'm too shagged out to come in today.'

But Turner knew the real reason why she preferred to stay out of the way: she did not want to be there when Ashworth was told of their affair.

'Tell them I've got a sore . . .' She giggled. '. . . stomach from yesterday and I'm taking a couple of days' sick leave.'

Turner entered the police station to find a state of confusion in the front reception. Uniformed officers were everywhere; most looked cold and battle-weary. He shouldered his way through the crowd to the main desk which was being manned by PC Fred Ritchie.

'What's happening, Fred?' he shouted above the noise.

'What isn't?' Ritchie replied wearily. 'We had a near-riot on the council estate last night. Drugs raid. Nicked three dealers and four pushers, but our lads got surrounded by a mob of about a hundred. They controlled it but only just.'

'Any of our lads down?'

'Two minor injuries but only sticking plaster, steak-on-the-eye jobs. I've got a message for you from the Chief Constable. He wants to see you as soon as you come in.'

The mood of Chief Constable Ken Savage was in direct contrast to that of Turner. A night of promised oblivion induced by six pints of lager and two large scotches had been snatched away by a telephone call from the station. As a result Savage had spent a long night sobering up and monitoring events on the other side of Bridgetown. This state of sobriety, especially one not arrived at via a period of sleep, was guaranteed not to bring the jovial side of his nature to the fore.

Savage stubbed out his half-smoked cigarette in the already overflowing ashtray. His office, his clothes, reeked of stale smoke; this, and the broken capillaries on his nose and cheeks, told that he, like many others who had reached the top of their professions, often sought relief from the stresses and pressures of his office in tobacco and alcohol.

He stood viewing the snow-covered rooftops of the town from his office window as he mulled over in his mind the happenings of the last few hours. This near-riot bothered him. When he had been stationed in London, before transferring to Bridgetown, Savage had gained some experience of this type of disturbance and knew how quickly one minor incident could spark off an orgy of violence and destruction.

The real world had caught up with this sleepy town far more rapidly than even he had anticipated, forcing him to face decisions which he had been avoiding for months.

'Come,' Savage barked in answer to a knock on his door. Turner walked into the office. 'Ah, Turner, yes.'

'Good morning, sir.'

'Take a pew, man.'

Turner sat down as Savage left the window and returned to his chair.

'Do you know what happened last night?' Savage asked.

'I've been filled in briefly, sir.'

'It was only the weather that saved us,' Savage confided. 'The heavy snowfall dampened it down; if it hadn't we'd have had a full-scale riot . . .' He snorted angrily. 'And we're not even equipped with riot gear. When are they going to realize that if they want the job done properly they've got to come up with the money?'

Turner, slightly embarrassed by the Chief's outburst, remained silent.

'Anyway, that's not what I want to talk to you about.' He pinched the bridge of his nose between thumb and forefinger. 'Why haven't you charged Steven Carway?'

'I'm waiting for Chief Inspector Ashworth to give me the go-ahead, sir,' Turner said stiffly.

'Yes,' Savage reflected. 'Turner, I'm going to take you into my confidence. CID is in for a big shake-up. Firstly you need more people . . . four would be the number I'd put on it. CID needs to be fully computerized and with a good man to lead it.' His bloodshot eyes surveyed Turner's face. 'A detective inspector is needed and I'm looking to promote from my existing officers. Am I making myself plain?'

'Yes, sir, very.'

'Good, now I want your opinion of Jim Ashworth.'

'He's a good copper, sir,' Turner replied stoutly.

'But?'

Turner shifted uncomfortably in his seat. 'I'm finding this difficult, sir. Obviously the promotion you're offering is attractive but I'm not willing to sell Jim Ashworth down the river for it.'

'Good man, but that's not what I'm asking you to do. I just want your honest assessment. Look, let me help you. Jim Ashworth has been a good copper, none better, and still could be. I don't agree with the consensus of opinion that says he's past it, but what he won't do is move out of the 1970s into the '90s . . . would you agree with that?'

'Yes, sir, I think I'd have to,' said Turner, realizing he was indeed selling Ashworth down the river. But it was true, Ashworth's excessive thoroughness and attention to detail often infuriated him.

'Good. Well, there's no need to involve you further at this point. Now Bridgenorton are lending us a couple of their DCs.

They owe us for clearing up the hit and run. I want them working with you on these burglaries and I want Carway charged with murder. Don't worry, I'll sanction it with Jim.'

Back in his own office Turner's conscience was not bothering him unduly. The decision to put Ashworth out to grass had not been his; it seemed that the decision had already been made, so there was very little he could have done to alter it. Besides, the difference between his current salary and that of an inspector was substantial and looked attractive with maintenance about to rear its ugly head.

The telephone on Turner's desk rang. He picked it up. 'Hello?'

'Hi, lover.' It was Kerrie. 'I'm still in bed and I'm thinking about you.'

'You're taking a chance,' he reproached. 'Ashworth could have been in the office.'

Kerrie's giggle came down the line. 'I just can't leave you alone, haven't you noticed?'

'Yes, I did get that impression,' Turner laughed.

Again she giggled. 'What I'm really ringing about is I've just phoned some friends of mine to break the glad tidings that we're together and they've invited us out for a drink and a meal to celebrate.'

The thought filled Turner with horror. He was basically a shy man, not at ease with strangers or skilled in the art of making small-talk. 'I was rather hoping for a quiet evening and a chance to catch up on some sleep,' he said, hoping she would agree.

'Oh, please, Owen,' she replied petulantly. 'Peter and Chris are great fun, you'll love them, and besides I've been stuck in this flat for weeks waiting for you. Now we can, let's get out and party.'

'All right,' Turner said reluctantly.

Ashworth's appearance interrupted the call.

'Okay, Kerrie,' Turner said quickly. 'I'll tell the chief inspector.'

'I take it the great man's in,' Kerrie whispered.

Turner did not reply. As he put the telephone down he addressed Ashworth. 'Kerrie won't be in for a couple of days, she's suffering from the after-effects of yesterday.'

'We shouldn't be putting women into that type of situation,' Ashworth said as he lowered his bulk into the chair. 'Now, Carway . . .' be began.

'Did you hear about the drugs raid?' Turner asked.

The interruption brought a hostile glare from Ashworth. 'Yes, Uniformed handled it badly,' he stated flatly. 'Too much surveillance. They'd been aware of it for three weeks, should have nipped it in the bud, crushed it before people got used to buying their drugs there.'

My God, Turner thought, you just can't win with this man; on the one hand you mustn't rush things, but on the other, delay also comes in for criticism. Kerrie was right, he decided: Ashworth had only one way of doing things, and that was his own way. The opinions of others were at best dismissed and at worst held up for ridicule.

'Right, Owen, today we interview Carway again. We want to know about Stella's circle of friends. The lesbian is in there somewhere. The Ratcliffe woman . . . that's something else we need to chase. She's got to have relatives, friends, someone must have a photograph of her. If we can get our hands on one we'll put out a TV appeal for her.'

Turner felt a surge of relief when a police constable put his head round the door and said, 'The Chief Constable wants to see you, Chief Inspector.'

'Let battle commence,' Ashworth sighed.

Although he would never admit it to a living soul, Ken Savage dreaded locking horns with Ashworth. It wasn't that he disliked the man – on the contrary, he not only liked him, he respected him into the bargain, appreciated his bluntness, it saved a lot of time. Ashworth didn't just call a shovel a shovel – should the need arise he would pick it up and hit you over the head with it.

In the past even his legendary stubbornness which, when he

thought he was right, could make him completely intransigent, had not particularly bothered Savage, but over the last six months that intransigence, that inability to adapt had begun to create problems. Despite what he had told Turner, Savage did see Ashworth as past his best but did not relish the task of telling the man it was time to retire.

When his secretary announced Ashworth's arrival he lit another cigarette. 'Jim,' he said, his tired face breaking into a smile as he indicated the chair in front of his desk.

As Ashworth sat down Savage fired the question, 'Why hasn't Steven Carway been charged? And mind . . .' He pointed a nicotine-stained finger in Ashworth's direction. '. . . I want a little more than gut feeling.'

'I've got more than that, sir.' Ashworth began to tell the Chief Constable about Stella Carway's lesbian affair and the alleged involvement of Susan Ratcliffe.

Savage listened for all of sixty seconds before shaking his head. 'Jim, Jim, all this is totally irrelevant. I've read the file . . . the case against Carway is watertight.'

'I disagree, sir.'

'Jim, the papers are crucifying us over this. Not a day goes by without them suggesting our incompetence.'

Ashworth could feel his blood-pressure rising. He leant forward in his chair. 'Yes, and those same papers will be questioning our competence in five years' time when it comes to light we put the wrong person away.'

'Charge Carway, Jim.' Savage's voice rose. 'That's not a request. Am I making myself clear?'

'Very clear.'

'Good. Now about those burglaries.'

'I've done some work on those, sir, and I think – '

'No, Jim, let me finish. Bridgenorton are lending us some manpower and I want you to put Turner in charge of the operation.'

'Turner?'

'Yes, Jim, I want to give the lad his head, see what he's capable of.'

'I see.' They locked eyes across the desk. 'I've known you for

206

a number of years, sir, and I think it's true to say we've had some battle royals . . .' Savage nodded as he stubbed out his cigarette. '. . . but of all the things I might accuse you of, being a liar isn't one of them so I'd appreciate a straight answer . . . are you telling me it's time to stop setting the alarm in the mornings?'

Savage shifted his weight in the chair and took another cigarette from the pack on his desk. 'Not in so many words, no.'

'Then what is it?'

Savage lit the cigarette. 'It's true I've got a dilemma. CID has got to expand. At its present size it just can't cope with the current workload.' He looked at Ashworth. 'And it needs to be computerized. Now I know your thoughts on computers . . .'

'I don't think you do, sir, because we've never discussed the subject, but I'll be happy to give you my views. Computers can be invaluable for forming links with other forces and for storing information but what they're incapable of doing is reasoning and detecting. They're only as good as the people operating them and in my considered opinion this total reliance on them which seems to be developing will be very harmful to the force.'

'These changes are not a matter for debate,' Savage snapped. 'They are fact. What I'm saying to you is, if you think you can head that sort of operation, fine, if not . . .' He left the sentence open.

'Thank you, sir,' Ashworth said as he stood up. 'And how much time have I got to make up my mind?'

'Take as long as you want . . . within reason, that is.'

'I think I can let you know within a week,' Ashworth said stiffly. Then he turned and walked out of the door.

Susan Ratcliffe swallowed hard in an effort to push the bile and half-digested food back down her gullet. Her stomach turned again, resisting its return.

Several minutes had passed but her eyes remained transfixed on the flickering television screen, unaware however of the weatherman's explanation that the north-east airflow was responsible for the arctic weather which was now gripping the British Isles.

The last item on the evening's news had brought the past rushing back to her, sweeping away the happiness of the last few days. The newscaster had said: 'And an item just in . . . A man has been charged with the murder of Stella Carway at her home in Bridgetown on October 29th. He has been named as Steven Carway, the murdered woman's husband . . .'

Suddenly the tiny flat seemed claustrophobic. Susan went to the dresser, rifled through its contents until she found a bottle of gin, her guilt-ridden mind all the time evaluating how this latest development would affect her safety.

In the kitchen she poured the neat spirit into a tumbler and gulped it down. How much did Steven Carway know? Did he know anything? No, he wasn't even aware of her existence, she told herself, willing it to be true.

There was nothing that could connect her with Stella Carway. Nothing . . . except the large policeman who had called at the flat.

She refilled the tumbler with gin.

16

Sarah knew Ashworth was troubled; his hale and hearty manner betrayed him. Over dinner he astounded her by announcing that he was thinking of retiring. This was followed by a rosy-hued description of the advantages such a move would bring: more time for the garden, hobbies, not to mention the opportunity for them to spend more time together.

None of this had the desired effect on Sarah though; she presumed that the speech was meant to indicate that retirement was his idea but she knew him too well to be taken in by subterfuge. In her wildest dreams she could not picture him in a beany hat, spending his days pottering about in the garden.

This man was a detective. It wasn't simply his livelihood, it was him. If you took away the trappings of his office, removed the mantle from his shoulders, you were left with a busybody who would always have his nose in the affairs of others.

No! If her Jim was moving towards retirement, someone or something was pushing him there.

His jovial mood prevailed. Even when he confided the news that Turner had split from Karen and had moved in with Kerrie he did so without his usual admonishments directed towards the young. Somehow that news only added to Sarah's worries.

The meal over and coffee consumed, Ashworth took the puppy into the garden. The toilet-training was going quite well but the fact that Peanuts seemed preoccupied with rolling in the snow did not bode well for this particular evening.

Sarah watched them from the kitchen window. The news of Turner's split with his wife had brought home to her the fragility of human relationships and that in turn caused her to dwell on the seemingly silly worry that had been with her throughout the day. It had started at the hairdresser's. One of the young assistants had attended to Sarah but just as she was going under the drier Ann Thorncroft had strolled over and said, 'Hello, Mrs Ashworth, how's Jim?'

Sarah had replied, 'I didn't realize you know my husband.'

Ann had smiled and said, 'I've met him a couple of times. He seems very nice.'

And that was the sum total of Sarah's concern. 'Nice' was not a term often used to describe her husband. Although she knew him as a kind gentle person, the years and his occupation had provided him with a hard outer shell which few people of short acquaintance could penetrate. 'Nice' just seemed to suggest some knowledge of him, that's all.

Sarah shrugged as she stared down into the bubble-filled sink. After all, she reflected, couples spend most of the day away from each other, their jobs and professions bringing them into contact with the opposite sex; fidelity had to be taken on trust. Even so, a chance remark could still lead one into a maze of uncertainties and insecurities from which there was no escape.

Ashworth returned to the warmth of the house, his feigned

209

mood of optimism slightly askew after fifteen minutes in the sub-zero temperature. After drying the dog on her towel he announced that he was going up to the study for ten minutes. Sarah knew this meant he would be absent for at least two hours.

'I've put the heating on, dear,' she called after him.

When, by bedtime, Ashworth had still not emerged Sarah climbed the stairs in search of him. The study was in darkness, Ashworth silhouetted against the window, his large frame a dark smudge against the white wilderness outside.

Sarah was concerned. 'What are you doing in the dark, Jim?'

'Just thinking, Sarah, just thinking. We have no time to stand and stare and all that.'

'Oh dear.' The slur in his voice told Sarah that Ashworth had consumed far more scotch than was good for either his mind or his liver. She switched on the light and drew the curtains.

'Funny how something so beautiful can cause so much damage,' Ashworth reflected as the vast expanse of white, dotted here and there with dead and decaying summer vegetation, was shut out. 'A drink, Sarah?' he asked as he crossed to the drinks table.

'No thank you, dear, I've had a sherry.' She wanted to tell him he'd had enough but instead she heard herself saying, 'I ran into a friend of yours today. Ann Thorncroft.'

'Hardly a friend,' Ashworth replied gruffly. 'I interviewed her a couple of times about Stella Carway's death. They'd been friends and she was very upset about it.'

Sarah relaxed as she sat down. That was it then . . . Jim was always kind and understanding when dealing with people who were upset or traumatized.

As Ashworth once again settled into his chair Sarah looked across at him; perhaps it was the harshness of the overhead light but suddenly he looked older, the sparkle had left his eyes. 'What is it, Jim?' she asked softly.

He gazed morosely into his whisky glass before saying, 'What makes you think there's anything wrong?'

'Well, Steven Carway's arrest is all over the television and yet you haven't mentioned it. Does this have anything to do with your retirement?'

Ashworth gave her a wan smile. 'Did he jump or was he pushed?' He took a drink. 'Let's say I was given the chance to jump.'

'Jim, that's awful. Is all this connected with the Carway case?'

'More or less. More or less,' he muttered tonelessly.

'Do you still think the husband's innocent?' Sarah asked urgently.

Ashworth looked up then. He said, 'That's the part that worries me . . . I don't know, and what really disturbs me is, I no longer care.'

To Sarah's ears that last remark did not hold a ring of truth.

Ashworth had always enjoyed the drive to work and he was determined that today would be no different; even with the hangover which refused to budge and the events of yesterday still fresh in his mind he endeavoured to find pleasure in the drive along *his* high street. Further along, the wintry scene of the open countryside filled him with an almost childlike wonder. But still he found it impossible to totally dislodge the sense of gloom which had been with him since yesterday.

He did still care about Steven Carway, passionately so, but he was no longer certain of the man's innocence. If he had stopped to think, he would have realized that his self-assurance, his solid belief in his own judgement, were being eroded; and they would be further eroded before the end of the morning.

Ashworth arrived at the station promptly at nine o'clock not knowing that by ten fifteen he would be unofficially retired. The events leading up to this were swift and painful.

One of the two detectives on loan from Bridgenorton turned out to be Darren Waters, a young man with a sallow complexion whose interpretation of the term 'plain-clothes' amounted to a leather jacket, grey slacks and an open-necked white shirt. The second officer was more conventionally dressed in a grey suit; he was immensely overweight with a jovial face which fitted his name – Trevor Jolly – perfectly.

On arrival Turner introduced him to the two men after which an awkward silence prevailed. Turner then began to brief Waters and Jolly about the burglaries, expressing the opinion that the best way to tackle them was by use of the computers. They were to compile a list of all juveniles previously involved in this type of crime; this list was to be whittled down to the most recent incidents, the perpetrators of which were to be interviewed immediately.

At this point Ashworth interrupted, putting forward the view that these burglaries were the work of an organized gang and not young opportunist thieves. His opinion was met with blank stares, then three pairs of eyes questioning his right to any involvement in the matter. It was at this point that Ashworth realized he was being side-lined, condemned to sit behind his desk with little to do until such time as he was willing to give into pressure and call it a day.

Ashworth moved to his desk as Turner discreetly dismissed the officers, despatching them to the central control room.

As soon as the door closed Turner rounded on Ashworth, stating, 'I've been put in charge of this case, Jim, and I don't feel inclined to tolerate interference from you.'

Ashworth, unable to believe his ears, countered with, 'May I remind you, Owen, that mine is the more senior rank and although you've undoubtedly been privy to the plot to remove me, until that process has been completed this is still my nick!'

'You're paranoid, Jim, do you know that?' Turner retorted before storming out.

Ashworth guessed that Turner was heading for the Chief Constable's office and was proved right when, some ten minutes later, he was summoned there himself.

A weary Ken Savage attempted to pour oil over the troubled waters but Ashworth resisted. He said, 'I'd like to know, sir, if I could retire here and now. I have absolutely no intention of spending the next few weeks having my decisions overturned by junior officers.'

Savage seemed relieved by this request. 'I think you're making the right decision, Jim,' he said. 'And in view of your long commendable service I can offer you four weeks' leave during which time the paperwork can be sorted out.'

At ten fifteen precisely Ashworth climbed behind the wheel of the Sierra which would be at his disposal for just four more weeks and drove home through the snow.

Susan Ratcliffe's boots left deep indents in the wet sand. An observer traced her passage from the harbour wall, across the sweeping expanse of sand and gravel, to a cluster of rocks in front of which she now stood. The formation afforded her some degree of protection from the cruel bite of the north-east wind which cut through her thick clothing, goose-pimpling the flesh beneath.

The roar of the grey hostile sea, the mournful cries of the wind and the inimical squawking of hungry gulls were all around her.

The observer paused only briefly at the harbour wall before jumping down on to the beach, his heavy weight causing his boots to sink into the sand almost up to the ankles. He followed Susan's footprints, his longer stride demolishing every other one as he walked along.

Susan glanced up as he approached the rocks.

'Hello, Susan.' The wind grabbed his words and threw them away. He saw her distressed look before she turned from him.

'What do you want, David?'

He made her face him as he said, 'An explanation. You just ring me, tell me not to come round and then nothing. You won't answer the phone or come to the door . . .'

Susan turned away and gazed along the beach. 'What about the bank? Why aren't you there?'

'Stuff the bank,' David shouted as he took her arms and roughly pulled her to him. 'You owe me an explanation, Susan.'

She was forced to look into his eyes, a blank dull expression was on her face. She said nothing.

'Look, just tell me you used me to relieve your frustrations . . .' he said with exasperation. 'Just tell me that and I'll go away.'

Alarmed, Susan said quickly, 'Oh no, it wasn't like that.'

'Then what is it? Have you met someone else?'

She shook her head. After a moment she said, 'It's something from my past. Oh, David . . .' She threw her arms around his neck and clung to him.

Gently David pushed her away and held her at arm's length. 'A man from your past?' he asked softly.

Again she shook her head, slowly, hopelessly, unable to meet his eyes. 'No, it's about a place called Bridgetown and a woman who was murdered there.' The tears came then. 'I should never have become involved with you,' she cried wretchedly. 'But I do owe you an explanation.'

'Not here,' he said, now dreading the revelation that was to come. 'Your place . . . my place . . . coffee? Let's just get out of this cold.'

David put a protective arm around Susan's shoulder and led her away.

Turner parked his car in the high street, the wheels crunching down the dirty snow in the gutters. His mood was mixed. The previous evening had been a disaster. He had found Kerrie's friends tiresome, they had found him boring.

Sitting there, watching them chatter unceasingly and laugh hysterically at nothing in particular, a sense of isolation had engulfed him. This had been his first chance to view Kerrie objectively, from a distance, and certain things had become blatantly apparent. Firstly, most of what she said meant very little in the greater scheme of things; she was superficial, her beliefs transient. And secondly, her inane incessant giggle, which made her sound like an overgrown schoolgirl, was beginning to irritate him.

After her friends had departed, they had gone to bed. Turner had been tired and as Kerrie began her love-play, he had murmured, 'Let's get some sleep.'

But Kerrie would have none of it. 'Come on, Owen,' she had coaxed, her hand sweeping down over his chest, lightly touching the muscles of his stomach as it continued its journey.

'You're not with that old hag now. I want it every night and there's something nice and hard under here that tells me you're not that tired.'

Due to his mood and weariness Turner's performance had not been good; he had applied little technique. After only a couple of minutes he had heard the petulant note in her voice, been aware of the slightly fishy smell of her body fluids as she had cried, 'No, Owen, don't come yet.' But he did and it had seemed a fitting end to a very unsatisfactory evening.

He was out of his car now and walking briskly along the high street. The argument with Ashworth had left a sour taste in his mouth. For God's sake, what was he supposed to do . . . tell lies, falsify his opinion in some futile attempt to stave off the inevitable? Not to mention delay his own advancement.

There were many plus factors in this new arrangement though: he enjoyed being in charge, calling the shots; it was good to be working with people closer to his own age, enjoyable using modern language – 'offensive slang' as the dictionary defines it. Ashworth would undoubtedly refer to it as simply 'offensive'.

Turner found Ann Thorncroft sitting in the middle of the salon. Two of the chairs were overturned but there appeared to be no other damage.

She favoured him with a radiant smile as he entered. 'Hi,' she said.

'Much taken?' he asked as he surveyed the room.

'Not really, some bottles of gel, two hand-driers. I've made a list.' She stood up and handed it to him. 'They came in through the store-room window. I haven't touched anything.'

Turner examined the store-room, noting the smashed glass of a small window where the thieves had gained entry.

'Any chance of catching them?' Anne called after him.

'We'll probably get the gear back,' he replied. 'But it looks like kids so even if we do get them all we can do is tell them off while they stand there taking the . . .' He stopped abruptly then, smiling, said, 'Laughing at us.'

Ann gave a deep throaty laugh. 'You nearly slipped up then,' she said as she came to stand behind him.

215

Turner found he was aware of the strong spicy fragrance of her perfume, the dancing teasing light that sparkled in her eyes, her ready easy smile, her body beneath the plain white smock which promised a lithe beauty. Moving away from her, he said, 'It smells a bit in here, doesn't it?'

'Yes, it's not a man's domain, is it? Would you like to come upstairs?'

Ann had made some advancement with the decorations to the flat: the floor was now covered with expensive autumnal-coloured carpet; the three-piece suite was the same but a coffee table had been added, together with a tastefully ornate standard lamp, and there was a television and video on a stand.

Ann sank into the settee, curling her legs up by her side. Turner chose to sit in an easy chair.

'How's Jim?' she asked as Turner studied the list of missing items. 'I was talking to Sarah on the phone and she mentioned something about retirement.'

Turner glanced up. 'Yes, that's right, in fact he's on a month's leave at the moment, then he's finished.'

'Oh, poor Jim.'

'Yes, it's sad. God knows what he'll find to occupy his mind. Do you know the Ashworths well?'

'Not really, Sarah's just started coming to the salon. She's getting me interested in some classes at the Women's Guild.' She allowed Turner to return to the list then after a moment she said, 'Sarah said it was something about Stella's murder that sparked this off.'

Turner made a few notes then gave her his full attention. 'That's right, everything was neatly wrapped up when it came to light she'd had a lesbian lover . . .' Ann remained silent, her face impassive. 'That doesn't seem to surprise you,' he commented.

'It doesn't,' Ann said frankly. 'Stel enjoyed life . . . if swinging both ways helped to fulfil her then she would have gone for it. Very interesting though. Do you know who the woman was?'

Turner shook his head. 'No, and that was the problem. To

dear old Jim every female within a fifty-mile radius became a suspect and had to be eliminated. He just couldn't see there wasn't time and that it simply didn't matter. I'm sure his mind's going . . . at one time he even had you in the frame.'

A look of astonishment passed over Ann's face and as she sat there laughing, hugging her knees, Turner began to realize that her presence, her bearing, her husky voice and appraising eye were beginning to act as a mild sexual stimulant.

She was still laughing as she said, 'Well, if Jim Ashworth doesn't know I'm not a lesbi . . .' As her voice trailed off her hand shot to her mouth and she said through a chuckle, 'Ah, ah, I'm telling you my secrets.'

It was Turner who now looked incredulous. 'You and Jim Ashworth? He's old enough to be your father.'

Ann's large green eyes sought and held his. She said, 'Flattery will get you anything you want.' Then she averted her gaze. 'Jim's a very attractive man, but nothing happened.'

'No, of course not,' Turner mocked.

'It didn't, honestly,' she laughed. 'Oh, this is so embarrassing. I'd blush if I could remember how to. I need a ciggie now.' She jumped up and crossed to the coffee table, took a cigarette from the packet and lit it with a table lighter. Finding Turner's eyes still on her she continued. 'He came here one night, we had a few drinks and it got a bit silly.'

'Jim Ashworth?' Turner said in a tone of disbelief.

Ann smirked. 'I think I frightened him to death.'

'Probably what turned his mind,' Turner quipped. 'Does Sarah know about this?'

'Oh yes,' Ann said derisively. 'I made a point of telling her.' She began to act out the scene. 'Sit down, Mrs Ashworth. What would you like, a wash and blow dry and perhaps a subtle colour? Oh, and by the way, I fancy your husband something rotten. Actually I made a pass at him . . . I wanted his body, you see.' They both laughed at her antics and then she said, 'Do I shock you?'

'No, you surprise me . . . and interest me.'

Ann watched as he openly studied her body. 'That's nice,'

she said softly, then her tone changed as she stubbed out the cigarette. 'Sarah tells me you and your wife have split.' She returned to the settee and sat down.

Turner nodded.

'And by the look on your face I'd say you're not very happy.' She laughed softly. 'Come on, it's your turn to confess.'

Turner shrugged and said, 'Out of the frying pan . . .'

'The grass isn't greener?'

'No, it's the same light brown colour.'

'Oh dear, I've spoilt things now,' Ann said with regret. 'I've got a gift for depressing people.'

'You haven't, you're very easy to talk to.'

'Thank you. I like people, I try to help them.'

Turner looked at his watch and stood up. 'I really must be going. I'll send – '

'What star sign are you?' Ann asked suddenly.

Turner looked perplexed; he said, 'Gemini. Why?'

'I thought so. If we had more time, a couple of hours, I could sort out your problems.' It was a thinly veiled invitation for him to visit her again and one which Turner knew he would be unable to resist. 'And I've got an idea for something that could occupy Jim Ashworth's mind. I'll have to put it to Sarah.'

As they walked down the stairs Turner said, 'I'll send someone from Forensics but don't hold out too much hope. As soon as he's gone I'd get the window fixed and look into burglar alarms.'

'Will do.'

They reached the hall and stood facing each other, their bodies almost touching.

'Tell me,' Turner said. 'Is the invitation to sort out my problems still open?'

'Yes,' Ann said simply. 'Can you make it this evening? Without getting yourself into trouble, I mean?'

'I think so.'

Susan stared at David's grim face over the kitchen table in her flat.

'What a mess. What an unholy bloody mess,' he groaned.

'I know,' Susan replied miserably. 'If you want to walk away and just forget me, I'd understand.'

David shook his head sadly. 'I think we both know it's too late for that.'

'But it'll be years before we can be together,' Susan said urgently. She was eager to offer him every chance to feel free of her.

'The best thing we can do is go to a solicitor and find out what your position is.' He paused. 'And then . . .'

'What?'

'Bridgetown. It's confession time, Susan.'

Fresh tears sprang to her eyes. 'I can't, David. I can't.'

'We must, it's the only way. We can't live with this thing likely to catch up with us at any time. Let's get it over with, Susan,' he pleaded. 'Face whatever comes from it and after that we can get on with the rest of our lives.'

Susan was shaking as she muttered, 'I know you're right, but I'm so frightened.' Then with an anguished sigh she cried, 'I wish I'd never met Stella Carway.'

Turner spent the rest of the day examining his soul. Despite sifting through the records of juvenile offenders and interviewing likely suspects, the break-ins continued. Although consoling himself with the fact that he and his new team had only been on the job for a short time, he was already beginning to feel the strain of responsibility which came with the increased salary.

His personal life had become shambolic and seemed destined to worsen. He had always viewed promiscuous people with more than a little distaste and was therefore disturbed by his own desires.

With hindsight he knew that he had been motivated by sheer lust for Kerrie's body and the new experiences to which he had been introduced, but shouldn't he, realizing the mistake, be attempting to rectify it instead of compounding the problem by forming an association with Ann Thorncroft? The fact that he seemed powerless to resist alarmed him considerably. On the other hand, was he misinterpreting the signs that Ann was giving out? She had said she had an idea that would keep Ashworth's mind occupied; perhaps she did simply enjoy helping people after all.

At five o'clock he telephoned Kerrie to inform her that he would be working late. She did not seem overly concerned and said she would go out with friends for the evening. Then at six thirty, praying there would be no further break-ins overnight, he left the station.

Ann was waiting for him and a smile lit up her face as she opened the door. 'Hi,' she said. Her white smock had been replaced by a simple jersey dress which clung to her shape, accentuating the curves. 'The window's been fixed and the burglar alarm people are coming tomorrow,' she told him as they entered the lounge. 'So that's another day I'll have to keep the salon closed.'

Her perfume overwhelmed Turner as she took his coat and motioned for him to sit while she poured drinks. He was feeling awkward, doubtful now as to why Ann had invited him. The first sip of scotch, as it warmed his stomach, reminded Turner that he had not eaten since lunchtime.

Ann was sipping gin and tonic on the settee and her huge green eyes seemed to mock him over the rim of her glass.

'Well,' Turner said, rather uncomfortably, 'have you sorted my problems out?'

She did not directly reply but said, 'I meditate.' She gave a deep throaty laugh which Turner found pleasing. 'That sounds like a ridiculous answer, I know, but most people's problems stem from the fact that they don't understand themselves.'

'I don't think that applies to me,' Turner said, disappointed with her reply.

Ann's eyes held that mocking light again as she asked, 'Doesn't it? I'd say you're a person who will always enjoy a change . . .' She paused to sip her drink. 'In between the sheets, I mean.'

Turner could feel himself becoming aroused and took another drink in a vain attempt to bring himself under control.

Ann was saying, 'Now you know that's true. If you'd just

admit it your life would be a lot easier.' She drained her glass. 'Morality is forced upon us every which way – parents, education, society; no wonder most of us are screwed up. Cigarette . . .' she murmured absently, leaning over the arm of the settee to rummage in her handbag. As she did so her legs opened and for a few tantalizing seconds Turner found himself looking at her smooth thighs and the satin crotch of her black briefs.

Ann found her cigarettes and stood up. 'Finish your drink and I'll get you another.'

'No, no, this is enough, I'm driving . . .'

'Relax, you won't be leaving for ages.'

Turner passed his glass and Ann strolled to the kitchen, saying, 'I bet you miss your wife and kids, don't you?'

'I wish none of it had happened,' he replied glumly.

'Now, can you honestly say you didn't enjoy one single minute of it?' Ann said mockingly as she gave him a fresh drink. She laughed when he hesitated. 'See what I mean about being honest?' Returning to the settee she lit a cigarette. 'The part you enjoyed is what you want, the rest you can do without.'

'So what's the answer, get visiting rights to my kids and screw around?'

Ann laughed. 'Don't be so intense. Get back with your wife, live a normal life . . . then find yourself an understanding mistress and be discreet.'

The scotch was beginning to cause Turner to feel light-headed. He said now in a mocking tone, 'So there are all these women out there who are going to say, just drop in whenever you can . . . I don't mind.'

'Not quite, but there are a lot of women who want some fun now and again but don't want anything to do with the rest of the package.'

Turner found it impossible to take his eyes from her face, even when she moved to the coffee table to crush out her cigarette. She stood in front of him and said, 'What you need is a woman who lives alone; a woman in business . . . say, hairdressing. One who won't be the least little bit demanding out of bed.'

The ache in Turner's groin increased. He placed his glass on the floor. 'I don't know whether to take you seriously,' he complained.

Ann's smile was seductive as she said, 'That's part of the fun . . . finding out.'

17

Sarah was worried about her husband, spending most of her time dissecting those worries and fears. Was she in danger of developing what everyone was accusing Jim of possessing . . . paranoia? After all, this man with whom she had shared the best part of her life had always been difficult; it was only natural that he would be totally devastated by the events of the last few days. Nevertheless, in almost thirty years of marriage she had never seen him like this: withdrawn, preoccupied, unable or unwilling to communicate his feelings to her.

His drinking was beginning to bother her too. Oh, he wasn't rolling about drunk or anything like that, just having a little more than was usual, but it was a worry; so unlike him. Sarah feared that if the overall pattern continued their marriage could suffer, and if it went on for too long she could see him heading for some sort of mental breakdown.

Looking down at the Christmas present she was attempting to wrap Sarah sighed and fought to free herself of these worries. All Jim needed was something to occupy his mind: once he became obsessed with something again he'd soon forget this whole dreadful business.

The ringing of the telephone broke her pattern of thoughts. She wandered out to the hall and picked up the receiver. 'Hello?'

'Is that Mrs Ashworth?'

'Yes, it is.'

'It's Sergeant Martin Dutton at Bridgetown station. Is Jim available?'

'Yes, hold on a moment.' Placing the receiver on the table she quickly went to find Ashworth who was still in bed, sitting up and staring moodily into the mug of tea she had taken up a good ten minutes earlier. 'Jim, Sergeant Dutton is on the phone.'

Without speaking Ashworth picked up the extension beside the bed. 'Hello, Martin.'

'Hello, Jim, I've got something, I think. A woman's just come in asking for you, says it's about Stella Carway.'

Ashworth felt a surge of adrenalin which brought his feet from the bed to the floor with such haste that some of the tea spilt over on to the quilt. 'Where is she now?'

'That's the thing, Jim, I've put her in the interview room . . . Dutton paused: Ashworth could hear footsteps hurrying along and Dutton shouting an acknowledgement to whoever it was. Then he was back, speaking in a low voice. 'I might be the only copper in this nick who doesn't know you're on a month's leave before you resign but I can only cover for half an hour, then I'll have to report it to Herr Turner.'

'Martin, I owe you one,' Ashworth said gratefully.

Dutton chuckled. 'Yes, I'll have it in a straight glass.'

Sarah heard the hiss of the shower then sounds of Ashworth dressing and moments later he came down the stairs. He seemed hyped up, preoccupied. 'Sarah, I've got to go to the station. Something's come up about Stella Carway.'

'But, Jim, you're on leave and Ann Thorncroft's calling in . . . remember? She wants to see you.'

'This is important,' he snapped as he put on his coat. Then without even a goodbye he left the house, muttering, 'I know they're wrong. I know it.'

When Ashworth entered the station he found Turner and Sergeant Dutton locked in a heated debate. As he approached the desk Dutton looked up. 'Chief Inspector,' he said with relief. 'I was just explaining to Sergeant Turner that I wasn't aware you were on leave so when this woman came in asking for you I rang your home.' Turner was glaring at the man.

Ashworth said quietly, 'It's all right, Martin, you did the right thing.'

Turner made no attempt to hide his anger. 'I can handle this, Jim,' he said roughly.

Ashworth gave Turner a look heavy with contempt as he said, 'I'm sure you can but let me remind you, I'm only on leave, I'm not dead yet.'

Rank had once again been pulled and Turner resented it; without another word he turned and strode off.

'She's in No.3, Jim,' Dutton winked.

On the way to No.3 interview room something nagged at Ashworth's mind. That smell on Turner, it wasn't a male fragrance; heady, spicy, it held associations for him. Suddenly the face and the name flashed into his mind simultaneously. It was Ann Thorncroft's perfume. Well, well.

Ashworth entered the room. Sitting at the table were Susan Ratcliffe and David Darlow who rose in an almost defensive gesture as Ashworth closed the door.

Susan's face was pale, her eyes were dark hollows. She hesitated for a second and then said, 'I don't know if you remember me.'

'Yes, I do, you're Susan Ratcliffe,' Ashworth replied softly.

'And this is my fiancé . . .' She stumbled over the word. 'David Darlow.'

'What can I do for you?'

She looked up at David who smiled encouragement. 'It's about Stella Carway.'

Ashworth pulled a chair to the table and sat down heavily. 'What about Stella Carway?'

Susan took in a deep breath and said, 'I lied. I did know her.'

Ninety minutes later Turner was still seething about his run-in with Ashworth. He had expected a minority of officers to stay loyal to the chief inspector but what he could not tolerate was the way Ashworth had marched into the station and taken over. Damn it, the man was judged to be no longer competent, scrapheaped. He had no right to come barging in.

The telephone buzzed. Turner picked up the receiver sharply. 'Turner.'

'Hello, Owen.' Ann's friendly voice soothed him somewhat. 'I'm twiddling my thumbs while the alarms are being fitted so I thought I'd give you a call. How are you?'

'How am I?' He laughed. 'I'm knackered, that's how I am.'

'I should think so too,' Ann teased. 'I don't know any of the women responsible for keeping you happy but they weren't doing a very good job.'

'You did, though.'

'And I can't wait for the next time.' She was quiet for a moment and Turner was about to speak when she said, 'I've been talking to Sarah Ashworth. She's really worried about Jim.'

'Don't mention that bloody man to me,' Turner said tersely, resenting the change in subject.

'No, listen, Owen, she seems to think he's heading for some sort of breakdown.'

'It wouldn't surprise me,' Turner huffed.

'And there's something about Stella's murder, some new witness turned up or something.'

'I don't know anything about it, Ann, because bloody Ashworth galloped in here like the Lone Ranger and just took over,' Turner said moodily. 'The man just doesn't seem to get the message.'

'So you don't know anything about this woman?'

'No, Ann, I don't and I'm not likely to until the interview's over.'

'Sorry, Owen, I'm just so worried about Sarah, that's all. Shall I see you this evening?'

Turner's mood softened. 'Yes, I think I could be persuaded to drop by.'

'Seven?'

'Seven,' he confirmed.

Sarah felt quite buoyant after her heart-to-heart with Ann who, in her opinion, was one of the kindest, most caring people she had ever met. Ann's enthusiasm had inspired Sarah and that inspiration was still with her as she telephoned her husband. It was Turner who answered.

'Hello, Owen, it's Sarah. How are you?' She was determined not to become involved in the feud between the two men.

'Hello, Sarah, I'm very well. You?'

'Fine, thanks. Owen, you don't happen to know where Jim is, do you?'

The irritation in his voice was unmistakable as he said, 'Yes, he's just this minute walked into the office. I'll put you over to him.'

'Hello?' Ashworth's gruff tone indicated to Sarah that things were not going his way.

'Hello, Jim, did the new witness reveal anything?' she asked tentatively.

'I thought so but as usual I'm in a minority of one.'

'Oh dear. Ann was sorry she missed you.' She paused, waiting for a reply, but Ashworth said nothing so she pushed on. 'Ann has this marvellous idea for your retirement. Why don't you write a book?'

'A book,' he said, and it was obvious that he did not share Sarah's enthusiasm for the idea.

'Now I know that tone but just listen, Jim, she's got the whole thing worked out. Although the book market's a bit flat at the moment, apparently the specialist book area is still doing well. Ann suggested calling yours *The Memoirs of a Small-Town Policeman*. She even knows a publisher.'

Ashworth thought, I'm sure she does – intimately, no doubt.

'She's so creative,' Sarah enthused. 'Her idea is to make the first chapter the Carway case because it received national coverage and it's still fresh in everyone's minds. You could call it, "The Christmas Bow Murder".'

'Did she suggest that?'

'Yes.' With relief Sarah realized that Ashworth was beginning to show some interest. 'There would be a lot of research involved – '

'Yes, all right, Sarah, I've got to go now. I'll be home late afternoon.'

Sarah was left staring at the telephone, surprised by Ashworth's abrasive manner. She was not overly disturbed though, guessing that perhaps he would prefer to discuss the venture in

226

private and not with Turner there to overhear his future plans. Still in optimistic mood she set off for the kitchen to prepare the vegetables for dinner.

Turner, now seeing no reason for subterfuge, parked his car in the high street. The thaw was well under way; the gutters were clogged with a dirty black sludge of melting snow and the thin layers of tightly packed ice on the pavements were made dangerous by a covering of water.

As he approached Ann's salon Turner thought back to his telephone conversation with Karen, earlier in the day; it had begun as a discussion about custody of the children and had somehow worked around to talk of reconciliation. Then in his mind's eye he saw Kerrie waiting for him at the flat, ready to 'party' . . . Oh God, his life was becoming so tangled; some day soon something would have to give, but not now. He looked at his watch; he had an hour and he was unwilling to think beyond that hour.

Turner did not share Ann's excitement about the newly installed alarms; as she showed him where the beams were positioned he was thinking about her body, longing to strip it of the blue jeans and baggy sweater.

Once upstairs he rather impatiently accepted her offer of a drink.

'What's this break on the Carway case?' Ann called from the kitchen.

'It's nothing,' Turner answered moodily as he sat watching the minutes ticking away on the clock.

Ann gave Turner his drink then curled up with her own on the settee. 'No, tell me, Owen, I'm interested. Sarah's becoming a good friend to me.'

Turner sighed impatiently. 'A woman called Susan Ratcliffe came into the station this morning. She used to live at Morton . . .'

'Stella's lover,' Ann said darkly.

'No, not from what she told us. Apparently, she and Stella were in care together years ago and had kept in touch. Her story was that the money Stella siphoned off from Carway went into a bank account in Morton. Stella was buying her an antiquarian bookshop in Devon.'

Ann leant forward. 'So I was right . . . she was Stella's lover.'

Turner sighed again. 'What does it matter, Ann? I've been thinking about you all day, for God's sake.'

'She must have been,' Ann insisted. 'You don't just buy a bookshop for someone – '

'What difference does it make?' Turner said sharply as he looked at his watch.

'It interests me,' she replied firmly. 'It's something to do with a book. Tell me.'

Things were not going the way Turner had planned; there were barely forty-five minutes left and he was beginning to fret. 'Ashworth's put entirely the wrong interpretation on it,' he began resignedly. 'He reckons there was a lover's tiff – '

'What do you make of it?' Ann asked quickly.

Turner finished his drink then said, 'Susan Ratcliffe has been to a solicitor and he's obviously arranged the facts to make her appear innocent. What I think happened – and the Chief Constable agrees with me – is this: Stella wanted to vanish, and God knows she had good reason. She wanted to get away from Watson, the hit and run, her husband before he found out where the money really went, and lastly she wanted to get away from the girlfriend. She'd told Ratcliffe about this woman, how she wanted to off-load her. The woman was a real bitch by the sound of it, jealous, possessive, made Stella's life a misery . . .'

'This is fascinating,' Ann said as she lit a cigarette. 'Go on.'

Without much enthusiasm Turner continued. 'In my opinion Stella wasn't buying the shop for Ratcliffe, she was buying it for herself, but she needed an address for correspondence about the shop, banking, that sort of thing and that's where Ratcliffe came in; Stella used her just like she used everybody.' Turner shrugged. 'Carway must have cottoned on at some point and murdered her. That left Susan Ratcliffe with a number of choices: keep quiet, go to the authorities and return the money or, more tempting, take the money and adopt the new identity.'

'Stella was a cow,' Ann said softly.

'What?'

'Nothing, just an observation.' She gave a cheerless smile. 'Stella did ruin so many lives. Anyway, what went wrong for this Susan?'

Turner glanced at the clock; half an hour left. 'The promised land didn't turn out as she'd expected. The enormity of what she'd done, the chance that at any time she could be discovered, was too much for her. I think the final straw came when she met a man – she couldn't cope with the thought of living a lie for the rest of her life.'

Ann looked pensive as she stubbed out her cigarette. 'And what did Jim make of all this?'

Turner's laugh had an unpleasant edge to it as he said, 'He went charging off to the Chief, and even though Ratcliffe has a cast-iron alibi for the time of the murder, he wanted that alibi examined, the case reopened.' He smirked. 'The Chief sent him home with a variation of "never darken my door again."'

He looked across at Ann who was staring vacantly into space. 'Poor Jim,' she muttered.

'Look, Ann,' Turner said gently. 'I know this isn't very romantic but I can't stay long . . .'

This brought Ann's attention back to him; she gave him a curious look, as if she were seeing him for the first time. Abruptly she brightened. 'You're right, I am delaying. I'm interested in what you've told me but not that interested.' She hung her head in an attempt at shyness, saying, 'Something happened this afternoon . . . woman's trouble of the monthly variety.'

With much irritation Turner said, 'You've made me go through all that because you've – '

'Now, now,' Ann chided. 'I know I appear brash but some things do embarrass me.' She patted the seat beside her. 'Come here.'

As Turner sat Ann kissed his lips, her hand traced the outline of his chest, toyed with the buttons of his shirt. 'What you've had in mind all day is out of the question,' she whispered. 'But there are other ways to reach the same result.'

Slowly her hand slid down to his belt buckle.

Sarah lay in bed, staring into the dark; now and then the lights from passing cars shot across the ceiling, illuminating its artexed surface. Where on earth could they all be going at this early hour? She sighed. Try as she might she could not go to sleep.

Turning on to her side she looked at her husband's sleeping form. He smelt of whisky again. As if able to feel Sarah's eyes on his back Ashworth moved in his sleep, muttered, 'She thinks she's got away with it . . . she hasn't . . . hasn't.'

Sarah despaired. She knew he was in fearful trouble but what could she do about it? The hoped-for interest in the book idea had not materialized; he seemed to be sinking deeper and deeper into his own private world.

Then it came to her: she would make an appointment to see their doctor, discuss it with him; he would know what to do. Eager now for the morning Sarah closed her eyes and tried to sleep.

18

Interview room No.1 always had a depressing effect on Ashworth. It was situated below ground level, and its small high windows allowed in little light, sound or sight of the outside world. The overhead fluorescent strip now cast its harsh glow around the room, illuminated every corner, created the impression that there was no place to hide.

Ashworth sat in wait, elbows on the table, head in hands. His stomach turned and gas that had been trapped in his digestive tract was now free, pushing upwards, vibrating in his throat.

He was nervous; no, it went deeper than that – what was beginning inside him was fear. This emotion was not entirely alien to Ashworth but by the same token it had never been a constant companion.

At first glance the loss of confidence in his ability displayed by his colleagues had developed rapidly but in retrospect Ashworth saw that this was not the case. As the rising tide of crime washed over society so the number of unsolved cases remaining on file increased. Ashworth supposed that, viewed in black and white, pitting solved against unsolved, his efficiency would be brought into question. In his present dark mood Ashworth imagined that over the last few years many of his fellow officers must have come to the conclusion that the only way to reverse this unwelcome trend would be to replace him with energetic new blood.

As he sat there, immersed in his soul-searching, Ashworth saw that his marriage was suffering because of this, indeed, all areas of his life were being damaged.

Over these past few days a tiny but growing part of him had wanted to walk away. But James Ashworth was not cast in that mould. He knew that happiness sprang from inner peace, when self-examination revealed dignity, integrity and self-respect. Failure he could live with, as long as he knew that he had done everything within his power to avert that failure.

Sitting back in his chair he rubbed his tired eyes and inhaled deeply. He was operating on emotion and endeavoured to swing the inner dial back towards his intellect.

What evidence had he got, bottom line? Very little. That terrifying thought echoed around Ashworth's disturbed mind. He was ninety per cent certain that he was right but as for tangible proof, well, he had none.

He did, however, have considerable knowledge of the human psyche. If his suspicions were correct then this woman had been living with her dreadful deed for weeks; every wakeful hour would have found it there in the centre of her mind, refusing to be dismissed. It would very likely slice its way through her sleep, bringing her awake, sweating and trembling.

Ashworth gauged that by now the strings connecting her network of nerve cells would be so utterly stretched, so taut that any additional pressure would cause them to snap.

There was a knock on the door. A tingle of apprehensive expectancy shot along Ashworth's spine. He inhaled, exhaled slowly, silently counted from one to ten, feeling his muscles relax as he did so.

'Come in,' he called in a firm clear voice.

The door was opened by a perplexed DC Jolly. 'Ann Thorncroft, sir,' he announced.

Ashworth rose to his feet as Ann stormed into the room, closely followed by a WPC who closed the door and stood beside it. DC Jolly, with his ambling gait, walked over to the tape recorder, a puzzled expression still on his face.

'What the hell is this, Jim?' Ann demanded. She looked spectacular in tight blue jeans and Aran sweater. 'Owen will be here soon so you won't get away with this farce.'

'Oh yes, the galloping sergeant,' Ashworth said with a savage smile. He looked at his wrist-watch; it was seven fifteen. 'If I've got my timing right, Ann, the good sergeant is meeting his wife from the early evening train. He's also having a little trouble with his girlfriend so it will be some time before he can be located. Whatever you've been led to believe, I haven't completely lost my faculties. Now, please sit down.'

With reluctance Ann crossed to the small table and sat. Ashworth watched her. For a few moments her hostile green eyes stared into his then she averted her gaze and studied the table top. Ashworth continued to watch her as he returned to his seat.

The near-silence in the room became oppressive and was broken only by the sounds of breathing, the hum of traffic, noises which seemed unnaturally loud, distorted out of all proportion.

Ashworth noticed tiny specks of burnished brown near the roots of Ann's hair before the black glowing mane began. In fact not one small detail of her was lost before his highly perceptive gaze.

He allowed another two minutes to tick away before he spoke, using a soft gentle tone.

'Do you know, Ann, when you made a pass at me I felt thirty years younger, but since then I've put those years back on and another thirty besides.'

DC Jolly glanced at the WPC standing by the door and his plump cheeks folded back into a grin as he cast his eyes upwards. The young woman constable put her hand to her mouth in an attempt to suppress a giggle.

'Do you know why, Ann?'

Ann made no reply, did not even look up. A niggling doubt began to grow in Ashworth's mind: was he right? He tried to stifle it as he went on, 'You see, I realized it wasn't because you found me attractive, you just wanted all the inside information about Stella's murder, needed to know what was happening, whether any of the trails leading to you had been picked up.'

His voice had taken on a rhythmic hypnotic quality. Ann remained immobile but Ashworth persevered. 'I picked them up, Ann, and they've led me to you.' Still no response. 'When your little ploy with me didn't work you tried befriending my wife and when you got nothing from her you seduced Turner.'

He changed tack quickly. 'It must be very difficult for a woman with your inclinations to go to bed with a man.'

This remark did bring a response. Ann looked up and stared at him through misty eyes; one mascara-stained tear travelled slowly down her cheek. She made a sound half-way between a sob and a bitter laugh as she said quietly, 'That certainly was a mistake. I'd only been to bed with Owen once and I couldn't bear him near me. I was already making excuses. It was a mistake.' She lowered her head and stared again at the table top.

'Not the only one you made, Ann, not the only one.'

Ashworth's words stung her ears. Her tightly drawn nerves snapped and pent-up emotion spewed from her in a torrent of rage. She sprang from the chair, kicking it across the room. 'You bitch, Stella,' she cried in a frenzy. 'You fucking bitch. I still hate you.'

The outburst was so sudden, so violent that Ashworth recoiled slightly. He was aware of DC Jolly moving towards her and quickly put up a hand to stop him; the gesture held such command, such authority that the man halted in his tracks.

Ashworth motioned for Jolly to switch on the tape recorder then crossed the room to retrieve the chair, his movements light for such a heavy man.

'Sit down, Ann, please,' he said gently, pushing the chair against the back of her knees. 'Tell me about Stella.'

As Ann fell heavily into the chair her whole body slumped, even her facial muscles seemed to sag. Ashworth studied the harsh set of her mouth, the vacant unseeing eyes as he returned to his seat.

'Stella,' he coaxed.

In the silence that followed he was aware of the rhythmic beating of his heart, could hear the rasp of his dry throat as he swallowed.

Finally, in a matter-of-fact tone, Anne began. 'I'd fancied her for years. She knew, of course, I'd made it very plain. She had a way of making "no" sound like "I'll see, let me think it over".'

She reached into her pocket for a tissue and paused to wipe her eyes. 'Then one night we were at my place, Stella got very drunk . . . and it happened. The next morning she hardly remembered it but I did. Then not long after it happened again and Stella loved it, said it was beautiful.' She looked at Ashworth and said fervently, 'Oh, Jim, I felt so good, so wonderfully good.'

None of this interested Ashworth but he knew it was the route Ann must take to provide him with the information he required so he made no attempt to interrupt.

'So happy,' Ann said wistfully. 'Oh, I suspected she was still having men, although she swore she wasn't . . . and I wanted to believe her so much.'

She fell silent then and Ashworth prompted her with, 'It went wrong, didn't it, Ann? Was it something to do with Morton?'

She nodded slowly, sadly. 'Yes, Morton. That's when it

started. When Stella began to go there she said it was just business but I didn't believe that. I followed and saw her with that Ratcliffe woman. They were in Stella's car, laughing, joking.' She shuddered at the memory. 'I felt devastated.'

'When was that? Which day?'

'The day of the drama group party at Stella's house,' she replied vaguely. 'She came home early for that.'

'The day Stella was killed?'

'Yes.'

'What did you do, Ann, after you'd seen Stella with Susan Ratcliffe?'

Ann closed her eyes tightly and fresh tears spread across her face. With a trembling hand she wiped them away, saying, 'I came back to Bridgetown. I was supposed to go to the party but I couldn't face it. I went home and just walked around, thinking.'

Ashworth decided it was time to cut through the emotional debris inside the woman's mind. He said, 'But you went to the house later, didn't you?'

'Yes.'

'You argued with Stella, didn't you?'

'Yes, yes.'

'And you killed her.'

'No. No.' Ann's voice quaked. 'It wasn't like that. It was an accident.'

'Tell me about the accident then,' Ashworth persisted.

Speaking quickly now, Ann said, 'I went to the house. I had this insane idea that if I told Stella I was finished with her she'd beg forgiveness. She just laughed, went upstairs and ran the bath. I followed her. I was still so angry. I realized then that she could do anything she wanted with me. She undressed me, made me get into the bath. She was talking to me as if I were a child, saying she would make me happy again, telling me to forget all this nonsense. I sat there loathing myself. I wanted to tell her to piss off but I couldn't. I felt so much for her . . . I couldn't.'

Ann broke down, buried her face in her hands, tried to blot out memories too painful to relive.

235

Relentlessly Ashworth pushed home his attack. 'What made you kill her, Ann? What happened?'

Slowly her hands left her face and she stared down at them as she said, 'Someone came to the front door. Stella went down. It was a man. He didn't stay long. I crept out on to the landing and I heard Stella trying to get rid of him, but she was laughing, telling him he couldn't have it tonight, leave it till the morning.'

She looked up, her eyes begged understanding. 'I don't know what happened to me, Jim. I stood there listening and all of a sudden it dawned on me that this was how it would always be, there would always be other lovers; Stella would always be lying to me. I can't remember what happened next, it's all so blurred. There was this rushing roaring sound inside my head and I was downstairs trying to hit Stella but she was too strong, she pushed me away.

'I think our legs must have got tangled and Stella fell over. I remember the sound her head made as it hit the floor . . . a dull thud. Yes, and when I looked her eyes were open but I could only see the whites . . .' She stopped abruptly; her breathing was rapid.

'Then you strangled her,' Ashworth said bluntly.

'I don't remember . . . I don't remember any more . . .'

'You do, Ann,' Ashworth pushed.

Ann's face was flushed with panic; she shook her head violently. 'I don't, I swear to God, I don't. There was a voice inside my head screaming, "Hurt the bitch." It got louder and louder . . . I couldn't stand it. Then it stopped and Stella was dead. I knew I'd killed her. I felt so calm . . .'

Ashworth leant forward and gently touched Ann's arm. 'There's no need to go on, you've told me all I need to know.' Looking at her tear-ravaged face he felt a strong surge of pity. He said kindly, 'Is there anything I can get for you?'

Ann looked at him and tried to smile. 'A large gin and tonic?' Then she shook her head as if denying her own request. 'Coffee and cigarettes perhaps.'

'I'll see to it.'

'Jim, how did you know? How did you find out?'

'Simple. It was when you suggested I call the chapter in the book, "The Christmas Bow Murder". The bow part had never been released to the media. I've just spent two days at the library going through back copies of all the newspapers. So, the only ones to know were the police and the killer.'

What he failed to mention was the fact that he had also spent an extremely uneasy time wondering if he or Turner had fed her this information.

There was a touch of hysteria on the edge of her laughter. She said, 'It's ironic, isn't it? I killed Stella for a non-existent affair and put you on to me by trying to lead you off a trail you weren't even on. Don't you think that's funny?'

'No, Ann, I think it's sad.'

For a few moments they looked at each other, both knowing there was nothing left to be said, then Ashworth left the office, giving Jolly a cursory glance on his way out. He had done his job – done it well – and now he wanted to be away from this place, these people.

Ashworth had almost reached the swing doors at the end of the corridor when they burst open to reveal Turner, who wore his newly acquired authority like an old comfortable garment. At the sight of him Ashworth felt a knot of anger in his middle but he harnessed it, reined it in.

Turner stopped in front of him. His face, still discoloured from the Watson incident, was pink with rage. 'Have you gone mad, Jim?' he asked, his tone strident. 'The Chief's on his way.'

'The Chief, eh? How American,' Ashworth commented lightly. 'Really modern, that.'

Turner spoke with exaggerated patience. 'Jim, you've been removed. You don't seem to understand that I'm totally in charge of CID, at least for the moment.'

'All yours,' Ashworth replied graciously. 'I was just tying up some loose ends.'

'You've hauled Ann Thorncroft in here behind my back . . . well, I just hope she's good-natured enough to let it ride.'

'Oh, I think the lady has other things on her mind, Owen, like waiting for you to go in and charge her with Stella Carway's murder.'

Pure shock registered on Turner's face and Ashworth savoured the moment. He said, 'It's all on tape. I've followed procedure to the letter.'

Ashworth, having made his point, knew he should leave it there but a part of him could not resist driving that point still further. With an acid tone he said, 'And of course someone who is totally in charge of CID will have to explain what he was doing going to bed with the accused person . . . not only to his friend, the Chief, but also to his wife . . . oh, and his other mistress.'

He grinned wickedly as he patted Turner's shoulder. 'Never mind, I'm sure you'll think of something. Anyway, I'll leave you to it.'

It was a light-hearted Jim Ashworth who emerged from his car at the station next morning; his head was clear, his eyes bright. He had made his peace with Sarah and on the strength of that peace had been allowed to breakfast on wonderfully unhealthy eggs, bacon, mushrooms and fried bread.

In the Chief Constable's office a rather uncomfortable Ken Savage greeted him. 'Jim, Jim, you cunning old dog. Come on, sit down,' he said with false heartiness.

Ashworth complied with the request. 'I take it Ann Thorncroft's been charged, sir.'

Savage nodded as he lit a cigarette. 'Make that Ken, will you, Jim, it's a familiarity that's long overdue. Yes, she's been charged and I've arranged for Steven Carway's release.' He busied himself with flicking ash off his shirt before saying gruffly, 'Right, let's get this out of the way. I never apologize, sign of weakness, but I will say there are a few red faces in this nick today.'

Ashworth remained silent.

'What's happened on this case has caused me to have a major rethink about our dispute, Jim, old son, and although I admit events have altered some of my opinions, I still feel that changes in CID are called for.'

'I couldn't agree more,' Ashworth said easily.

Savage's face brightened. 'That's music to my ears, Jim, now – '

But Ashworth had not finished. He said, 'There's something else I've realized over the last few days . . . I've always felt sorry for people who can't express themselves without the use of four-letter words, felt it sad that they needed them to make a point, but I've come to realize that at times, when feelings are so strong, they can be used in a very effective way to convey those feelings to others. This is one of those occasions because at this moment in time I've an almost overwhelming desire to walk round this desk, open my flies, and piss in your lap.'

Ashworth saw the full impact of those words on Savage's face; whatever colour there was beneath his slightly yellow skin drained away, then came flooding back in a bright flush of anger. 'Watch it, Jim,' he snapped. 'You're going too far. I could have your job for that.'

Ashworth shook his head as he stood up. 'I don't think so, you've already asked me to resign once.' He reached into the inside pocket of his coat and pulled out an envelope. 'A second request won't be necessary,' he said icily.

A glowering Ken Savage took the envelope, sliced it open and withdrew its contents. The letter was addressed to the Chief Constable of Bridgetown. It read:

Dear Sir,
Recently you informed me of the changes being implemented within the Bridgetown CID and asked if I felt able to fit in with these changes. After giving the matter considerable thought I find myself unable to be part of a system which through its lack of efficiency, ability and, may I respectfully suggest, leadership, allows a perfectly innocent person to be charged with murder and then places every obstacle in the path of a senior officer who is attempting to prevent this miscarriage of justice. Yours faithfully,

James Ashworth (Chief Inspector)

Savage looked up at Ashworth in total disbelief. 'Jim, you can't put this in.'

'I have,' Ashworth replied before turning and walking to the door. 'Happy Christmas, Ken, old son.'

He left the office without looking back.